T0158875

Invasion!

Invasion!

A Story of Historical Science Fiction

Norm O'Banyon

INVASION!
A STORY OF HISTORICAL SCIENCE FICTION

iUniverse books may be ordered through booksellers or by contacting:

iUniverse
1663 Liberty Drive
Bloomington, IN 47403
www.iuniverse.com
1-800-Authors (1-800-288-4677)

Because of the dynamic nature of the Internet, any web addresses or links contained in this book may have changed since publication and may no longer be valid. The views expressed in this work are solely those of the author and do not necessarily reflect the views of the publisher, and the publisher hereby disclaims any responsibility for them.

Any people depicted in stock imagery provided by Thinkstock are models, and such images are being used for illustrative purposes only. Certain stock imagery © Thinkstock.

ISBN: 978-1-5320-0326-4 (sc)
ISBN: 978-1-5320-0343-1 (e)

Print information available on the last page.

iUniverse rev. date: 07/27/2016

Before the Beginning

The woman worked her way through the shallow water seeking any sign of food, completely unaware that she was both hunter and hunted. For many days the men had left the camp in search of meat, only to return empty, more hungry than when they left. She had resorted to collecting the eels that hid in the reeds. They were small, but any nourishment was better than gnawing a dry bone. She waded a bit deeper. A tiny movement caught her attention and she stood still, waiting. A medium sized eel feeding on the green slime on a reed stem rose near the surface. In a perfectly timed grab, the woman grasped it, crushed the skull of the fish, and dropped its slippery body into her gathering basket. She continued searching, for she knew the men would need food.

The Seerier explorers had crossed vast emptiness of space, seeking a new home since their solar system had become dangerously hostile. They were in search of an oxygen based atmosphere. Generations had been spent searching with no successful results. Riding the gamma pulse wave on a timeless journey, they were nearing the end of their resources, both for their craft and themselves. The third small planet in a equally small solar system had given them hope. For where there was oxygen, and hydrogen, there would be a liquid base in which they could recover.

The frozen cap of the planet was unapproachable, but the warm tropic belt was perfect. The Seerier ship, less than ten centimeters in length configured into its landing shape, slowing gently. The touchdown in a mineral and microbe rich lagoon hardly made a splash at all. Concealment was no chore for the nearly transparent craft, in the shadow of a stone. Now the next step would be to find a compatible DNA strain with which they could connect. The challenge was the fact that nearly every creature they came upon was much larger than they were and also hungry. The Seerier had found a wonderfully nutritious home, but one filled with predators, most of which were cold-blooded.

The woman placed another eel in her gathering basket, and watched for more. The explorer had followed her heat signature in the water, and its sensors had indicated that this was a warm blooded primate. Steadily it closed the distance between them until it found a hairy leg. It needed a portal to attach the growth cells. Less than a centimeter square, with four tendrils, the transparent explorer worked its way toward the surface. There it was! An opening that could receive...first the cells were attached to the moist inner lining...then the DNA strand....and then the endorphin stimulus. To the host it had been no more irritating than a stray weed floating against her skin, but with good fortune, in three days the cells would be released in something like a sticky mucous and three new Seerier explorers would be born. The endorphins would increase the probability of the host's return to this watery nursery. The DNA attachment would appear in the next primate birth, when a North African descendant of a Neanderthal, a Homo erectus, would give birth to a smooth skin, enlarged brain and skull, slim upright Homo sapiens. The story of mankind was about to take a monumental stride. The explorer swam away in search of another host.

The inevitable march of evolution migrated the humans east, eventually crossing the ice bridge to the North American continent, then south, south, south. The Seerier explorers migrated west through the Mediterranean Sea, through the Strait of Gibraltar, then west, west, west on the Atlantic current, into the lush Caribbean Sea. Regardless of the speed of their progress, it was inevitable that the two bands would meet again.

The Beginning

The Ojibwa, a strand of the Atakapa people of the Cherokee Nation, had lived in this territory for ten thousand years. Even their ancient stories could not remember a time they were anywhere else. They had foraged short distances to establish one hunting camp or another, but this warm flat region was theirs. Finally they had agreed that Calcasieu, as they called it, was their sacred place. Comfortably situated near the shore of the sheltered water of Vermillion Bay, they would enjoy a full life and bury their honored dead. No longer would they build scaffolds where carrion would feed on their forbearers, or thieves remove treasures. Now for many generations, they covered their dead with clean soil from the river, twelve to a row, and six rows to a level. Then a layer of clay was added for stability, and they began again. Age, illness, occasional calamity and infrequent hostility with their neighbors, had developed a burial mound three meters high and thirty meters square. Calcasieu would be a gift to their descendents.

Then the Spanish explorers arrived with their diseases, and another level was added to the mound. The strangers were finally chased away with spears and arrows. The people wanted nothing but their own privacy. The French, however, were even more stubborn. They too brought more and worse illnesses; but they also brought muskets and the claim that everything west of the Mississippi River and north to the Yukon Territory was theirs. Yet another layer was added to the mound, and then another. Finally a remnant of the Ojibwas abandoned their ancestral Calcasieu, moving north.

An explorer named Robert Cavelier de La Salle named the region Louisiana in the year 1662 to honor the French King Louis XIV. The first permanent settlement, Fort Maurepas, was founded in 1699 by Pierre Le Moyne d'Urbervilles, who received a significant land grant for his effort. The French military officer from Canada had no interest in developing the land, so he lost it in a gambling wager to Joseph Brussard from Acadia. While the new owner had no interest in the land either, he was creative enough to divide it into one hundred parcels, and sell them to men who did have an interest in developing agricultural opportunities. Evan Cossindale inherited one of those parcels from his grandfather, and with his new bride, Clarice, set out to become a farmer.

There is just one more facet to this history lesson: Napoleon Bonaparte harbored secret ambitions to construct a large French colonial empire in the Americas. The dream faltered however, after the French attempt to quell the Saint Dominique revolution ended in failure. Two thirds of the more than 20,000 troops were slain. A year after the French withdrawal in 1803, Haiti declared its independence as the second republic in the western Hemisphere. As a result of his setbacks, Napoleon gave up his dreams of a new empire, and sold the Louisiana Territory to the United States for $15 million dollars. That's how Evan and Clarice Cossindale became American land-owners.

Cossindale Parcel

The young deputy rode along beside the wagon so he could sound wise to the fresh settlers. "They call this here 'Live Oak Road.'" They had been following the twin tracks for the past three hours. "Your place is at the very end of it. I think we are gettin' pretty close. Have you been travelin' long?" After four hours in the saddle, he was eager for any conversation.

The woman answered, "We left Acadia, what you call Nova Scotia, on the tenth day of May. We made it to the Bermuda current by the fifteenth and it took us two days to get around the tip of Florida, and two after that to get to New Orleans, and another day on the train to get to Lafayette. By the time we found a wagon with horses, and all the goods we feel we need, we had used four more days. I do believe this is Saturday May 24th of the year 1814, and we are very anxious to see the plantation."

"Yes, ma'am, it is the 24th, right enough; but you know this is raw ground you purchased and not a plantation, so to speak."

She wore a bright smile, "Raw now, but there is a beautiful plantation waiting for us to awaken." Her husband nodded. She was repeating what he had told her repeatedly, until she had started to believe it.

Within an hour they found the end of the road, and the large pecan tree that marked the corner of their land. "Now your parcel goes 850 paces due west, and 850 paces due south, or until you come to the bay. I've heard there is real good fishin' in Vermillion Bay. You probably'l need a boat though." The deputy was quiet for a bit, and then said apologetically, "Your place has the mound. It's not quite a

5

mountain, but an old Indian ceremonial site. It would be smart to build your house on top of it. That way no flood could ever get you." There wasn't much of a smile to suggest he was offering a good idea, or that even a mention of a flood had been in his plan.

In some ways that first night was wonderful. They were at their journey's end; they were sleeping on their own property. On the other hand they had to empty all the boxes from the wagon so they could spread their blankets on the wagon bed and try not to hear the wild noises from the woods around them. Evan hoped the two fires he had made would create enough smoke and light to keep the night critters away. Privacy was a non-existing privilege, but on the other hand, they were sleeping on their own property.

In the morning, Clarice was frying a skillet breakfast, a potato, an onion, some fat back and two precious eggs stirred together, while Evan used the shovel to continue clearing the weeds from around their site. She had requested a latrine trench away from the wagon. So the first planning decision was made: where to put the outhouse?

All the while, Evan was talking about what they needed to get from the general store, or the lumber yard. It sounded to Clarice like he was planning a trip back to Lafayette.

Finally she asked, "Evan, are you planning to return today?"

His mood had been buoyant since arriving at this their home site. "Yes there is so much to get before we can begin. I feel like a windstorm of ideas. If we leave soon, we can be back before nightfall."

She smiled a wistful look at her husband. "How could we start our lives in this new place by forgetting the fourth commandment?" she asked. "We might save a day before our start here, but the neglect of remembering the Sabbath, and keeping it holy would be sorrowful to me. I hoped we could read the scriptures and sing a bit, and offer God our heartfelt thanks for safely arriving here."

Her soft words were all he needed to hear to be reminded of the promise they had made to have a holy marriage and a Christian home. "We can get an early start in the morning," was his way of agreeing completely.

Their first stop was the lumber yard. Evan negotiated for almost an hour to get material enough to build a small house and a barn, finished material to make furniture, and six framed windows, to be delivered within the week.

On their way to the general store they had to pass the auction yard, where slaves were being sold. After much discussion, Clarice had convinced him that while unpleasant to their sense of justice, it would be necessary for a working farm to have slaves. They watched as three were sold. "I can't imagine reducing a human life to $30," she whispered in his ear.

Slave Auction

"Next I got a healthy buck," the auctioneer announced. A nearly naked man was pulled into the ring by a chain around his neck. His body had several bruises and scabbed wounds. "He is a bit contrary," the auctioneer advised, but strong enough to be a prized worker. Someone in the back offered $10 and someone else raised it five. Another bid or two, and there were no more who wanted to take the risk.

"Fifty dollars," Evan said clearly. The auctioneer immediately hammered the sale.

"Now we have his women," the auctioneer said with an insinuating slur. "One's mostly grown and the other is six years old, a future house slave for sure." Evan felt Clarice's fingers dig into his arm, as the two naked figures were paraded for the buyer's inspection.

"Twenty for the both of them," an opening bid called. The bidding spiraled up, and up. Clarice's grip became nearly painful, so Evan continued bidding, and didn't stop until the auctioneer's hammer sold him the two for $375. He paid for his purchases, wondering a bit what he was to do with three slaves, and one of them a child.

He was guiding them toward their wagon when an angry voice said, "I want the girl." Evan ignored the words for he did not understand their meaning, nor to whom they were directed. A bit louder, he heard, "I want the girl! I'll pay fifty dollars for it." A scruffy man with well worn clothes was standing near the wagon. "I said I want the girl. Do you hear me? Now are you are going to sell her, or I am going to take her?" He took a threatening step toward

Evan. Clarice stepped in front of the slaves, who were as confused with the situation as she was.

"Sir, you are not going to take the girl, and I don't think you will hurt me either. We still live in a humane world," Evan said with conviction.

"Stuff it, you foreigner. I said I am taking her now." One more threatening step drew him nearer.

Evan shouted "Acadia, aidez, aidez!" At least a dozen nearby men turned in instant response. The scruffy man hesitated. Again Evan spoke loudly, "This man wants the little girl for his own pleasure. Even in this barbaric land, there must be some laws against that. And he wants to forcibly take her!" Now the scruffy man was looking about somewhat nervously. This was not working as he had imagined it would. He was encircled by angry men, some of whom carried weapons.

The man jerked a long knife out of a sheath on his belt, which was definitely a thoughtless move. Instantly he was clubbed unconscious by one of the bystanders. A Marshal of sorts was rushing to see what the trouble was all about as Evan said, "Merci, my fine countrymen. My Name is Evan Cossindale; if I can repay your kindness feel free to call upon me. Our home will be at the end of the Live Oak Road." From that day, "Cadians", or "Cajuns" as some called them, would be known as a strong and loyal sub-group of Americans citizens.

At the general store, Evan purchased clothes for his new slaves. The woman and child were especially happy to be able to cover their nakedness. Perhaps nothing could have generated gratitude more quickly than that simple act of decency. The unexpected expense was nothing compared to the idea that now he was a compassionate slave-owner. And it had happened so suddenly. Evan would need much prayer to understand God's hand in this day. They revisited the lumber yard, adding enough material to build a home for their help. Finally they loaded a tarp to make another tent, extra tools, and food in the wagon. Then began the trip home that would soon become familiar.

The summer was spent building: first the main house, where they shared a common evening meal; then the "help's," then the barn for the horses. All the while they worked on communication skills. They learned the name of their slave was Moesh; his wife's name was Tchidore, which was shortened to Dory, and their child's name was Tchamalli, which was shortened to Molly. Mr. Evan and Miss Clare became the owners' usable names. One evening Dory told them how the slavers had attacked their village. Many of the elders were shot or bludgeoned to death. As she described how their son, Mistan, had tried to resist, he had been severely injured, and eventually died in the hold of the ship that brought them to this land. Tears were in their eyes with the painful memory. Again her conversation concluded with sincere gratitude for saving them at the auction.

Another task of summer was delineating the property boundaries by planting over a hundred pecan starts. The west line hid two hazards: poisonous snakes, which Moesh was quick to dispatch with a shovel; and down near the beach, an area of quicksand, which they carefully marked. The east line was hiding two happy discoveries. There were a host of volunteer Taro plants, perhaps left over from long ago trade with the Caribe. They became a constantly renewable source of food, and a future profit-making income. There was also a small fresh water artesian spring. When Mr. Evan suggested using shovels to dig out a straight boundary streambed, Moesh said, "Maybe use plow?" A half mile trench was easily accomplished in one day following the careful markers.

The plow had been used to turn over the soil across the property to allow sugar cane starts to be planted. With Moesh and Dory's help, Mr. Evan had planted enough to insure a profitable harvest next summer. The Taro plants, much to Mr. Evan's delight, were dug, cleaned, and cut into small strips; when fried in grease and salted; they were a snack that could carry them through the workday. The crown of the plant was split into quarters and replanted, soon to make four more savory meals. An area west of the barn became designated as "Taro Row." Soon it had grown to more than a half acre in size, and the large roots were taken into town once a month to barter at the general store in Abbeville, where they also had a mailbox.

The most enjoyable part of the summer, however, was the afternoon leisure in the shallow water of Vermillion Bay. Molly would gladly spend as much time as her parents would allow there. With a full half mile of sandy beach, they found that the area where the spring water flowed into the bay was the most comfortable and available to the houses. Whether swimming, or sitting in the gentle water, or wading, looking for shells, the time seemed to drift by; and they always felt rejuvenated and happy, eager to return. They had no way of understanding that the Seerier had long been very active along this section of the beach.

One rainy evening, as they lingered at the shared table, Miss Claire asked an important question, "Moesh, do you think we should visit the auction again? Is there too much work here for just the four of us?"

He was still, thinking about the answer. "It is not an answer I can give. There is not a day that goes by without some expression of our great good fortune in your visit to the auction. You have made it possible for our little family to continue." Both Clarice and Evan were aware how quickly and competently Moesh had gained those language skills. "If it were up to me I would wish you could buy all the slaves. Our lives are that good. But it is not..." he searched for the word, "practicable." They understood he meant practical. "You might want to hire some temporary help when the sugar cane is harvested. But that will be only for a short while. Our eight hands can do great things here." Then giving a bit of an afterthought, he added, "If you are asking are we lonely for our own people, I would ask, 'Are you?'"

Dory finished his thought again by saying, "We do not live like slaves here in your house. We are blessed, and would like to learn more about your God, to whom we see you pray." She was thoughtful for a moment before adding, "Especially those nights when the loud storms come, I wish I could pray like you." The subject would come up again.

Mr. Evan and Moesh were taking a wagonload of Taro to the Abbeville general store, the best harvest to date. It was only an hour away, but their conversation had been of special interest to Moesh.

Mr. Evan had explained that a section of garden area adjacent to the Taro Rows could be used by them to grow vegetables for their table, or Taro for trade at the store. "You mean that I can have it for my own use?" Moesh asked incredulously.

"That's just what Miss Clare and I have in mind. We don't think you will abuse the opportunity, nor neglect our other chores. It just seems right that you should also receive something more." It was a difficult subject if pushed much further. "I don't suppose Mr. Lester will be open minded enough to do business directly with you; but if you can tell me what you want from the store, and how many Taro in the pile are yours, I'll take care of the bargaining. Do you agree with that?"

"Yes sir, wholeheartedly, sir. I would so like to be able to buy a bit of tobacco, and a little pipe, or a small whittling blade." His smile was born on the wings of unexpected hope.

Mr. Lester was tallying the load, "Fifty four Taros at 35 cents apiece is…$16 dollars." He glanced at Evan.

"Mr. Lester, I brought these to you thinking you are an honest merchant. You told me you would pay 35 cents apiece, which comes to $18.90. It's only a couple hours to Lafayette where they may not try to cheat me." He started to climb back onto the wagon. "I might as well keep these. Good day, sir."

"Hold on," the embarrassed merchant called. "I said I would give you 35 cents in merchandise. That's a better rate than cash." When Evan paused, confused by the lack of logic, the general store owner added, "I remember that you have been looking for a small used row boat; I just got one in this morning that I would be glad to sell you for $10 dollars in Taro."

By the time the wagon was headed home, a pile of groceries, a boat with oars and a shrimp sock were in the wagon. Moesh had a small pouch of tobacco with a cob pipe, and a small folding pocket knife. The most significant consideration was the envelope that had been in his mailbox; Evan had a letter from his cousin Philip. He reread the letter to make sure he understood its contents: "Dear Cousin Evan. I hope this finds you and your lovely wife well. The endeavor you have undertaken is very large, and your family wishes you only the very best. I have not quite found the success I know is near for the boat building business. I have good employees and several companies are interested in our productions; we just need more building materials. Here is the reason for this letter. I received the same sort of inheritance from Grandfather as you did. I cannot attempt both this business and a brave relocation into the wild Americas as you have. Are you interested in acquiring the parcel of land adjacent to yours? I am three years in arrears on the property tax. If you will pay that dept and tender $7,500 dollars for purchase of the property, I may be able to finish our first blue water freighter. Please let me know as soon as possible. It would be a great boon to me. Yours sincerely, Phillip Cossindale.

That request was so important, Evan overlooked the irritating accounting at Mr. Lester's. He wondered at the marvelous turn of events. He was convinced of one thing. Clarice would surely want to pray about this a lot, because she had just missed her period.

There were only three pecan trees mature enough to produce nuts. But the three of them produced a lot! Evan pondered what they would do with a hundred more trees. With the help of Moesh, Dory and even little Molly, they were able to collect, peel and dry five gunnysacks of the tasty nuts. Mr. Lester offered Evan eight dollars in barter per sack, which guaranteed a supply of eggs, condensed milk and Moesh's favorite, hot sauce.

More Land and More Slaves

By Christmas the details had been worked out for Phillip's parcel. Evan and Clarice went to Lafayette to the county registrar to file the deed and pay the back taxes. Their plantation had just doubled in size, and they found a general store in Lafayette that would pay 50 cents a head for all the Taro heads, and ten dollars for each bag of pecans, they could haul. Evan said they would need to plant another hundred pecan trees around the new property. Clarice said it was also time to stop at the auction yard, even though there were no slaves currently to be sold. They would probably need more help soon. Evan spoke to the callous auctioneer.

"If the *Duc de Maine* or *Aurore* brings more slaves from the Senegambia coast area, and if there is a young man with a wife, I will buy them both, if the price is right."

The auctioneer, who had become liberated from any humane feelings, looked at this slim man with a stout spirit. "There are few things in my world that cause me to smile," he said. "I still remember how your wife protected those slaves as you stood up to Claude Patrice. You were either so confident in doing the right thing, or you were sure your friends would stand with you, you scarcely blinked at him. I still smile when I think how he pulled his big old knife, and fell like a bag of manure. I like what you did that day, and I will keep me eyes open, although there are fewer and fewer ships coming in any more, now that England has outlawed slavery. Will you pay $300 dollars for the pair?"

Evan held out his hand in agreement. "If you send the deputy for me, I will be here the same day. He was aware that the bank balance was under $5,000. But they were prepared to start putting deposits back in it.

A fortnight later, the deputy showed up late one afternoon. He greeted Evan and said, "There is an auction at noon tomorrow with a couple darkies you might be interested in. The thing is, she was banged up on the way here, and …" He wasn't sure what more to say. "Mr. Roberti wants you to look at her before the start of the auction. She might not be worth much." Evan paid the deputy two silver dollars for his service, and Clarice invited the deputy to join them for supper. If he would like to share the barn with the horses, they could go in together first thing in the morning. It was too late to start for Lafayette now.

The sun was just coming up when Clarice whispered to Evan that she was not feeling up to an eight hour ride in the wagon. "Do you mind taking Moesh in my place?" It was actually a relief to Evan, for he had worried about a long arduous day for a woman who was now definitely pregnant. If he trotted the horses part of the time, they could easily make the auction yard before noon.

Mr. Roberti, the auctioneer, shook his head in disgust. "Damned sailors must have picked her out for sport. She was beat up and raped a lot on the way here." They were standing in the shed, looking at a man and woman in chains, both naked. Her left side was entirely bruised, from armpit to waist, and her arm was also bruised, swollen and crooked. "With that broken arm, she's not worth a damn to me. I'm going to have to shoot her, unless you'll take her. If you'll pay me $200 for him, I'll throw her in free."

Evan stared at the man in unbelief. How could a person so lose their soul, that another injured human being could become just a nuisance thrown into a deal?

"O.K. a hundred and a half, but that's as low as I go," the auctioneer growled. There was no satisfaction on his face, nor on Evan's.

Evan had tossed some worn clothes into the wagon, in the hopes that he would be able to cover the nakedness of two people who were in great confusion. One of his shirts worked as a smock for the woman. And trousers were gratefully accepted by the man.

Fortunately Moesh could speak a bit of their dialect. He tried to assure them that the worst of their ordeal was over, and they could trust Mr. Evan.

The first stop was a doctor's office who would treat people of color. On his second try Evan found one, Dr. Andrew Bell, M.D.. The compassionate doctor bound the woman's ribs, and as carefully as possible set and splinted her broken arm. A grimace clouded her stoic face, and a small whimper was her only response to the pain. Dr. Bell was trying to wave off any expense when Evan insisted on at least paying ten dollars. They would become life-long friends.

The last stop was the general store, where he purchased a bolt of blue cotton fabric, with some thread to match, a shovel, cooking pot and bucket. They had discovered how effective the shrimp sock could be. Moesh especially enjoyed rowing in the bay, pulling the scoop along.

On the ride home, Moesh learned that her name in Senegambia was that of a flowering tree, not familiar in this new world.

"May I tell her that 'Lily' is a flower of great respect for us?" Evan asked Moesh.

The slave smiled genuinely, saying, "You own us, and can call us by any name you choose." Their friendship had grown to nearly bridge the unnatural condition of slavery. "But I think Lily is a fine name, there is honor in it." There was considerable conversation between the slaves before Moesh could explain, "His name meant "winner," or "champion." It was a very proud name, but I think inappropriate for a slave, for it suggests dominance." He looked at Evan with a steady gaze. "I suggested to him that we might call him "Link," recalling not the chains of bondage, but the strength we offer each other. We are each a link in a bold new effort to live fully and with dignity, which you allow."

"Moesh, you must have been a scholar, or a teacher in your homeland. Your insight and understanding is refreshing in this primitive place."

"I was a hunter," he said in quiet reply. "But perhaps understanding is welcome whatever our task. Speaking of task, may I ask a question?"

"I always welcome your questions. They lead us to good choices."

Moesh hesitated, then said, "The new space is equal to what you already have, is that correct?" He waited until Evan nodded, then went on, "Sugar cane is a more profitable crop than Taro, but it is only harvested once a year, while Taro is harvested at least twice. Is that correct?"

"You're correct. In the long run, though, I'm not sure which is the more profitable. The sugar mill will always buy the canes, but they try to negotiate the price down if it's a productive year. And it is costly initially to purchase the cane roots, which take a year to mature. Taro, on the other hand, is either a cash or barter crop with many more opportunities to market it. We also multiply," he paused to make sure Moesh understood the word, "our number of plants; each time we harvest one Taro we wind up with four more new ones. And they grow all year long, which provides food for us. So they are more dependable. I think a good farm would have a balance of both." They chatted all the way home about the use of the new property and the convenience of two more willing workers on it.

Miss Clare and Dory watched the wagon approach the house, Everyone was delighted with the success of the day, although two in the wagon bed weren't sure how to express it. As soon as Miss Clare saw the splinted arm, she wanted an explanation. The account she heard caused immediate feminine attention.

"Dory," she directed, "take her down to the beach so she can bathe herself. Let her get clean and comfortable before we eat. I have a small bar of lilac soap she can have. A lady likes to have a pleasant fragrance when she meets new folks."

The five slaves made their way to the familiar beach, each with a different intent. Molly was there because she could once again frolic in the water. Her playfulness underscored the message that Moesh and Dory had given. This was not a place of pain or shame. Moesh was there to make sure the new folks didn't decide to make a run for it. He had stressed that in this new world, run-away slaves were either shot or hung. Survival for an escapee was not a possibility. Dory was there to try to comfort and assure this new woman that whatever she was dreading was not going to happen. Life here could be more than expected. Link was there to make sure no further damage was done to his wife. The experience on the ship had been pure hell for her, but for him as well. It was physically for her, emotionally for him; they had been completely victimized. Lily was there to get clean. Regrettably the horrible memories lingered, but she could at least cleanse her body. The appreciation she felt for the gracious mercies of this day was surprising and puzzling. There was a lightness removing the ugly guilt. She would need to think about this more.

The Seerier were there because this beach had become a popular nursery for them. The hosts came frequently and lingered long enough to receive several administrations. They, however, did not need the DNA attachment, for the Seerier recognized their own, administered eons ago. One host in particular, however, had needs this day not commonly encountered by them. The host was damaged! So each administration was accompanied with a cell replacement boost and an immunity stimulant. The endorphin signal was repeated several times. It was all they could do to repair their host.

It was only Dory's promise that they could return to bathe tomorrow that persuaded Lily to finally get out of the water. To the surprise and enjoyment of the other four there was a bright smile on her face, the first since her arrival. All five of them, under the influence of multiple endorphin boosts, felt a joyous new unity, a bond only hours old but as strong as any they could remember.

Miss Clare had made a kettle of soup from last night's shrimp, caught, cleaned and cooked by Moesh. She had diced Taro, and onion; boiled with a couple quarts of fresh water, then added a couple cans of condensed milk and a bit of spice. Oh, my! That was so very tasty. They lingered at the table, beginning the communication process and planning tomorrow's chores, which were few this time of year.

Two days later Lily was shocked when she began to dress for the day and noticed that not only were her bruises no longer painful, they were no longer evident at all. The swelling in her arm was gone, and her ribs were barely tender to the touch. Healing was miraculous, if not quite complete. Four days after that, a menstrual flow began signaling no pregnancy had eventuated from the attacks on the slave ship. Her mind could release some of the fears.

The lower half of the new property was plowed and planted with sugar cane starts by the end of February, which guaranteed some sort of a harvest this year. After considerable conversation, Evan and Clarice agreed that while it would be a risky gamble with their dwindling savings, they would begin construction on the main house. It could possibly be finished by the time the baby arrived. Evan took out three thousand dollars for materials, and a thousand dollars to hire a carpenter to plan and build the frame with their help. Clarice requested that the beautiful structure might be built on the mound, facing Vermillion Bay.

The Legend Begins

The first step was building the stairway up the side of the mound. They scoured the nearby woods and selected four stout trees with straight trunks, They became the pillars, drilled and bolted together with timbers. Two landings, one a third of the way up, and another a third of the way higher, made the stairway reasonable to climb. Evan was grateful for the other two backs that could hoist the long planks to the top of the six meter mound, once he had secured a rope to the end. Bit by bit the graceful home began to take shape.

They were just placing the final rafters on the peak when Moesh heard a startled cry, then a scream of pain. Link was already moving toward the crisis. They found Charles their carpenter laying on his tool chest. He had fallen off the top of the mound, slid down the side, and impaled himself on at least two wood chisels, one through his arm, and the other deep into his thigh, Fortunately there was no arterial bleeding, but the wounds were open and terribly deep. As Mr. Evan was extricating one of the razor- sharp tools from Charles' arm, he asked Link to get Miss Clare. "Have her bring some towels and a strong needle and thread. He was pretty sure what must be done, just not who would do it. By the time she arrived at the side of the mound, he was gently lifting the carpenter off the large chisel in his thigh that must have hit the bone. There was considerable blood on him, on Charles, and the ground under him. Evan had no idea how much it would take to bleed to death, but this looked seriously close.

Mr. Evan asked if there was anyone else who would try to stitch closed these nasty wounds. When no one else would, he set about it, knowing that it was urgently important to stop the bleeding. On the leg first, he was afraid he was about to feint, but reminded himself that this man's life depended on closing the wounds. He took about a dozen stitches that pulled the edges together firmly. The arm got four or five on each wound. He then directed the others to get a blanket that they could improvise into a litter, to carry him down to the beach, Salt water would help cleanse the wounds, and clean the patient, who had only groaned with each stitch.

They pulled his britches off; then got him into water about two feet deep, gently sitting him down. Mr. Evan asked Molly if she would fetch a pitcher of fresh water from the spring. "I'm afraid it's the strongest thing we have to drink here," Evan said, trying to fight the shakes he was feeling.

Charles looked up with fearful eyes. "When I saw that chisel coming through my arm, I was pretty sure this was my last day. You were a fast thinker to save my life. Thanks." He was surprised at how calm he was, in fact he could almost say that he was feeling better. No one knew that he was surrounded by a mass of Seerier, offering their microscopic assistance. The carpenter was carried back to the house where he was made as comfortable as possible on the floor. Once again Miss Clare had worked her magic with a pot of Taro and some of the raccoon Moesh had killed last night. The Gumbo was hardy and very flavorful. If it helped the healing process so much the better.

With the first light of morning, Evan was on his way to Lafayette driving the carpenter's wagon, with Charles resting in the wagon bed, and Evan's horse on a lead behind. Once there, he went directly to Dr. Bell's office, where a professional examination could happen.

"You say you put these stitches in yesterday?" the interested doctor asked. "Look at the healing that has already begun. I don't need to do anything but watch your progress. Mr. Evan, your work may not be sufficient for a school of medicine, but it certainly saved this man's leg, and perhaps his life. I'm very impressed." Looking closely at Charles he asked, "Have you taken anything for pain?"

"Only that spring water from the pitcher. You know that was about the sweetest, purest water I can remember."

"I am amazed. If you will come back in about a week, I will remove these stitches. Then we'll see what more needs to be done." Surprisingly, Charlie came back in only three days because the scabs were getting itchy. The doctor said a couple more days would have been problematic at this rapid rate of healing.

"I've been telling everyone I know that the spring water was miraculous, a healing fountain," the gratefully carpenter said through a grin.

By the time Charles was strong enough to return for his tools Moesh and Link had installed floors both up and downstairs, and carefully covered the roof with tongue and groove lumber. He brought with him the fourteen windows for the first floor, and the beveled glass door looking out at Vermillion Bay. He also brought the incredible wonder at his rapid and complete recovery from what the "experts" were calling a crippling injury. He should not be expected to walk naturally with a severed thigh muscle. Again and again he attributed his miraculous recovery to the spring water.

Now the Legend grows

Two weeks later, Evan was returning from visiting two sugar mills, getting instructions for harvesting and preparing the canes, as well as price quotes. There wasn't much difference in their bids, but one was a mile closer, which made it a favorite choice. As Evan approached the end of Live Oak Road, he noticed a carriage standing near his property.

"May I help you?" he asked the driver of the carriage.

"I'm looking for… the Cossindale plantation. Might this be it?" The man's voice was reedy and his breath labored.

"I'm Evan Cossindale; how can I help you, sir?" The puzzle seemed extreme.

"I am a desperate man, sir. A friend of mine… heard that your… carpenter had a …near-death accident, …but by drinking your spring water… he was miraculously healed." The man had to gasp during each phrase. "I am hoping you will… allow me the same courtesy."

"You came all this way just for a drink of spring water?" Evan repeated mystified.

"If that's all you… did for the carpenter,… that's enough for me. But I think he… also bathed in it." Evan ached for the laboring man's breath. "I'll pay you fifty… dollars to give me the same… treatment."

"Sir, I make no claims to anything but a salt water dip, and a pitcher of spring water" Suddenly Evan had the feeling of the snake-oil hucksters who made incredulous claims to innocent people.

"I understand that. The doctors say… my lungs are filling… with a fluid my body …cannot handle and I …have a very short time to live. If this does not work,… I hold you completely fault-free. But it is my only… hope at this stage. Will you do it… for a hundred dollars?"

"Let's get you wet, and see how you feel in the morning, Then we can speak about gratuity. Please follow me to the house." He was thinking how he could possibly make this into a meaningful and still honorable experience for this stranger.

The first challenge was to inform Clarice that there would be an additional plate at the table for supper, and some sort of sleeping arrangement needed to be made. He also asked her for that bath robe she had made for him from the bolt of blue fabric.

Then, when their guest had completely disrobed and had put on the bath robe, Evan asked Moesh to accompany the gentleman to the beach, precisely where the carpenter had been seated in the water, and finally he asked Molly to take a pitcher of spring water to the man with a drinking glass for his comfort. During the hour he waited, quite unknown and of course, unseen, a horde of Seerier were at work. Their instant diagnosis was that here again was a damaged host. They did their microscopic duty, stimulating cell replacement, and an immunity booster. The increased endorphins were immediately realized; the visitor felt blissfully content. The man felt younger, lighter, and more healthy than he had for years. When Evan came to rinse him off with another pitcher of spring water, the man started to protest the waste. When his host explained he was following the exact footsteps he had with the injured carpenter, the visitor was yielding and still. The "treatment" model had just been cast.

When the visitor was dried and dressed, he sipped another glass of spring water, He announced that the cure had already begun, for he was breathing more freely. Clarice announced that she had prepared a family favorite: fresh shrimp with Taro chowder. She offered it with fried Taro sticks. All eight sat at the table together. Molly may have had the largest smile because she had been given an opportunity to serve.

Evan and the visitor strolled back to the beach to watch the sunset. Evan explained what a frantic year they had experienced just to get to this stage. The first new crop of Taro was ready to harvest, as was the first sugar canes. Hopefully the big house would be finished by the time their first child arrived.

"It seems to me you have the... two ingredients for success young man," the visitor said, obviously breathing more freely. "You have vision, and focused energy. I believe you will accomplish... great things here. Would you mind if I give you... a little help? I publish a small paper in Florida. May I tell my readers about your gracious... hospitality and fabulous spring water?"

"It is a vain man who believes he needs no help in this world. I am happy you feel that your time here was well spent, especially now that I understand how far you have come to visit us. I welcome your help."

"May I say that you have also given... me a refreshing view of the slavery issue. It is apparent that your slaves... understand their position. But they also... have your respect, which gives them a unique dignity. I find this wholesome and quite rare."

The visitor was offered the bed, but asked where the carpenter slept before he could be taken to the doctor. When Clarice answered quietly that he had slept on the folded wagon cover, the visitor smiled and said, "Who knows, that may be... the most crucial part of the healing. May I?" He took off his coat and shoes and pulled the thin sheet over his shoulders. This warm evening had little need for a sheet, other than privacy. He was still soundly sleeping when Clarice entered the kitchen in the morning to light the stove fire. When he raised his head, she said quietly, "I'm sorry if I woke you. I'll have coffee brewing in the shake of a lamb's tail."

The man stood and took a deep breath; "Oh, thank you Jesus!" He exhaled and did it again. "It really did work. I feared it was a pipe-dream. But I can breathe! Praise God from whom all blessings flow!"

A pan scramble got their morning started on the very best foot. It was obvious that Clarice was nearly full term pregnant, yet as gracious as any hostess might be.

"Son," their guest began his leave-taking by shaking Evan's hand, then kissing Clarice's, "you have refreshed my body and perhaps more important, my mind. My name is J. Henry Higgins, and I pledge to you that we will see one another again." He presented Evan with five gold double eagle twenty dollar pieces, and then gave a ten dollar eagle to Moesh, and another to Link. He even gave Molly a silver dollar, much to her surprise and joy. Finally, he added an eagle gratuity to Clarice for her gracious hospitality even at full term. "It is clear to me that you have something unique here, and the humanity of it is beautiful. God bless you." He started to climb into the carriage, then paused and asked, "Do you think I could take a jar of that spring water with me? I know I have already consumed a pitcher of it this morning, and will probably have to stop in the brush three times on the way back; I just love the purity of it." Molly was running toward the kitchen to fetch him one.

Clarice spent her ten dollars on a baby crib from Lafayette, on Evan's next trip. Evan spent his on hiring a local sugar cane grower to transport the harvest in his large wagon with side braces. Five large loads earned enough from the mill to replenish the savings account. Both Link and Moesh put their coins in secure cups in the cupboard. Having even a bit of money helped them feel empowered.

"Mr. Evan, may I ask a favor of you?" Moesh rarely was this talkative.

"Of course. What would you like?" Evan was curious where this may lead them.

"I wonder if you will let me pick up the bent and discarded nails around the big house. I would like to make a blow pipe for hunting squirrels and birds. It would work better if I had a nail as a sharp point. Some of the spikes could be for a throwing spear. I've seen tracks of deer and hogs nearby. A good spear shaft could work better than throwing a stick at them."

"Take all you want. I would like to see the spear when you have it made. That would be a wonder to me." Nothing more was said about it, but Moesh had a project that would serve the future for them, in many ways.

"Link, I'll need you to ride with me into Lafayette to deliver these Taro." For two days they had dug, cleaned and trimmed the large heads. There were almost three hundred in the wagon. That meant twelve hundred new plant starts for Moesh to get in the ground while they were gone. "Then we can get the windows for the upstairs, and the crib." Evan was looking forward to the day.

As they were passing through Abbeville, Mr. Lester saw the wagon and stepped out into the road to greet Evan. "Hello! I'm glad to see you." Then looking at the large mound of Taro, he added, "but I'm not sure I can use that many. I am out, so if you will just take then round back, we can work something out."

Evan had slowed the wagon, but not stopped. "Sorry, Mr. Lester, these are going to Lafayette. The general store there wants them all, for 50 cents each. I might be able to get you a handful tomorrow to barter. You squeezed me a little too hard, sir."

The merchant walked beside the wagon, "But I need some today. I'm out."

"Yes, sir. I heard that. Our deal is barter for merchandise, and I need cash today not groceries." He flipped the reigns so the horses sped up a bit. "I'll bring you a few tomorrow." The merchant was reminded that he was not the only one doing business today.

Link stayed with the wagon as Mr. Evan went in to deposit the income from the first harvest. He said that his bare feet would not be comfortable on that shiny marble floor. A surprise was waiting for Evan as he made out his deposit slip for $2,725 dollars, the teller told him there had been a voucher to his account, sent to the bank from Mr. J. Henry Higgins in the amount of one thousand dollars. The teller handed him a letter that accompanied the draft.

"Dear Mr. Cossindale. The pleasant memory of our hours together has not faded, I am happy to report. If anything, my health continues to improve daily, which is a delightful mystery. With this deposit into your account, I have made an investment in our future. I trust this is not too bold of me. Please recognize this as a positive aid to finish an upstairs bedroom for your future guests. I consider it pre-payment for when I get to visit again. I eagerly look forward to that day. Yours, cordially, J. Henry Higgins."

Charles the carpenter was delighted to be invited to do the finish trim work inside the big house, and planted nine Mulberry bushes around the base of the mound. He was finished before Clarice went into labor. There was a progressive move in the housing arrangement; Evan and Clarice moved to the wonderful but mostly empty mound house; Moesh, Dory and Molly moved next door, and Link and Lily finally had a house all to themselves. It was an ideal and permanent situation.

When the labor pains began, Evan admitted he was of little use, except to pray. He looked in on her regularly, but it was Dory and Lily who attended Miss Clare during the birthing hours, and welcomed baby Rebecca. Two days later, while her baby was swaddled and sleeping, Miss Clare went to the beach to bath. If it worked for a carpenter and an editor, she was confident that healing comfort would be hers as well. She was not mistaken.

The Tallahassee Herald carried a provocative editorial: "Juan Ponce De Leon was not wrong, merely misdirected. The conquistador, explorer, governor of Puerto Rico who named our state as La Florida, (the flower) was looking for gold, some say; others contend that he was seeking the fountain of youth. This editor contends he would have found the latter had he gone a bit further west.

"I was in what my doctor called the final stage of lung failure when I followed a friend's advice to search out a young plantation owner near Lafayette. I was told of a miraculous healing, experienced by a construction worker who could have easily bled to death, save for the administration of the fountain's pure medicinal water. Reader, I can see the smirk on your face for I wore it too, until my body was restored to full health. Yes, even at my age. I was welcomed graciously, treated tenderly with respect. Twelve hours after arriving, I departed a healed man, and a fervent believer in what Juan was seeking. You must have an appointment to go there. Write to Mr. Evan Cossindale in care of Abbeville Louisiana. If you pay your $100 dollars and are not completely comforted, I will refund your money. I so believe it is a safe offer, for the fountain continues to flow, sweet and pure."

The letters started arriving; one or two a week at first, then sometime as many as four or five a week. The requests were from the ill and injured, from young and no longer young, from women and men alike who were desperately seeking health. Evan made every effort to accommodate them as they came season in, and season out. Dory assumed cooking duties so Miss Clare could take care of Rebecca. For greater privacy for the visitors, Evan and his crew built a small cottage dressing room with a bed and easy chairs adjacent the beach. With Moesh to guide them through the model, the people came and sat in a wooden chair partially submerged in the comfortable water. They drank deeply from the fresh stream; they were welcomed with hospitality, and they went home convinced that new vigor or health or healing had occurred.

Trouble

One terrible exception to that occurred on a spring evening. Two horsemen sauntered onto the property just about dusk. Casually they approached the big house, giving the other buildings a careful look. "Hey Cossindale, are you home?" one of them shouted. "We figured out what kind of a house you got goin' here, and we want some of it. I want to dip my wick in something young and sweet! Cossindale, do you hear me? I want a woman!" They waited for an answer like conquerors.

Evan came down the steps carrying a small double barrel shotgun. "Gentlemen you are misguided. There is nothing here for you, please leave."

"Yeah, you still talk like a foreigner. I said I want a woman, a young one, tonight or I might hurt someone. You don't have your Cajun kin around to help you this time." He started to dismount, but hesitated when he heard Evan cock the shotgun.

"I said you are not welcome here, Mr. Patrice, not now, not ever;" Evan spoke calmly and quietly.

"O.K. we tried this the nice way," he pulled his pistol from its holster, "now I'm going to shoot your…" The sentence had no conclusion for a short lance drove through his chest and out his back. His mouth moved to gasp, but made no sound as his lifeless form folded, and slid to the ground.

"What the hell did you do that for?" the other rider shouted as he pulled his gun ready to fire at Evan. Another lance hit him precisely as the first, squarely in the chest and out the back. His eyes rolled back as he died in the saddle. Moesh stepped out of the mound's shadow carrying another short lance and a throwing stick of some sort.

"Some people just never listen to a warning," he said quietly, perhaps mindful that this man was the one who wanted Molly on the day of the auction. "I'm sorry to take such action, Mr. Evan, but I thought you were about to be hurt. May I get rid of these before the women become upset?" He relieved the bodies of their holsters and guns, and anything they had in their pockets. Then he draped the dead bodies over their saddles and led the horses back toward Live Oak Road.

In the morning the horses were in the barn and Evan was eager to know what had finalized the evening. Moesh said he had gone about a mile from the house, left the men's clothes neatly on the edge of the road and taken the bodies deep enough into the brush that is was most unlikely they would ever be discovered before the animals consumed them.

Evan was determined to go to the deputy, however, and report something. He would work on that on his way to Lafayette. He rode the horse with the least blood on the saddle. The deputy was given only a skeleton of the truth. Evan said the horses had appeared in the morning, rider-less, but obviously after some trouble. The weary deputy agreed to go back with Evan. At the point they found bloody clothes but no bodies, however, the deputy was ready to return to his office. He murmured something about hearing an old Cherokee legend about an Ojibwa Chief's ghost that haunts the roads during a full moon, which must have been last night. He asked Evan to keep the horses, unless some kinfolks come by to claim them. Moesh never shared with Evan that there had also been two double eagle twenty dollar gold pieces in the pockets of the dead men.

Easter was a beautiful time of celebration. With the windfall of income from the beach visitors, Evan wanted to do something special for Clarice who had endured a huge risk coming into an unknown world, had gone without many comforts or conveniences since they were first married. Now she could begin to enjoy the house of their dreams. On a trip into Lafayette, Evan stopped at the second hand store. He was looking for a real dining room table, and found one. It was mahogany with carved legs and leaves that would expand it out to seat a dozen; the chairs were upholstered with a burgundy fabric. The price was a little too steep, he thought, so Evan switched his interest to a small upright piano. Clarice would be charmed by that. The shop owner tried several times to steer him back to the dining table, then lowered the price a bit. Finally, after an hour of gentle negotiation, Evan purchased both at a reasonable price. The store owner also threw in a box of music books. There was even a Book of Common Prayers for the Worship Leader. Their Sabbath devotions would have a bit of structure to them now. Evan wondered just a bit how many it would take to get that piano up the stairs into the house.

Clarice was charmed, especially by the piano. Each evening she enjoyed playing the songs she had learned as a girl. Her mother had patiently introduced the classics to her, and now they gave serenade to the twilight. Those who listened from their homes below, were also serenaded by melody and harmony. When Miss Clare invited Molly to learn to play the piano, she was eager to say, "Yes!"

One thing often leads to another. Miss Clare offered to teach Molly how to read and write, as well. Perhaps it was a latent missionary motivation, but while she was at it, why not teach Dory and Lily as well. If the men would learn, they could have their chance as well. One good thing does lead to another.

The spring Taro harvest was more abundant than Evan could imagine. Moesh made side rails to increase the capacity of the wagon. They took just over a thousand heads to the Lafayette store, and two hundred to Mr. Lester for merchandise credit. On the way home Mr. Evan explained to Moesh, "I want to give a gratuity to both you and Link of twenty dollars each, and Mr. Lester has given you permission to come into his store as long as you are accompanied."

Moesh was so happy hearing that, he clapped his hands and said, "Praise your God!"

A New Dear Friend

O nce again Evan was surprised to see a carriage next to the house when they turned into the Vermillion Plantation lane. As the wagon approached, the smile of doctor Bell appeared from within. He waved and walked toward the wagon as Moesh stepped off. "Hello Mr. Cossindale," the cordial physician said in greeting. "I'm sorry to bother you at home, but I have a rather urgent request. I recall the amazing recovery your carpenter experienced, and I wonder…" He didn't know exactly how to finish his request. He was a medical doctor in search of a very nonmedical cure.

"Dr. Bell it is always an honor to greet you, especial if there is a kindness I can offer in return for your many. How can I help you?" As Evan stepped up to the carriage he became aware that the good doctor was not alone.

The doctor explained his purpose. "My nephew, Captain Cal Perry, is a member of Col. Thomas Hindes' Mississippi Dragoons, an elite military strike force. Out here in our haven, we haven't been aware that England has been trying to retake the Louisiana territory from the United States. In January there was a vicious battle at Lake Borgne, for control of New Orleans, which the Brits lost soundly. However, in defense of his country, Cal suffered three near-fatal injuries. His leg was to be amputated, but his Dragoon comrades brought him to me in a last-ditch effort to save him. He also has gun-shot wounds to his side and chest. I have removed the bullets and controlled the bleeding, along with most of the infection, but his fever returns. There must be some infection that I have not been able to find." The doctor looked down at the ground rather than meet

33

Evan's gaze. "Is it possible we might try the spring water treatment that saved your carpenter? I'm at a loss what else to try."

Evan turned toward Moesh, "Would you fetch Link and the wooden beach chair, so we can move the Captain to the water? And I'll bet Lily would like to greet the doctor that fixed her arm."

The four men had little difficulty moving the heavily sedated patient to the shore. Dr. Bell helped remove his robe and he was gently situated in the shallow water. Molly agreed to hold his head to prevent him from inadvertently taking in water.

"There is no guarantee any of this will work on this brave man" Evan quietly said. "We have usually let folks soak for about an hour, but that may be more than his condition will allow. Let's see how he is faring in about half that time. He is welcome to stay in the cottage, and we can give him a bit more water tomorrow." He then offered the doctor accommodations in the big house. "The upstairs bedroom overlooks Vermillion Bay, if you would like to spend the night."

As they walked back to his carriage, the doctor replied, "I'm embarrassed to say that I must hurry back to Lafayette this evening, leaving you with his care." Then more seriously, he added, "and if Cal is too weak to make it, I will pay for his treatment and the return of his body, so the family can bury him with honor." He set a suitcase beside the carriage. "In the good fortune that he needs clothes, there are some in here."

In the shallow water the Seerier had discovered another seriously damaged host, and were busy with a cell replacement boost and an immunity stimulant. The endorphin signal was repeated several times. The rest would be up to Captain Perry.

For two days his life hung in the balance. Molly faithfully administered the glasses of cool spring water. When Lily brought him a bowl of gumbo broth in the evening she was prepared to find a dead body. When she brought a bowl of gumbo broth in the morning, she still had the same expectation. Moesh and Link moved the Captain into the water each day, and gave him outhouse breaks when he was not in the water. Molly's pitcher was emptied several times

On the fourth day when the men came to help him into the water, Cal was able to shuffle along under his own power, as long as they kept him steady. He assured them he was strong enough to return to Lafayette.

"You know, the last two weeks are kind of a blur for me," Cal said quietly. Moesh had folded a comforter as an extra soft cushion for the wagon seat. He rode in the wagon bed as Mr. Evan drove. "I remember the start of the battle. We were giving them a pretty good whoopin'. Then they brought up some artillery on our flank and it got real mean, real quick. The next thing I knew I was in Uncle Bell's office getting fixed up. Then I woke up in the cottage by the beach. That was real nice of you, Evan. I can't believe I feel this good, even with some aches. It's like I am getting stronger by the minute." His genuine smile was a great part of the morning.

"I don't know much about medicine," Evan said with a chuckle, "but I was pretty worried for you when you arrived. It makes me want to sing or something when I see that you are recovering." He held up his hand saying, "Don't worry I won't spoil the morning by barking a tune. I'm just looking forward to the look of joy on your uncle's face in a few minutes."

They chatted about the pleasant area, the privacy and the possibilities a man might have in starting a place of his own. Cal was surprised to know that Evan and Clarice had only been here for a couple years. He knew that his feelings were magnified by the buoyant mood he was enjoying. None the less, he wanted to talk with a certain lady named Rose, who would be relieved to learn that he had first of all survived his wounds, and secondly that he was seriously considering becoming a Louisiana farmer, maybe tobacco or cotton. His future felt only rosy!

"You haven't told me how much I owe you for this fantastic care I've received." He patted his obviously empty pockets.

Evan chuckled at his humor. "You know, we are pretty relaxed about that. I just want you to get healed first. Then you can send something to your uncle for me. We can work it out."

"There is a buzz of things going on in my head this morning... good things, even great things." The smile on Cal's face grew wider.

"I'm pretty sure my military days are over. My family is pretty well off, so I think my dad will be very happy to help me get a farm of my own." He became serious, "Evan, I think I want the sort of life you have made here. I want to be your neighbor. I know it sounds selfish as the dickens, and please forgive my avarice; this is the sort of life I have dreamed of." Impulsively he turned around and gave Moesh a pat on the back. "This is how we were meant to live! I'll get well and bring you my payment in full."

Moesh to the rescue

On their way back to Vermillion Plantation, Evan stopped at the Abbeville general store to let Moesh use his twenty dollar credit. He found Mr. Lester in a more grouchy mood than usual. He informed Evan that he had to throw out most of the Taro that were recently delivered. They were all culls, he said. Because of that, the credits were no longer on his account. Evan pointed to the large box still displaying perfectly good heads, and said, "That is the third and last time you have tried to cheat me." He spoke quietly so Moesh, who was fascinated at the items available to him, could not hear the encounter. "Moesh hates snakes. He cuts off their heads and dines on them. You are a grocer, Mr. Lester, but also a snake. You will honor those credits, or pay the consequences." Evan was surprised at the intense emotion he was feeling.

To his surprise, the merchant nearly collapsed. "Please help me," he nearly sobbed. "I don't know what to do. I'm just about broke, but still he comes to rob me."

"Who is robbing you?" Evan realized there was more to this situation than an irresponsible merchant.

"I don't know; I think he's a colored. He is hooded and wears white gloves. He has a shotgun and a bag. He just walks in when everyone is gone and tells me to put the money in the bag or he will kill me."

"This has happened more than once?" Evan asked in amazement.

"Yes, six times. About once a month, usually on Saturday, but once on Friday," the shopkeeper groaned.

"Have you reported this to your deputy?" Evan seemed shocked that a crime could be repeated without punishment.

"We don't have a deputy, and the Marshal is two hours away in Lafayette. I just don't know what I can do." His plaintive eyes searched Evan's face as though waiting for an answer to his dilemma.

"Moesh," Evan called. "Will you help us?" Of course he responded immediately. Evan told him briefly of the situation and wondered if Moesh would be willing to protect the store owner for a couple evenings until the robber returned.

"Shall I kill, or capture him?" was all Moesh asked for clarification.

"It would be best if you can capture him so we can find out where Mr. Lester's money has been hidden. But he must be stopped in any case." The slave nodded in understanding.

Evan suggested that since there was not enough time for Moesh to go home for his weapon and return before the store closed, perhaps Mr. Lester would close early and lock the door. Moesh would return tomorrow afternoon and each Friday and Saturday as needed.

Before they left, Moesh was intent on a purchase. "May Moesh buy some tobacco, and a white Sunday shirt, and one for Link too?" His soft voice warmed the hearts of the other two men. "We want to honor Miss Clare's God with white shirts."

On the third Saturday afternoon, Moesh rested in the back storeroom of the general store. He heard a voice shout, "Put the money in the bag!" He rose silently and went to the door, hoping that Mr. Lester had remembered not to block the way. Moesh peered through the ajar crack. Not five paces from him, a hooded man pointed a shotgun at the merchant. When Mr. Lester stepped to the cash drawer, the hooded man's head turned away from the storeroom, which was all the time Moesh needed to step out with his short lance and throwing stick. It was a whisper of rushing air, and the lance struck the back of the shoulder of the robber and passed through, protruding from his chest. There was a scream; then the shotgun fell to the floor, followed immediately by the skewered man. Moesh had a second lance prepared to hurl if it was needed. Fortunately for the robber, it was not needed.

Moesh drew the lance out of the wounded man's shoulder, and then stepped over him to secure his ankles together with a light rope. Using the same rope, he then fastened the man's hands behind his back, trying to ignore the groans of protest. "If you have a wagon or carriage, we can get him to the Marshal and be back by dark," he said nonchalantly to Mr. Lester.

The storekeeper, now fully confident of his own safety, pulled the hood off the head of his robber. "Well damn it to hell! That's Luis Nunez, one of my best customers. He has the tobacco plantation just at the edge of town!"

Softly Moesh said, "It seems to me he was one of your worst customers." He dragged the wounded man outside the store, to bleed in the street.

Nunez confessed everything to the Marshal. He was a careless gambler whose plantation couldn't keep up with his losses. Eventually the judge sentenced him to ten years at hard labor, and ordered his wife to pay restitution of $700 dollars to the storeowner. It might not have been all of Mr. Lester's losses, but certainly most. He was no longer afraid of going broke. Moesh had hero status at Mr. Lester's store, and Mr. Evan asked Dr. Bell to forward the news to his nephew that the tobacco plantation was going into a distress sale.

Evan found himself asking a philosophical question. "How can time pass so serenely, and at the same time so quickly?" The Taro harvest was again the best ever. With Link's help, he took almost sixteen hundred heads into Lafayette, and another hundred to Mr. Lester. Then it was time to harvest sugar canes, which produced another big crop. There were never less than three visitors a week at the beach. The pecan trees were starting to produce. Two full wagon loads of bags were taken to Lafayette, and the dried husks would be cook stove fuel for months. Lily gave birth to a healthy son, whom they named Adam, for he was like the Bible story of the first man. Clarice was pregnant again. How quickly time carries us along!

"Evan, Love, may I ask you a question?" He flinched, because that had become Clarice's way of opening a serious discussion. When he nodded, she asked, "How is our bank account. The plantation is earning money these days, is it not?"

"We've had a most satisfying year," he answered with a smile. He had no idea what was on her mind, after all, she was already pregnant again.

"I know I should leave the big decisions up to you, so forgive me if I am out of place. We receive more requests for our beach treatments than we can oblige, due to our limited hospitality space. What do you think of the idea of building a larger facility that might welcome four or five at a time? It could rest on the other side of the mound. If we cleared the brush down to the beach it would have easier access to the water, and take up no crop space. She had said all that she had planned. The seed was planted.

On his next trip to Lafayette, Evan had a meeting with Charlie the carpenter to discuss design, and construction of another addition to Vermillion Plantation. Weather permitting, construction would begin in the new year, 1818. He had a stack of letters waiting for him at the Abbeville store, most of them inquiries of the beach treatment. Mr. Lester joked that they would need a bigger box to hold them all. One of the letters, however, was of prime interest to him.

"Dear Mr. Cossindale; my prayers are that this finds you as well as I have come to be, completely healed and fit. No longer in the military, I am seeking your assistance in locating property in Louisiana. My uncle has informed me of the possibility of a tobacco plantation near you. Everything about those prospects seem ideal to me, and the brightest part is that Rose has agreed to become my wife. I will arrive in Lafayette via train on the 6th day of November, and wonder if you would have Moesh meet me and transport me to Vermillion Plantation, where I would like to revisit your splendid beach and drink again of the life-changing spring, the fountain of health. If it is not possible for those arrangements to fit your schedule, I will impress my family ties upon Uncle Bell. In any event, I will see you very soon. My heart is eager to be in your presence again. Cordially, Cal Perry."

The westbound train came to a stop amidst a cloud of steam. Evan watched the crowd of folks offloading. He reminded himself that the Cal Perry he last saw was a very wounded man. Then he saw him, tall and firm in stride, and beside him a man of color who had the bearing and intensity of a guard dog. Evan waved until he received one in return.

"You look much better than when we were last together," Evan said brightly. They shook hands, then embraced as brothers might .

"Thanks to you, I am completely recovered," Cal answered. "And this quiet man is Cain, my father's personal attendant. When father can't be with me, but wants me kept safe, Cain is my companion." They each carried a suitcase, but Cain's seemed considerably heavier, perhaps because his had a substantial amount of gold coins. A small rug was tied to it. Evan studied the facial markings trying to be a little less than obvious. Cal explained, "Those are tribal scars that identify him as part of the king's guard. When other slaves see them he usually gets a wide berth. Soon you will forget he is even with us." Cal was climbing onto the wagon, obviously eager to leave.

"Do you want to stop and greet your uncle, or be on our way to Abbeville? It's about a two hour ride, if you haven't consumed too much water."

"I've been on that rattling train for two days, and am very enthused about seeing a plantation that might be for sale. I'll look in on Uncle Bell before I leave." The agenda for the morning had been set. Once in Abbeville, they stopped at the general store to get directions to the Nunez plantation.

The rows of harvested tobacco plants looked barren, but the fields were very large, twice as big as Vermillion. "I wrote Mrs. Nunez a letter saying we would stop by today. Before I let my heart get too far into this dream, I need to make sure it is even available. Someone may have beaten me to it." Cal had a wide smile, in anticipation.

As they drove in the short lane, they studied the plain modest house, which was clean if less than impressive. There was a large drying shed for the tobacco leaves and some frightful huts for the workers. They were neither clean nor attractive. There was a general atmosphere of neglect to it all.

Cal said with a wave of his hand, "At least it has plenty of room for improvement!

They were welcomed into a home that smelled heavily of tobacco smoke and sweat, which made the glasses of tea taste like dirty water.

Benita Nunez welcomed them cheerily, thanking them for their interest in acquiring this very productive plantation. "I already have a handsome offer," she said brightly. "But I am open to others. There is a big demand for a place like this."

Cal thought to himself, "Let the games begin." Calmly he answered her, saying, "Well, Benita, within an hour's ride from here there are forty sections of land available at eighteen thousand per section. In fact we are on our way to one that has a lovely plantation five bedroom home with outbuildings, and a mile of beach. It is growing sugar cane, Taro and pecans, so it is hard to compare with tobacco." He shook his head as though in thought. "With the back taxes you owe, and the robbery restitution lien, I thought you might be interested in a way out of this." He stood as though to leave. "Thank you for your time. My counsel is that you take the offer you have. God's blessings to you, ma'am."

"But wait" Benita urged them to stay. "You haven't told me what your offer would be. You seem to know everything about this place. How much do you think it's worth?"

"With livestock, I would offer you thirty thousand dollars, knowing that those cribs must be torn down or burned and replaced, maybe the same with this house."

"The only livestock we have left…" her voice broke and she began to weep, "is the seven darkies, five men and two women. Luis lost everything else gambling." Her face was in her hands.

Speaking more gently, Cal said, "It is not my intention to capitalize on your misfortune. Neither is it my intention to give support to a careless man who has no business trying to run a plantation. Out of Christian charity, on top of that offer, I will pay the back taxes and the $700 to Mr. Lester. That is my top and final offer." Cal walked to the door with Evan right behind him. "Thank you for your time today Benita, and the sweet tea. Good luck selling this place."

Halfway to the wagon, he whispered to Evan, "I'll bet she accepts the offer before we get out to the road." It didn't even take that long. Before Evan had the wagon moving a tearful Benita Nunez was standing beside it saying, "Your offer is very generous. I accept it." She held out her frail hand for Cal to shake, binding the agreement.

Cal got out of the wagon to open his suitcase. Using the tailgate as a desk, he produced a purchase and sales agreement, upon which he made an addendum of $700 restitution and a blank line for back taxes. He signed his name, and Benita signed hers. He would take it into the Lafayette courthouse in the morning to see what else had to be done before money changed hands.

A few minutes later as they were following the twin wheel ruts toward Vermillion plantation, Cal said, "It's hard to believe. I spent two days getting here from Hattiesburg, and in less than two hours I have purchased a section of productive land for my bottom price. I had sales agreements made out for forty and fifty thousand dollars as well." Looking at the driver, he added, "And once again I have you to thank for it. You got the announcement to me, and helped me find my way to it. Thank you Evan. You truly are a once in a lifetime friend. And I haven't forgotten about the services debt I owe you from my first visit here.

Evan had been thinking ahead to the morning. "Cal, you can take the wagon in to Lafayette if you choose, or we have two saddle horses that would save you considerable time." Then he told his friend about the evening that Moesh had sent spears through the two unmanageable men. "I'll throw those horses and saddles in as part of whatever you think you owe from our first meeting. But if anyone asks you, it would be safest to say that they were part of your purchase from Luis Nunez. He is already in prison and can't deny it."

"You say he used a wooden assist to throw the spear?" Cal was interested in matters of weaponry. "The Persians had something they called an 'atlatl.' A strong man could hurl a spear a hundred paces, with reasonable accuracy. It sounds like Moesh picked up some international skill. I would love to see a demonstration of that"

Cal was happy to see his old cottage, although to tell the truth, his memories of it were fleeting. He had been so very weak. When Evan asked if Cain would want a separate room, Cal chuckled and told him that Cain slept on the floor in front of the door. "He is Moslem," Cal explained, "three times a day he uses his prayer rug, and at night it is his sleeping rug. It works for him." There was time before supper to have a leisurely soak, accompanied by a pitcher of spring water. Cal couldn't remember feeling better, save for the ache in his heart from missing the closeness of his Rose.

All the legal stuff was cared for in three days. Cal owned a section of prime tobacco land, and with some prayer and conversation with Rose, he would figure out what to do with the house and help. As he was preparing to leave he gave Evan thirty $20 gold coins. "I still feel in your debt, since my horses are in your barn," he jokingly told his friend. "But in just a few months we will be close enough to share a meal now and then. I'm going to need help."

"I'm really good at helping other people with their problems," Evan answered, equally moved by the moment's tenderness. They shook hands, then embraced as brothers sometimes do.

The Hospitality House was finished by Easter. Facing the bay, it had a wide covered porch the width of the house, with a sun deck on top. Either place was a wonderful opportunity to watch a sunset over Vermillion Bay. Bougainvillea plants began to cover the north side of the house with bright blossoms in spring. Inside there were two guest rooms downstairs and four upstairs, with access to the deck. The parlor dining room had twelve foot ceilings, and crystal wall lamps. Dory continued to do the cooking in the main kitchen, and served the food at the convenience of the guests. Lily's job became laundering the linens and swimming robes from the guestrooms. They were a contented and efficient team.

Evan was thrilled at Clarice's easy delivery of a second daughter, Suzanne. The labor pains had begun on Friday evening, and early Saturday morning their family had increased; a sweet daughter and mom were resting comfortably.

Evan talked with Moesh about an important decision. "The Lafayette store has asked me to double our production of Taro. When I look at our farm there is only one available place for more plants." He had given it serious thought and was intent not to encroach on the main house or hospitality house. "Do you think we could make our east boundary line a double row of Taro?" He valued Moesh's opinion.

"Yes, Mr. Evan," the answer was given with a gentle smile. "If we are careful with exact pacing, two plow lines, down and back, should loosen the ground. When we harvest in a while, we'll have enough starts to make… over three thousand new plants." He raised his eyebrows in happiness. "That's enough for double, and more left for the house." There was a small pause as though he was carefully choosing his words. "And if we are very cautious around the quicksand, we could do the same thing with the west boundary, perhaps even more when we clear it from the brush." He was careful to never mention the bonus that Mr. Evan always remembered at harvest time. This might mean extra bonus too.

Being a man who liked to live without a debt, Evan recalled a lingering obligation. He wrote a letter to J. Henry Higgins at the Tallahassee Herald: "Good day to you Mr. Higgins. It is a lovely spring day here in Vermillion Plantation. We have recently completed our expansion of the Hospitality House and would like to open it with honor. It has been nearly four years since you were last with us, and our records show that we owe you a deluxe beach treatment." He smiled as he wrote such syrupy lines. "Our accommodations now include three meals and unlimited views of the sunset. All silliness aside, it would be an honor to welcome you to our home again. I believe you have an investment in the progress of this lovely slice of heaven. We have constant availability so you can arrive at your convenience. Cordially yours, Evan Cossindale." He really didn't expect an answer.

Perhaps he was still thinking about the letter when he saw the carriage coming down the lane. His first assumption was that it carried Mr. Higgins. But to his surprise and joy, Cal stepped out; then helped a lovely lady with dark hair and brown eyes. He waved as both Evan and Clarice came out to welcome them.

After he introduced Rose, Cal said, "We just dropped by to see the new Hospitality House. Charles told us about it. He has agreed to build a new home for us at the tobacco farm." They strolled around to the front porch. It was a very inviting building. Inside they commented on the twin stairways to the upstairs rooms. "He also told me about the fireplace. What a smart idea to build a security vault into it. I have asked him to do the same thing with ours." Evan wasn't sure how he felt about others knowing about the secret vault.

Molly served them sweet tea in the parlor. Clarice took advantage of the moment to tell them that Molly had been an outstanding piano student and was ready to perform her first recital as soon as Evan brought the new grand piano to the parlor.

"I didn't know we were getting another piano," the innocent husband said.

"I think I just told you, my love," she said with a twinkle in her eyes. "Wouldn't it look outstanding there in the corner?" Obviously Clarice had given the idea more than a little thought.

"As long as we are making new plans," Cal also took advantage of the moment, "I've been wondering about shared labor. We are about to top the tobacco plants to force larger leaves. If we could have the help of Moesh and Link, I would be happy to send our darkies over to help with your sugar cane harvest. That way we wouldn't need to hire help." Obviously he had also been giving the future some practical thought too.

They chatted until Dory brought out bowls of shrimp chowder. She had mashed the Taro making a thick and rich soup, made creamy by the canned milk. Rose felt more than welcomed; she had the comfortable inclusion of long-time friends. When Clarice said it was time for her to relieve Lily from the nursery and feed Susanne, the guests agreed that there would be many such lunches. "As soon as our place is built we will return your courtesy."

Evan was quick to say, "But don't wait that long before you come back. Our house is always blessed by your presence."

Cal replied, "Then would you mind if I fill a jar of spring water for the ride home? I brought my own jug." The four friends found humor and laughter in his appreciation.

It took two years for Evan to find that piano for the Hospitality House. He finally found an estate sale that also provided chairs and occasional tables that made the parlor more receptive. During that time Clarice filled the nursery with another daughter, Esther, and Lily had another son as well. They named him Noah, because they liked the Bible story of survival.

Mr. Higgins returns

Evan looked up from his chore of sharpening the harvesting blades. The sugar canes were full and tender, ready for another gathering. The carriage that came down the lane was unfamiliar to him, and there were no visitors scheduled. He walked out to greet the arrivals.

A well dressed man of color stepped from the driver's seat. "Good morning sir. Is this the home of Evan Cossindale?" His accent was European of some sort, and his bearing was that of a gentleman's attendant.

"It is," Evan said warmly. "How can I be of service to you?" He noted that the other person in the carriage was bundled in a travelling robe, even on this warm summer morning.

"My name is Sydney, sir. I am in employ of Mr. Henry Higgins who has most recently returned from a lengthy stay at a European Palsy Clinic. The doctors there finally gave up hope for his recovery. Mr. Higgins remembers fondly the successful recovery he experienced here at your fresh water spring, and hopes he may have another attempt." The man looked closely at Evan, and then said, "Frankly I believe he has also given up hope of recovery. The palsy has affected his face. His eye droops open so he is troubled with dry irritation. He must wear an eye-patch for protection. His mouth is also affected. He has trouble speaking and he cannot control the drooling. I so hope you can help him." Sydney seemed ready to cry. "His hands tremble so violently that he must be fed. It is really quite sad to see such a strong man brought to this end."

"This is not a clinic of any sort, neither is it an end," Evan said quietly. "It is a place where folks come to relax and receive refreshment. I will be very glad if that can help Mr. Higgins." He turned and called for Moesh and Link, who could use one of the wooden beach chairs to carry Mr. Higgins to the cottage to change into a beach robe. Then he could be safely and comfortably seated in the shallow water.

"Molly Honey," Evan directed, "will you go with Mr. Higgins. He has trouble swallowing, so just give him little sips of the spring water. Be careful that he doesn't choke on it." It may not have been a perfect plan, but it was a workable one.

In the following hour Mr. Higgins felt again the comforting warm water of Vermillion Bay, and tasted the pure sweetness of fresh spring water. Of course he was unaware of the cloud of Seerier who identified another broken host in great need of repair. Their administration of a cell replacement boost and an immunity stimulant began its healing work. The endorphin signal was repeated several times. When he was finally dried and redressed by Sydney, he was helped into Hospitality House for a pleasant lunch.

"I'b feehing mu bett," he said brokenly. "bery mu bett." While his mouth and face couldn't show signs of refreshment, there was definitely a new sparkle in his eyes. "Ma I sta for a cup more day?"

Sydney was quick to offer an interpretation, "Mr. Higgins would request a couple more days here in your splendid care." There was an attempt at a nod from Mr. Higgins. They were shown to the two lower bedrooms, which provided easy access for the chair transportation to the beach twice a day. On the fourth day Mr. Higgins said he was feeling strong enough to make his own way without the strong assistance of Moesh and Link. On the morning of the ninth day he finally admitted that he had obligations in Tallahassee that could no longer be put off. Amazingly, however, he no longer was troubled by either a drooping eyelid or mouth, and his hands were practically calm.

"Mr. Cossindale, if I had accepted your invitation three years ago, I would have saved myself eighteen months of frustration and thousands of dollars of doctor's expenses. I really don't know how to thank you. There will, of course, be a money transfer into your account, but that seems much too shallow. I have been wondering if there is something larger that I could also offer to you. I have been most impressed with Miss Molly. Last evening she played the piano beautifully. I remember her playing 'Love Divine All Loves Excelling;' when I asked her if she knew what the song meant she gave me an insightful and very faith-filled answer. In Tallahassee we have a normal school, a collage that teaches teachers. Two of the faculty members are in my employ and reside in my home with light duties. They would be delighted to tutor Miss Molly for a couple years if we have the permission of you and her parents. She has received excellent grounding here from Miss Clarice. Now she might be instructed in a wider understanding of literature, mathematics and geography."

Evan was aware how improved Mr. Higgins' speech had become, and how symptom free he was this morning. "But she has no wardrobe for such an opportunity," he offered.

Smiling sincerely, Mr. Higgins said, "My daughters, Meg and Lisle, who are the tutors, will take care of that with pleasure."

Finally, when Moesh and Dory were told of the offer, she wept, thinking it was a permanent separation of their family. Mr. Higgins assured them all that he would bring Molly back regularly, so he could enjoy the gift of renewed vigor from the spring water. Without knowing the impact on the future, the decision was made to expand Molly's education, formally.

Tallahassee School

She sat on the floor behind the carriage seat; it was the first time in ten years that Molly had been off the plantation. The scenery for the first three hours was modestly interesting. There were a couple new home sites being developed, but mostly they were passing brush and trees. Then as they approached the town, she was delighted in the variety and number of homes. In Lafayette, they boarded a train, which was a totally fascinating experience. She was guided to a compartment which had rich carpeting that felt wonderful to stand on. There were upholstered chairs, and windows from which she could watch people or countryside glide by. In New Orleans they remained in the compartment while some passengers departed and others boarded. Sydney quietly shared with her that New Orleans was the center of the slave trade, perhaps the largest in the world. She had seen many in chains.

"It seems strange to me," she shared quietly. "I have only a faint memory from the trials before Mr. Evan came to the auction yard. I understand that he bought us; I am a slave. But the kindnesses we have received makes it hard for me to relate to that." She pointed to a line of nearly naked people in chains. "The very first thing he did for us was buy us clothes, and then Miss Clare cooked delicious food for us. They have always protected us, even from the first day."

"You were, and are, very fortunate," Sydney said, remaining in that quiet voice. "Very few slaves could say that their treatment is even as good as an animal's." He shuddered, perhaps in memories better left unvisited. "Rest assured, in Mr. Higgins' care, you will continue in comfort and care."

The train slowly pulled out of the station toward Tallahassee.

Taro harvest, sugar cane, Taro harvest and then decorate the Hospitality House for Christmas, the time passed so swiftly that the Vermillion Plantation lost count of the dozens of guests who visited the beach treatment. A year fluttered by as silent as a great moth, and then another. Before Christmas Clarice announced that she was once again expecting.

It was Lisle's idea to have a spring graduation party where Molly could experience the grace of a social gathering. It would be a perfect conclusion to her two years with them. Meg immediately warmed to the idea, offering three or four names for the trusted guest list. They agreed it would be a grand way to conclude their instruction time together. Molly saw little value in a dinner, but because her teachers seemed so excited about it, she knew she could learn something from it. In reality she was so anxious to get back to Vermillion Plantation that she knew she could endure any last ritual. It had been over two months since she had seen her family, and the prospect of the early Taro harvest was exciting for her.

"So, let's invite John James, Senator Stanton's assistant, and his lady friend Amelia Knight; Jacob Post from Florida Security Bank, and I think it would be fun to seat Elizabeth Pease next to him. They both have some strong notions about the future of Tallahassee. I'll sit next to John Beaumont, who just graduated from Virginia Military Institute, and you can sit next to brother Daniel. Let's ask Danny to do the blessing." Now all they had to work out was the menu, and set the date so all might attend.

The night of the party Molly was a vision of beauty. Meg had found a pale yellow velvet dress that highlighted her rich brown skin. Lisle had offered a strand of pearls that complimented the neckline. The shoes were more uncomfortable than Molly was used to, but Meg assured her that the Italian men who put the heels under the shoes did it to force women to stand very erect and show off their chests. That made Molly smile and endure the discomfort. A comb with a gold accent flower was in her hair. All in all, she could hardly recognize the lovely woman looking at her from the mirror.

Before the dinner was served, Lisle asked Molly if she would consider playing a couple melodies on the piano for the guests. The low opinion these socialites had about slave girls, was instantly challenged by a lovely piano sonata, and then two or three familiar church tunes. Familiar, that is, to the women who attend church. For the men they were just nice tunes.

During the meal Molly enjoyed the happy conversation as folks shared their current concerns about city growth, or worries about the spread of crime, or the discussion about the increase of French speaking Acadians. Lieutenant Beaumont turned to Molly and asked about the first selection she had played for them.

Happy to be included, she answered, "That was Mr. Beethoven's Piano Sonata Number 14."

"I haven't heard that before," Miss Knight said. "Is that a new composition?"

"I believe it is about twenty years old, played mostly in Europe. He is a prolific composer."

Before she could say any more, the Lieutenant asked, "You say the second one is a church tune? Which church?" It didn't sound like a dangerous question.

"I believe he is an Anglican clergy named Charles Wesley. The tune is 'Soldiers of Christ Arise, and Put Your Armor On.'"

Now he had something to smile about. "I like that; it sounds militant."

"Well, sort of," Molly said, also with a smile. "The armor in question is described in Ephesians 6, as the whole armor of God. They are spiritual tools to assist in the battle with evil." She was wise enough to say no more. But perhaps she had already said too much.

"I suspect that slavery is the evil with which you would do battle. Perhaps you would join with the abolitionists." His smile grew wider. "Molly, I confess that you are the most talented and informed female slave I have ever known." The young Lieutenant's crassness was a perfect reflection of the standard social order. None the less, it made the other table guests most uncomfortable.

Lisle's voice was soft with concern; "Molly, since our callous friend has brought up the subject, is there anything you want to say about how you arrived in America?"

With near reverence, Molly answered. "Not a day goes by without my parents reminding me how fortunate we were to be purchased by Mr. Evan and Miss Clare. Our lives are full and happy."

Not wanting to leave the social correction hanging, Lieutenant Beaumont pressed, "Do you remember your home in Africa?"

"Not very well," Molly admitted. "I believe I was a happy five year old, with an eight year old brother, when the slavers attacked. There were very many of them with whips and guns. Our defense of spears and knives was little help. The old were bludgeoned to death. I do remember my brother, Mistan, was trying to protect me when he was struck down. His wounds were too serious for him to survive. He died in the hold of the ship as we were crossing the Atlantic." Just recalling the past had a way of twisting Molly's speech pattern in a way that made her want to be quiet.

"That's why I am always armed," the Lieutenant said with bravado. "Today it is necessary to be protected."

Daniel asked in surprise, "John do you mean you are carrying a weapon now?"

"Yes, of course. I don't go anywhere without a sidearm." His military bluster should have been a warning, not a source of curiosity.

"May I see it?" Daniel asked, not completely convinced of the presence of a weapon at the table.

John reached inside his dinner jacket and produced a silver derringer, saying, "It's only a single shot; but one is usually enough."

Daniel reached across the table toward him. "May I see it, please?"

"Yes. Of course. But be careful it is always loaded." It made him feel empowered to display something that was potentially lethal.

No one could tell for sure which one caused the accident. The simple truth is that the gun slid off Daniel's hand, and did a half turn in the air. It struck the table on its hammer. Even though it was not cocked, the tiny firing pin hit the cap hard enough to detonate the powder, which caused the pistol to fire directly at Daniel's chest.

With shock, the young man looked at the growing blood pattern on his shirt, saying, "You shot me." His face slumped onto the table as he fainted.

Molly may have been the first one to stand. "May I help lay him on the floor?" she asked. Servants came running to the emergency, and Meg told them to remove Mr. Daniel's jacket and shirt so they could understand the injury. Mr. Higgins burst in dressed in a night robe, saying, "What's all the … Oh Jesus!" Quickly the dinner guests made their way out of the dining room toward the door. Obviously, none of them had any experience with wounded folks, or motivation to assist.

Lisle noticed there was no exit wound. "The bullet is still inside him." Then on closer examination, they could see a bluish bump on his back. "There it is, but how can we get it out? It will poison him if we don't!" There was some discussion about getting him to a doctor, but no available care seemed timely. "We must remove that ourselves," Lisle said with conviction, even though the prospects made her tremble with dread.

Molly said in a soft voice, "I saw my father remove snake venom from Link's leg. I would try to help if you choose." It was a ray of hope in a moment of urgency.

Meg almost wept, "Oh, Molly, please help Daniel."

Mr. Higgins asked with a panicked voice, "What do you need?" Molly was standing in a circle of people who didn't have a better idea.

"Do you have something very sharp, and an empty bottle?" The absurdity of it seemed that this was approaching an unbelievable moment. But one of the kitchen help produced a brandy bottle nearly empty. Mr. Higgins quickly offered, "I have a razor?" Molly agreed that would be the best. In just another moment one was provided.

She asked Daniel if he could hear her. When he nodded, she propped his head on her lap and offered him a swallow or two of the brandy. Then she asked the kitchen folks to empty the rest, and place the bottle in hot water.

Her hands were trembling a bit when the razor was offered to her, but calmness was necessary. She prayed a silent prayer, asking for courage and guidance. Placing Daniel face down on the floor, she felt the hard protrusion with her fingers. "Daniel, sir, I am so sorry to hurt you. Please forgive me." She carefully drew the sharp edge across the bulge, feeling the flesh part. Daniel groaned a bit, but lay still. She repeated the process across the other way, making a clean cross opening. She wiped a bit of blood off and asked for the heated bottle and a cool wet cloth.

"Lisle, I will hold the open bottle firmly over the wound if you will wrap the cloth around it to cool it off there should be suction." It had worked when her dad did it! There was an awkward moment when their arms were in each others' way, but when Lisle wrapped the wet cold cloth around the hot bottle, tightly pressed against Daniel's back, an amazing thing happened. The wound widened slightly. A dark lead sphere appeared, and then popped to the surface.

"I've never seen anything like that!" Mr. Higgins murmured.

Using the edge of her fingers, Molly massaged the projectile the rest of the way out, as Daniel once again moaned from the discomfort. Then with the back edge of the razor, she rolled it away from the wound. It had worked! "Now if we can reheat the bottle and do all that again, we can draw out the bad blood that has collected inside." It had taken only three or four minutes, so why was she feeling shaken, and close to tears?

Meg knelt beside Molly and embraced her graciously. "You are so much more than I ever expected. God has used you to save him. Thank you Molly. Thank you!" She was also trembling, and in tears. The second evacuation brought out a black clot and more blood. Now he was ready to be bound with bandages. "Captain Perry had this sort of wound when they brought him to Vermillion Plantation. He enjoyed a full recovery," Molly reported. "How soon can we get Daniel there?"

In answer to her question, the west bound train chugged out of the Tallahassee station just after dawn, carrying Sydney, Mr. Higgins, Lisle, Molly and a semiconscious Daniel. By the next morning they were in New Orleans, and by noon in Lafayette.

Before supper, Molly cradled her wounded friend in Vermillion Bay, now assured that he would survive such a nasty wound.

The Higgins group remained at Vermillion Plantation for eight more days. It was a time of shifting attitudes for them. Mr. Higgins grew ever fonder of Molly, willing to sit all evening with her, listening to wonderful music and discussing its meaning. Lisle struggled with her feelings, which had first known Molly as a student, then a lifesaving hero. In this new peaceful setting, however, she was a servant who brought them pitchers of water while they lounged beside the bay, or who helped serve every meal. There was a deep social fracture here that seemed unnatural to Lisle. Daniel had only known her as a lovely dark skinned woman who was complex, yet endearingly humble. He recalled how tenderly she had apologized for hurting him, as she saved his life. Each opportunity he had to be in her company he admired her more, and more.

As they were preparing to take their leave of the Plantation, Mr. Higgins said with a catch in his voice, "This is the third time I have been here, and each time was life changing. How can I ever thank you?" Sydney was about to help Lisle climb into the carriage, but she turned so she could also have a farewell word. She embraced Molly tenderly saying, "You have shown me how flawed my Christian faith has been. I hope we see one another again, But if we don't, I pledge to you that many women of color will know of you, and be blessed by the lessons you have taught me. Thank you." She was weeping again.

Daniel took the longest to say goodbye. First he embraced Molly and gently kissed her cheek. While still holding her in his arms he said, "I must return to this place; it's like an Eden. I don't know how, but soon, real soon I will return. Thank you from the bottom of my heart." His voice also broke, and he kissed her cheek again.

That summer there seemed to be more mosquitoes, and more storms than usual. One even blew the waves of the bay up the beach to the Hospitality House stairs. Was it her imagination, or were there more irritations for Molly? She was very careful not to give expression to them, but Dory seemed to understand. One evening in their house, she sat down beside Molly and said, "It is very hard to be a servant, then an honored guest and student, then a servant again." She was quiet for a moment then asked, "What is the best lesson you learned in Mr. Higgins' house?"

"I learned," Molly took in a ragged breath, "that we all have value, slaves and whites. We all can learn, and become better people." Her mother was about to add to that insight, but Molly continued. "We all have fears, and make stupid mistakes that we wish we could take back."

Her mother's hand seemed more wrinkled than Molly remembered. It held Molly's hand and she asked softly, "Did you make mistakes there?"

A tear formed in Molly's eyes, and she nodded. "I forgot for a little while that I am a slave. I was asked if I remembered anything from my African home. If I had declined, or told some simple story, instead of the slavery account, perhaps there would never have been a mention of a gun, and Mr. Daniel wouldn't have been hurt."

Dory looked deeply into her daughter's eyes, eyes that seemed wise for her nineteen years. "It is easy here in Mr. Evan's care, to forget that we are slaves. He never harshly reminds us." She patted Molly's knee and said even more tenderly, "But we must never assume fault for other's mistakes and sins. I believe you so admire Mr. Daniel that you are grieving his injury." Then with a knowing smile, she added, "and perhaps you are missing him especially."

Molly had an embarrassed smile. "He kissed me on the cheek… twice."

"I saw that," her mother nodded. "And I believe that he is missing you very much at this moment. You are an extraordinary woman."

But Molly wasn't the only one irritated that summer. In Tallahassee, it was Daniel's job to write editorials for his father's newspaper. He had been aware of a growing tension in the slave-owner's world. There was very nearly as many slaves as there were owners, and management was an on-going issue. To be sure, slavery was an economic necessity, yet increasingly it seemed unjust and abusive. Some of his articles, especially since his injury, had been critical of the plight of slaves and the hopeless prospects for any redemptive change. That made for polarized discussions, and brisk newspaper sales, both of which his father welcomed.

Some of the irritations were much smaller. Mr. Evan had to rid the big house of two bats that completely terrorized the children, and a very pregnant Clarice was less than happy as well. Link agreed that there were more bats than usual, because there were so many mosquitoes for them to forage at night. "Bats are looking for a place to sleep after they have eaten," he suggested. "If you will allow me to use a few scrap boards and a burlap sack, I can put a nice resting place on the side of the barn that will keep the bats out of the house, and there will be more of them to eat the mosquitoes."

"Link, if you will do that, I'll bet Miss Clare will give you an extra slice of pie for supper," Evan said with a big grin. When it was installed, the flat shelter had an opening at the bottom which allowed the bats easy access to a dark space, and the burlap allowed them to easily climb up inside it. At twilight when they took flight, there were dozens and dozens that made an impressive sight. There were fewer insects, and no more invaders in the big house.

Daniel returned just before the sugar cane harvest. He rode down the lane on a rented horse, with a small bundle tied behind the saddle. Moesh was the first to recognize him and called out a cheerful welcome, alerting those in the big house. Before he could dismount, there was a circle of friends sharing their happy greeting, none smiling more radiantly than Molly.

"I feel as honored as a politician," he said brightly as he slid down. Evan noted that he still favored his right arm, so the healing had not removed all discomfort from the wounded young man.

One by one each person shared their happiness to see him again. "How long can you stay with us?" Evan asked. He was grateful that the Hospitality House had more than enough room to host Daniel for as long as he wanted.

"That sort of depends on you all," he answered with a boyish grin. "If I could have another cup of that delightful spring water, I'd like to make a proposal." Molly was already headed for the pitcher of fresh water.

As they sat in the shade of the porch, Daniel told them of his request. "You must be aware that there is growing tension in the plantations that have many slaves. The Abolitionists are more and more critical of the treatment those slaves are receiving. Vermont has already outlawed slavery, and has been the center of a growing debate. I see big trouble on the horizon, and it is coming our way. So the purpose of my visit is threefold; I want to see you good friends again, and secondly, my injury could benefit from a beach treatment, I believe you call it, to finish the healing. That can be accomplished in five days if you have room for me. The third purpose is less defined. I want to be a spokesman in the slavery discussion, and I know very little about it." He paused, very nearly blushing with the audacity he was feeling. "I'd very much like you to help instruct me on the subject; to allow me to live with you through the harvest season, to see how your slaves are treated and how they function in this idyllic setting. If you can introduce me to Captain Perry, I would like to see how his slaves are treated as well." He took a deep breath, suggesting that he was nearing a conclusion. "My father is interested in publishing an account of my time on the land, as it were. He would be glad to compensate you for my time here, but does not want me to be afforded the comforts that a typical guest would receive, but suggests I live either in a small tent, or in the barn, if you will allow it." There, it was said, and each person who heard the proposal had a different notion of it. No one thought it was inappropriate, but they wondered how they could allow one who they already admired and treasured, to be debased or denigrated in any way. The porch was quiet as each person considered the request, but all eyes were on Mr. Evan, who would do the right thing.

"Daniel, you are always welcome in this place. What you are suggesting is unusual, but based on the nobility of information. I believe this will be a great time of instruction for you. Use a corner of the barn for your bed, if you like. Since we will be topping the canes next week, you could make a right comfortable mattress with the leaves. Mr. Cal's folks will be here the following week to chop canes, and another group of drivers will transport them to the sugar mill. That will be an ideal time to hear from other slaves. We also need a load of Taro to go into Mr. Lester's store in Abbeville, and a big one to go into Lafayette. I think we can keep you pretty busy for three or four weeks."

Link explained that initially he and Lily had their evening meals in the big house with everyone. But now that there were two toddlers, who were both noisy and messy, they had started eating in their own house, bowls of food from the big house kitchen. If Daniel would like to join them, he was always welcome.

Dory explained that she tried to have supper prepared to accommodate guests who might want to have some beach time before supper. Dinner was prepared to be served, eaten, and the dishes done by sunset. That way no special lighting was necessary in the dining room or kitchen. That also allowed time for Molly to serenade the guests before it was time to retire for the evening. Clarice added that with their children, she liked feeding them a bit earlier, so she could enjoy dining with guests, and having the privilege of adult company.

Moesh invited Daniel to accompany him on his shrimping excursions three or four times a week, as Dory had need for them in her menus. Dragging the shrimp sock along the bay bottom for a bit usually produced an ample supply of the seafood, and on those days when a morning trip to Mr. Lester's allowed for some sausage to add to the pot, it was doubly delightful.

The porch conversation only reaffirmed Daniel's initial notion that here was a group of people who were functioning in efficient harmony and maximum productivity. While slavery was present in this grouping, it was secondary to trust and respect that out shown any injustice. Molly's smile had not faded since she heard that Daniel would be with them for more than a brief visit.

The following afternoon Daniel was rowing the small boat as Moesh paid out the thin rope that connected to the trailing contraption. "Go just a little slower, Mr. Daniel sir, so the trap can sweep along the bottom of the bay. That's where the shrimp live. They try to escape, but just swim into the open sock and are trapped. It is the easiest hunting I have ever enjoyed." He turned to study the angle of the trailing line.

"You asked me what I feel about slavery. At first I hated the slavers and all white men. Slavery opens the lid to reveal what's in a man's heart. Slavers were cruel, evil, greedy, ugly men. The sailors on the ship were the worst. Only by hiding behind me was Dory spared the mischief of their lust. Lily was not so lucky, and the consequence of their cruelty was such that they were ready to destroy her because of her injuries. Because we were captured slaves, their hearts were shown to be evil. But Mr. Evan did not know what to do with a slave when he bought us. Every day we give thanks for his wonderful heart. In Africa we lived in a mud hut with no stove or bed, wore skins and frequently did not have fresh water or enough to eat. Here he gives us clothes, a fine house to live in, and a large garden to grow our own vegetables. We even get to visit a store, which we had never seen before. There are very many wonderful things in this new land for us, all because of Mr. Evan's loving heart. We will die in his defense; we love him so much." Moesh's voice quivered in the tender feelings he was sharing.

"Moesh, are you suggesting that slavery has been a good thing for your family?" Daniel couldn't imagine a positive answer to that question.

"No not slavery! I had to watch the dead body of my eight year old son dragged out of the ship's hold and thrown over the side like trash. I had to endure a man bidding to buy my lovely wife and six year old daughter so he could have bed sport on her. By the way I had the opportunity to take the life of that evil man when he came a second time for Molly." Moesh was quiet for a moment as though reflecting on the truth he was trying to make plain. "But when Mr. Evan purchased us, our world was corrected, because he is correct. Miss Clare has taught Molly to read, to play beautiful music, and carry herself like a princess. None of that could have happened to us accept the auction yard. Slavery shows the heart of an owner, many are evil, harsh and ruthless. I am grateful that some have honor, and treat theirs with kindness." He pulled up the shrimp sock and nearly filled a bucket with the delicacies.

Daniel was still thinking about Moesh's words as he floated in Vermillion Bay. It was his beach time. Regardless of what the day might bring, this time was his very favorite. His body was surprisingly refreshed. He was not only clean, but in less discomfort from his wound. The very best part of this experience was Molly's attention with a pitcher of cool spring water. As always, they were not alone. Surrounding them and doing their unique interaction, the unseen Seerier were busy making ministrations of mercy.

The days that followed were without a doubt the most demanding physical labor Daniel had ever done. But they were also the most entertaining. For example, as he watched four year old Adam staggering to carry a ten or twelve pound Taro head to the wagon, Daniel laughed with delight. He asked Link if that heavy work might not injure the boy. "It will make his back and legs stronger," the father said with equal delight. "I think he will become a strong worker for the plantation." Daniel's laughter ended as he realized that slavery was handed down to the next generation, even though Adam had been born here in Louisiana.

The labor became intense when the sugar cane harvest began. It was easiest to strip the leaves off the canes while they were still standing. Once bare, the canes could then be topped and chopped to be loaded on the wagon. Daniel looked at the long row of canes in front of him. The others were already far ahead on their rows, and they were working without the comfort of gloves. He reached up to strip off another cane. Moesh's soft voice whispered advise, "Mr. Daniel, sir, if you have a lighter touch on the cane, the leaves come off without effort. I think you are working harder than the rest of us, and making us look lazy." He demonstrated how a looser grip around the cane could easily strip the leaves.

"Thank you Moesh. I thought you were stronger than me, now I see it is a matter of skill. I will work smarter." He followed the example and was surprised how easily the leaves separated from the cane. "Now I have it, I believe." He was fairly certain he would still be slower than the others.

At the end of the first day of labor, Mr. Evan asked the folks from Mr. Cal's plantation if they would care to have a bit of a swim before going home. At first there was reluctance from the men for they feared it was some sort of a test. But when Moesh assured them it was an acceptable offer, they fairly frolicked in the warm water. Daniel was shocked to see the severe scars on their backs and knew he had to discover the cause. Perhaps after a bit more labor with them he would earn their trust, and they would tell him their story.

The happiest surprise in the afternoon, however, was the offer from Mr. Evan of a small pouch of smoking tobacco and a cob pipe for each man, including Daniel. It was his way of expressing gratitude for their help. As the five men set out on the road home, there was little sign of fatigue from their labor, just the happy voices and lingering waft of smoke of rewarded men. Daniel was convinced that this opportunity to share in the basic labor was of immense value. He was also convinced that these lessons in dignity and appreciation would be poorly received by those who wanted to maintain the harsh institution of traditional slavery. When Daniel asked Evan about the expense of his gratuities, the answer was bright and easy, "What expense? I traded two Taro heads for the pipes and tobacco. By the next harvest those two heads will develop eight more. I just think it is good business."

The day the large cane wagon rolled in was pretty well organized. Moesh and Link had chopped about a hundred feet of the second row so the wagon could straddle it as the men on either side chopped and loaded their canes. It went smoothly as long as Moesh and Link could stay ahead. Daniel realized he had been left out of the assignments intentionally. His job was to accompany the wagon to the mill, to guarantee an accurate weigh in. Those hours began with little conversation; but by the time they had unloaded and were headed back to Vermillion, Daniel was learning more than he expected about slavery.

"Yes sir, our Master uses the whip sometimes. I guess I know why, but it seems to give him as much pleasure as it gives us pain. He uses the young women for his own pleasure too. There are a couple young men who are products of that, part colored and part white. I suspect they will have more trouble than any of us."

When Daniel asked about slave sales, he sadly learned more. "Yes sir, the Master gets rid of anyone who causes trouble after a few beatings. Mostly he sells strong young men. He probably knows that they are the ones most likely to fight back. He also sells some of the women who are too old for his bed sport. He sold my wife and daughter because he was mad at me. I spoke out of turn and he beat me, then broke up my family. You see how Moesh and Link have their families? That's not the case very often." Just listening to the driver's story, made Daniel sad.

By the time the wagon was loaded for the second time, it was time for Molly to bring out a tray of gumbo bowls, and all the men enjoyed a pipe of tobacco. That scenario was repeated in the afternoon, and then again the next two days. When the work was finished for the day and they were smoking by the beach, Daniel made a point to ask Mr. Perry's men about their experience of having a new owner. The one with the scarred back was sullen until Moesh assured him that Daniel would respect the information. There would be no trouble. Then the words tumbled out.

"Mr. Nunez was the meanest white man I ever met. He beat us, but he also beat his little wife. He was worse than a wild animal. When he gambled and lost, we all knew that trouble was coming, and he most always lost. He would swear at us, then out came the whip. He even beat his horses, until he lost them too. Then it was more grief for us. We're happy that Moesh speared him. We just wished he had killed him outright. It would have been better to have him dead in the ground than alive in prison." Daniel didn't know about that story, but was sure there was a proper reason behind it.

"Mr. Perry is sure enough a different kind of owner," the man continued. "He treats us more like Mr. Evan treats his. There's never been a sign of a beating from him. The first thing he did was burn our huts. He even gave us some big sticks to knock down the burning walls. That was the first fun I ever had on that place. Then we got a new house with our own room, with a bed and a dresser. He gave us new clothes, and soap to scrub with. I feel a lot better about the new plantation he is going to make. I'm proud for the first time in my life." A shy smile suggested the conversation was complete, and finished.

The twelfth wagon was finally piled high with profitable canes. It was their best production so far. They were also advised that by saving the cane leaves to dry, they could be fed to the horses. That would be better for next year's production. Instead of burning the leaves and scraping the ash into the soil, they could scatter the manure from the barn. It would be the same leaves but in a more useable form.

One morning as they were turning over the cane leaves to dry, Moesh asked Mr. Evan, "May I ask a question?"

"Of course, Moesh," Evan responded. "I value your wisdom. You have taught me ever so much."

"Are you pleased with the amount of canes you have grown, or would you like to grow more?" The gentle voice suggested a well considered idea.

"Moesh, I am pleased with what we have done, and yes, I am always interested in ways we could be more efficient. What are you thinking?"

The strong man stood up, and stretched his muscles. "If we have a row of canes, then a straddle row, and another row, we have extra room for the wagon. If we planted extra canes on the straddle side of row one and three, the wagon could still get through with care, and production would increase by at least a quarter. That would mean sixteen loads instead of twelve. Would that be good?" His expression did not change, but his voice had a boyish playfulness, for of course he knew it would be good.

It took Evan only a moment to understand and make a decision about the good suggestion. "Moesh, that is a fantastic idea. Our friend Daniel is preparing to return to his home. Perhaps this will keep him here for a day or two longer. Do you think Molly will think that is a good idea?" There was an equally playful tone to his voice as well. "I'll get some money, if you will get the wagon ready to go to the sugar mill. I believe they have ample cane starts."

In the big house he chose a small leather bag to hold the twenty five $20 dollar gold pieces, which would purchase three thousand cane starts. He then found Daniel sweeping the barn. Upon hearing the opportunity to spend a couple hours in the wagon with Moesh, the young man quickly agreed to ride along. Evan smiled thinking, "Who knows what a day might hold?"

Robber!

The seldom used road was nothing more than twin wheel marks through the weeds. Moesh was explaining that they were probably the only ones who used the road, and that only for the trips to Mr. Lester's store, or the infrequent trips to Lafayette or Mr. Perry's. It was a large surprise to both of them when a man rose out of the weeds, pointing a double barrel shotgun at them. He had a rag tied around his face. It was obvious they were being robbed. Since the robber could see no weapons, and nothing of value in the wagon, he demanded, "Give me your money, and I'll let you live another day!" He pulled back the hammer on the shotgun.

Moesh answered quietly, "We have no money."

"Shut up, slave!" The shotgun was pointed at Daniel's chest. "Give me your money," he snarled, "or you are a dead man." The second hammer was pulled back and the man took a threatening step toward them.

Daniel knew that conversation was useless, so he tossed the leather bag off to the side, the sound of coins could be clearly heard. As the man moved to the bag, Moesh urged the horses to gallop away from the robber. Curiously there was no attempt to stop them.

Moesh ran the horses until they were out of sight of the robber, around a bend in the road. Then he quietly pulled them to a stop. From under the seat he revealed his throwing stick and a quiver of lances. "Please guard the wagon Mr. Daniel, sir. I'll be back in just a bit." Without saying anything more, he stepped into the brush and was gone.

Silent minutes passed. Daniel expected at any moment to hear a gun blast, but instead could hear only the sound of birds and his own breath. After about a quarter hour, he began to wonder what he would do if Moesh didn't return. A deep foreboding set in. Would he go look for Moesh? Would he return with an empty wagon to Evan? Was there any other help nearby?

Then as casual as a man out for a stroll, Moesh appeared from around the bend in the road, leading a saddled horse. In his hand were his weapons, a leather bag, the shotgun and a couple hunting knives. He fastened the horse's reigns to the back of the wagon, handed Mr. Daniel the bag, which had a bit of fresh blood on it, and placed his weapons, along with the shotgun and knives, under the seat. "I think we should be on our way," was all he said. "We might be late for supper." They had only gone a short distance when Moesh explained, "The fool didn't even have a loaded gun." A half smile suggested he found wry humor in the bold robber's bravado. Or perhaps the half smile was focused on the two $10 dollar gold pieces he had found in the robber's pocket, and the gold ring with the red shiny stone, all of which were now in his pocket.

At the supper table Daniel was telling the story again, how frightened he had been by the robber's gun, and how quickly Moesh had gotten them to safety. The story ended there because Moesh was not present to give his account of the conclusion. As soon as they had returned with the cane starts, he had become absorbed in their care, and that of a new horse in the barn. The quiet man was not to be found for the evening meal. In respect for his courage however, from that day both Moesh and Link were invited to carry the robber's hunting knives as utility tools.

Daniel announced that he had overstayed the time he thought he would remain with them. 'I think I will be able to catch the eastbound train if I leave at first light tomorrow." His eyes held one after another of those at the table, until he found Molly's. "I have learned a great deal about our world, and my place in it," he said with conviction. "I have learned lessons I could have found only here with you." He shook his head, and said, "I feel like Captain Perry. I want to be your neighbor. I want the sort of life you have here.

There is honesty and affection as you have made this a productive plantation. But for now, I must be part of very large conversation about the future of our nation. We are approaching a critical time of change. However," he took a ragged breath, "I pledge to you that I will be back again soon."

Dawn had not spread across the eastern sky when Daniel rode out the lane. He had not given Molly a hug or the kiss he intended. He hoped that she would remember him on his journey. Three days later Clarice gave birth to a healthy baby boy. They named him Jonathan, which means "Jehovah's gift".

Riot!

The Tallahassee Herald became the lightning rod of social debate through the autumn and early winter. Henry Higgins had tried to maintain an open and fair attitude about all issues. Increasingly, however, the Abolitionists became more vocal, and the slavery owners had become more militant. There were more incidents of terrible brutality than there were examples of humane treatment of slaves. Finally in February a group of protesters gathered at the City Hall, speaking loudly against the Abolitionists. A curious crowd soon became an angry one as accusations were made and unsubstantiated claims declared. Stores that welcomed people of color were targeted with eggs, and splashed with paint. Someone in the crowd, perhaps from the competitor newspaper, shouted that the Herald was the cause of this trouble.

The mob surged the three blocks to the Herald Building and threw some of their torches through the windows. The fire that started small soon became uncontrollable. Before the firemen could get it out, six other businesses on the block were damaged or destroyed, and the fire had leapt across the street to devour eight more. The angry people had joined the chaos, and their frustration and discontent was not satisfied. Someone shouted they should get the bank, and someone else shouted, "No that has our money in it! Let's get the bankers!" They turned as a body of fury into Kearney Estates, and found along with other prominent citizens, the home of J. Henry Higgins.

There were some voices of reason calling for rational minds, but the bloodlust was stronger and louder. Torches were once again hurled through windows, both downstairs and upstairs. The wood frame buildings were tinder-dry and the flames were almost immediately out of control. The intense heat caused the crowd to back away. For some it was a moment of realization of what they had done. Unknown to them the residents had made their safe escape out the back of the burning buildings. Also unknown to them the voices that had called for reason were those of law enforcement, who were recording names of those involved in the arson. By morning Tallahassee had lost two square blocks of their main businesses and eleven luxury homes. The battle lines had been established in an uncompromising conflict. It would brood and boil for another thirty years. In the meantime, more than forty of the city's outstanding citizens were brought to trial as conspirators of arson and the destruction of property. Along with prison sentences, their properties and holdings were seized to satisfy the debts of their destruction. The lawyers were having a field day.

By the time the ink was dry on the final settlement papers, Mr. Higgins owned 51% of the Times newspaper, his competitor, and agreed to print both the Herald, as a morning paper, and the Times as an afternoon. The newer equipment made the jobs very workable. He and three others also owned two square blocks of ashes of the burned out businesses. Georgia had their statehood in '88, Louisiana in '12, Mississippi in '17, and Alabama in '19; it was a timely discussion that the Florida Territory should have a capitol. If it had a capitol, it could become a statehouse. What better location than Tallahassee? And what more appropriate situation than two square blocks of empty prime business property in the heart of town? It didn't take long for that idea to generate region-wide support. It would take another twenty years to be realized, but Mr. Higgins was in it all the way. He also had a lovely plantation mansion on the western outskirts of the city. All things considered, that fiery night of panic had been a gigantic blessing. Henry Higgins would be a prominent voice in the disposition of the region for the rest of his life.

At Vermillion Plantation, the crisis was much smaller, and furry. Nine year old Rebecca's chore was that of feeding the horses a can-full of grain every morning. They whinnied their greeting with excited verbiage, and she sang right back to them. Her task was nearly complete when she noticed a small ball of fur near the door. As she bent to examine it, she was startled to see it move. Needing more reinforcements, she ran for her dad, who admitted he had no idea what it could be. Together they went to Moesh for an answer.

"Show me, Miss Rebecca", the hunter asked softly.

The furry ball was still near the door when the envoy arrived. Carefully Moesh held a bit of the nap of the animal's neck. A squeaky growl and something short of a snap of needle-sharp teeth tried to ward off the intrusion. When the head moved, however, a bloody wound was evident, and an eye seemed damaged, or missing.

It was not difficult to surmise what had happened. Moesh told them, "This is female Weasel." He pointed to the small but full milk teats. "She has babies nearby. Probably last night as she was hunting, an owl was hunting her. It got a grab of her head, but she fought free." Looking at Mr. Evan, he asked, "Do you want me to …..," He sought the gentle word that would not offend a young girl. "...end its misery?"

Rebecca cried out, "No Daddy, No! We can't kill her! She has babies. Let me try to help her!" Tears of panic were spilling out. "Please?"

Moesh said softly, "Weasels eat mice, voles, birds or bats. They eat just about any fresh meat, maybe even shrimp. If you would like me to help, I can provide something for her to eat."

"Oh please, Daddy!"

Evan understood that the decision had already been made, but he needed to appear in control. Perhaps this could turn out to be a learning experience for his daughter, something small to grieve. "Alright, you two; Moesh will you move it into the far corner of the barn, perhaps on some dry cane leaves. Becca, remember that those tiny teeth can bite very hard. That helpless looking animal can inflict a vicious wound. You be careful. Maybe Link has an old glove you can use to handle her. There's a bit of left-over sausage in the chill box in the kitchen. That might be an easy first attempt at feeding her. But after that, she can't have our food. Do you understand?" Both Moesh and Becca nodded happily.

It took Becca about fifteen minutes to persuade the Weasel to try a bit of the meat. But after a tentative sample, the injured animal gained enthusiasm for it. It took Moesh about two hours to find the den of babies. His keen listening finally located their plaintive cries. Three babies with their eyes still closed were curled in a den in the root of a tree. Carefully Moesh placed them next to the momma Weasel. Without considering the implications to the future, Becca beamed with satisfaction. Her patient was feeding, and the babies were nursing. All was well! There was never a lack of food for Miss Becca's Weasel. While it was most often seen only by her, she reported that the playful creature was getting plump, and she didn't think it was because she was about to have another batch of kids, but maybe.

Molly loved to watch her father hunt. Moesh could be as still as a stone, waiting for a cautious squirrel to make its way across the canopy of branches in the pecan trees. Sooner or later it would work its way into range, which was a fatal mistake, With a puff of the blowpipe, a dart would find its target nine out of ten times. Or he could turn into a shadow in the brush, soundlessly tracking his prey. He never returned with an empty capture bag. One evening he even carried home a big old wild hog! After he and Link cut it into strips, they filled the smoker completely. Mr. Evan suggested that Moesh could take the front shoulder over to Mr. Perry's so those folks could have a roast too. It was a good time, of abundance and joy.

More Land!

Evan had paid little attention to the balance in his bank account. He was convinced that there had been far more deposits than withdrawals, but at his justification, he was pleasantly surprised. So much so, that he stopped in at the county assessor's office to find out the ownership of the adjacent property to his. There had been no new building activity anywhere near Vermillion Plantation. He was interested to learn that all the plots like his grandfather's inheritance were in arrears, soon to go up for auction. If he wanted to pay the back taxes, the parcels would be added to his current holdings. After a lengthy conversation with Clarice, he agreed to double the size of their property to one full section, a mile square. The price was staggeringly low. Now the challenge would be how to pay the taxes and make it profitable with Taro, sugar cane, and Pecans.

Working as a team, Moesh, Link, and Mr. Evan had cleared the brush from over half of the new property. Mr. Evan had directed them to attach a long rope to the pulling harness on the horses. The other end of the rope had a double hook that could be forced under the roots of unwanted bushes and small trees. It was an easy pull for the horses to unearth the unwanted brush, and loosen the sandy soil for planting new sugar cane starts at the same time. When the hooks discovered the charred timbers, Evan decided that was a good sign to stop for a season. They would plant what was available and look more closely at the buried timbers later.

That good time sped by marked only by the birthdays of the children. Suddenly Molly was twenty four, Becca was fourteen, Suzanne was twelve and entertaining the guests with her lovely voice, Ester was ten and a solid helper in the harvest time. Adam was nine, and with seven year old Noah, had chores around the barn. Jonathan was six; his father's pride a joy. Finally, one early summer morning, Mr. Daniel returned from his long journey.

His carriage slowly made its way down the lane, as though he was remembering each moment with new delight. Moesh was the first to call out a greeting. In a voice that could be heard by those in the big house, or Molly at the beach, he called, "Good day, Mr. Daniel, sir. It is a pleasure to see you again." Before the carriage came to a stop, there was a gathering of happy smiles, none brighter than Molly's, who had never doubted this happy reunion.

"Welcome back, Daniel," Evan said with a delighted voice. He stretched out his hand to a dignified man wearing a black velvet business suit. "It looks like you have been a busy man since our sugar cane harvest." As they made their way toward the Hospitality House porch, and a pitcher of sweet tea, Daniel explained that he had first visited Vermont, to understand their initial law against slavery. "That turned into a six month stay, which was very enlightening," he said with a sigh. "Then I was in Philadelphia for another stay through the winter. Compared to our pleasant warm December and Januarys, that was fierce. But I did meet some dynamic people who are in the Abolition Movement." Looking at Moesh, then Molly, he said, "I thought of you folks every day." After a moment to collect his thoughts, he finished, "I got back home for a brief visit, but have been a lobbyist in Washington for the past three sessions." His sip of tea tasted like being home indeed.

"How long can you stay with us, Daniel?" Evan asked. "We haven't seen your father or sisters for years. Are they well?"

"I would like to stay until the first Taro harvest, but reasonably, I'd better only use two or three of my available days. The family is well, physically," he answered with a grin. "I'm not sure of their mental state, however. Father is pretty serious about selling his interest in the Herald, and going to Washington to start a political newspaper. He has been referring to the 'Post,' as though it is already a reality. I know he is very ambitious about it. Meg and Lisle have turned the mansion into a school for girls, especially girls of color."

Looking fondly at Molly, he added, "You had a very profound effect on them."

"Are either of them married," Clarice asked. She had a rather large bias in favor of married life.

"Nope, I think we all are focused on issues that preclude the warmth of hearth and home." Daniel said, again looking at Molly. "Which brings me to the business part of the reason I am bothering you folks again; I am still gathering information for the Abolition debate. First, I must have some beach time, for sure. But I would also prize a conversation with you, Evan, and with Mr. Perry, about options to slavery in the agricultural aspect of our nation. What would you do if the slaves were all freed? Would it mean the end of plantations? You must know that I already have a strong notion about the answer, but I would treasure your thoughts. You after all, are the foundation of the discussion."

Evan and Clarice heard those words as an interesting philosophical position, while the five slaves who listened to them also, heard those words as puzzling and problematic. They hoped Mr. Daniel would allow them to share thoughts too.

Evan offered, "The barn is available, but you are definitely over-dressed for that. We have one guest upstairs and another down. You are welcome to any other room for as long as you'd like to stay."

"You know, what I had in mind was the beach bungalow. May I stay there a couple nights?" Within a very few minutes, Daniel was lounging in the warm bay water, receiving its ministrations, and remembering how rejuvenated he felt here. Molly brought him a pitcher of spring water, which made the moment perfect.

Supper was a special meal, prepared just for Daniel. Dory created her Jambalaya with shrimp and smoked pork. Daniel would have easily eaten a third serving, but to maintain a shred of dignity he held back to only two big ones. After the wonderful meal he chatted with the families until Susanne began to serenade them. Then he listened to a pure voice gracefully sing songs of faith and affection. He was captivated by her young charm. Finally when the Hospitality House was quiet, Daniel sat with Evan on the porch watching the fading twilight.

"Evan, I am delighted each time I visit to discover a new depth of charm here," Daniel said quietly. The evening had been so full he was hesitant to disturb it in any way. "You have found a way to share hospitality on a supreme level. I continually want to thank you for these gifts." The young man looked at his host who was only a few years older than himself. "You have accomplished what most would call the dream life."

"It does seem amazing on one hand," Evan answered in appreciation. "On the other hand it just seems like the right thing to do daily. It is just the way we are here."

"So, if you don't mind me asking a serious question this late in the day, how would you answer the possible changes if slavery were to be outlawed? I do think something like that is coming for our country." The thoughtful friend looked deeply into Evans expression.

"Well first of all," Evan began a large answer, "if it becomes the law, we will obediently deal with it as best we can. I think what we have going here could be reconsidered without a lot of trouble. There are two working families on our property. If they were not slaves, they would be free to live somewhere different, and find work to pay for their expenses, or stay here on a similar relationship. I think if I could determine an affordable wage to pay for the farm work and the housework, it might balance those expenses of housing them, paying for their food and clothing, and providing them a small garden plot to grow their own vegetables that they enjoy now. It would probably take a lot more book keeping, but I'll wager they would be about where they are today, except technically emancipated. I have already made arrangements for them to have an account with Mr. Lester's store. They both grow and deliver their own Taro heads for barter goods. They both receive bonus gratuities after a successful harvest. In many ways these folks have forgotten long ago their slave status. I hope you will allow them to affirm or correct my observations before you leave."

A wide smile spread across Daniel's face. "You have just verified the opinion I have treasured from you. It is the ideal arrangement you have quietly crafted in an unjust situation. I am so fortunate to know you, and so eager to spread this sort of peace across an increasingly divided country. You are my hero! You have defined the issue as one of economics, rather than race." He pointed into the gathering darkness. "By the way, have you noticed the exceptional amount to bats you have flying around the house?"

In the morning Daniel enjoyed a leisurely soak before there was much going on in the kitchen. Rarely had he been able to witness the morning begin so gradually. Colors and sounds blended in a soft pastel of beauty. The Abolition voices had seemed so demanding, but chatting with Evan in the evening had made the challenge seem more manageable. He wondered why he felt so happy, so optimistic. Gradually, his thoughts focused on Molly. Like the morning, she was a joy to see and hear. Near her, he felt more rooted in the pleasure of the world around him. It was something that deserved much more thought. But then he caught the aroma of perking coffee and he knew it was time to dry off and get dressed for another splendid day.

Daniel joined the other two guests who were already seated in the dining room. While they were being served plates of breakfast scramble, he learned that Mr. Porter was a dock worker in Beaumont, Texas. Three years ago, as a barge was being slid up into the dry dock, a Hauser had snapped and he was on the receiving end of the whiplash. His leg had been broken and severely shredded. Doctors had no way of repairing the damage and had recommended saving his life by amputating his leg. "Lucky for me," the smiling man reported, "some folks at the newspaper had heard about this place and I gave it a try. It took a week the first time to give me a lick of hope. But sure enough, I've still got a leg instead of a stump. I come back every year, just to make sure." It was a testimony of healing.

The lady at the table had an equally inspiring account. "I teach music in the Baton Rouge schools, and play violin in the city orchestra. My hands began to twist awkwardly by Arthritis. For a couple years I thought I could manage, but then I had made the decision to retire. That's when I also heard about Vermillion Plantation, and the hope they offer for new health." She wiggled her fingers lightly. "I know I still have some challenge with flexibility, but I continue to work and play. I was inspired the first time I heard

Molly play. Now to hear little Susanne sing is truly marvelous. This is my second visit, and I am sure there will be many more."

Daniel introduced himself. "My story is very similar to yours," he told the other two. "I arrived here after an accidental gunshot wound threatened my life. My father had been here twice before; one of the early visitors. I believe this is my third visit, and like you, I am completely convinced that something miraculous happens here." They toasted one another with glasses of pure spring water.

Daniel was listening to the jovial voices of men working outside. One baritone voice he thought he recognized as Brit, one of Mr. Perry's men. When he went to investigate, he found three of them picking Mulberries. There seemed to be an unusual amount of humor. "Good morning girls. Do you need any help with those heavy buckets?" he joked.

Hooting laughter greeted him. "Yes sir, we do, if we could just find a man strong enough to do a little work," Brit replied. "It is good to see you, Mr. Daniel, sir." It was one thing to be playful, but quite another to forgo propriety. "Will you be here long enough for a bit more sugar cane harvest?"

When Daniel noticed three more buckets of the berries, already picked and in the wagon, he said, "No, once was just fine for me." Changing the subject he asked, "That's a fine bunch of Mulberries. Do you eat those on toast?"

There was more laughter. "No sir. Cap'n Perry," he used the military distinction, "believes he can make these into a fine table wine, if he adds a bit of distilled mash. We're have'n a bit of a wager to see if it is ever going to be drinkable. Do you want in on the bet?"

"No thank you, but I would very much welcome a sample of the end product." Laughter and teasing followed that it would take more courage to drink a sip than put money on the bet. The day was beginning better than average for sure.

By mid-morning, Daniel had driven the carriage over to Mr. Perry's plantation. He had not seen the new mansion. It was gracious and large, with a veranda the entire width of the upstairs. "There are four bedrooms upstairs and our big one is in the back corner downstairs, where we can't hear the kids," Cal joked.

Are you planning a big family?" Daniel asked.

"Well that's the idea of four bedrooms upstairs. We figure seven or eight kids will have plenty of room."

Smiling broadly, Daniel replied, "That's pretty vigorous. Do you have Rose's permission for all that?"

"As a matter of fact, she's working on it right now. Our first born will be here by Christmas."

"Congratulations to you both!" Then Daniel explained the purpose of his business. He was eager to be a part of the growing dialogue between slave holders and the Abolitionists. "If slavery should be outlawed, Cal, how would your plantation be affected? Would you still be able to grow tobacco?"

The owner nodded in understanding, then said, "I've given that a lot of thought. Growing up in Hattiesburg, it's not a new subject, but a way of life. And it seems to me that the size of the farm sets the attitude for the answer. If a farm is small and struggling to make ends meet, then slavery is almost a necessity. It's seen as not just cheap labor, but free labor. Those are the disgraceful conditions that Abolitionists will point to, and rightly so. If the place is larger, however, more productive, I believe they could get along with hiring labor. In fact, that might be better business."

He continued, "I've always liked the rancher model that has a bunkhouse where the year-round hired hands live. During the cattle drive they might hire on a few extra hands, and during the winter they may only have a skeleton crew. It's a matter of management; that makes sense to me. I believe as long as there is not a war going on there will be a sufficient workforce available."

"That brings up another question," Daniel broke in, "if you don't mind me asking." When Cal nodded in agreement, Daniel asked, "Suppose you had a job with a bunch of willing workers to hire. Would you choose a white man over one of color or would that make any difference?"

"You know," Cal chuckled, "that's more of the same answer. It depends on the manager's ability. I know men who won't have anything to do with a Spaniard, or an Irishman, regardless of their abilities. Others might shy away from a yellow man or a red one or a black one. This tobacco plantation will be a success, I believe, if I can find the right workers to do the job. If I allow personal preferences to let me overlook some strong knowledgeable laborer, I'm only hurting myself. I have a neighbor who has taught me the wisdom of seeing the talent of the man before I see the color of his or her skin." They both nodded in agreement of that truth. "And if, because I can, I use free labor instead of skilled ones, I'll do the same crappy job with this place the last owner did."

Daniel had heard more than enough to dwell upon for one day. By the time he returned to Vermillion, he found a warm bowl of Jambalaya waiting for him. He ate alone, then headed for the beach, remembering the gentle calm of a morning swim. In his bungalow, he found that Lily had already refreshed his robe, which was dried and folded on his bed. It was not until he was comfortably resting in the shallow water that he saw Molly swimming at least a hundred paces beyond him in the deeper water. At about the same time she noticed him quietly watching her. She swam in slowly, perhaps looking for some unobtrusive way to get off the beach without passing near him. When she was about ten paces from him, she stood up and began to wade ashore. Her thin cotton dress clung to her wet body; the sun shining through the thin fabric revealed her slim shape and feminine softness. It was an unexpected moment of awe for Daniel. Her loveliness was innocent and powerful at the same time, and he could not look away. Her hands brushed the water from her curly hair, which only accentuated the trim shape that was trying to become invisible.

"Please excuse me, Mr. Daniel, sir. I didn't know you were going to have a second beach time today." She was aware how revealing her wet dress clung to her, so she shyly turned to walk away. It only enhanced the captivating moment. "I'll bring you a pitcher of spring water, as soon as I am presentable." She hurried toward her house.

Daniel pondered the exceptional moment. Had he uttered a word? He was speechless, but not without revisiting her splendor. Molly was a beautiful woman! There were thoughts tracing through his head that were in violation to his friendship to his hosts, and inappropriate as a guest here. He tried unsuccessfully to think of anything else, as he lounged in the water. Before she came back with the pitcher, he had gone into the bungalow to dry and dress.

He was the only one in the dining room for supper. Dory had prepared a creamy mashed Taro with shrimp and smoked pork, It was delicious but as Daniel ate, the food was tasteless compared to the recollected vision of a lovely woman rising out of the water. He did not seek out Evan for more conversation, but went to the bungalow intent on an early morning departure.

Perhaps he was dreaming. As he tried to recall it, the night was perfectly still, with no sounds from the other buildings. He was awakened by his door closing. Did he actually hear something? Was there a moving shadow in his room, or was it just a wish? His eyes were still closed when he felt the weight of another on his bed, and the warmth of a body next to his.

"Mr. Daniel, I do not want you to go away as you did before. I want to be able to say 'goodbye.' I want you to remember Molly wherever your many travels take you." The weight shifted more onto him and he felt her lips, soft and moist upon his. There was no demand, no agenda, just a long passionate kiss. And then the weight was gone. The shadow drifted across the room and the door quietly closed. Daniel was weeping for the wonder of it; tears ran down his face for the sheer beauty of the moment. Without passion, or fumbling lovemaking, his heart had been completely captivated. He experienced an ardent love like none he had ever known. Amidst all the complicating impossibilities, the torrent of reasons why this could never happen, he knew without the shadow of a doubt, that one day he would give his body, his heart, his very soul to that marvelous woman. One day he would!

It was still very dark when Daniel rolled the carriage out to be harnessed to the horse. He was being as quiet as possible, but suddenly he realized that he was not alone. Moesh stepped from the darkness and helped with the final straps.

"She loves you like none I have seen before," Moesh said in a hushed voice. "She honors you above all others," he said quietly

"And I receive her love as a gift," Daniel whispered. "I pledge to you, as to my father, that I will never dishonor her or cause her grief. With your blessing and her agreement, I would take her as my wife one day." His hand rested on the strong shoulder of the shadow before him. "I'm not sure when I can return, but my pledge to you and to her is that it will be as soon as I can."

It was the second week of June when Evan received a letter from Lisle Higgins. He reread it to make sure he understood the importance of it, and knew that Clarice would be thrilled. "Good day to you at Vermillion Plantation. Each time our brother returns from visiting you, he is more vibrant, and this time is no exception. In fact, from what we can gather, he may have lost his heart. He is quite smitten by Molly, which we completely understand."

"The purpose of this letter is to advise you that a double tuition has been paid for your daughters, Rebecca and Susanne, for the coming school year. Their ages are ideal to enter our finishing school. Rebecca seems to be a candidate for our normal school, completing her preparations to become a teacher. Our music program is eager to determine if Susanne's voice is as cherubic as Daniel described. Our staff are all professional musicians in the Tallahassee community, with worldwide acclaim. Our school term is from September through May, with two intermissions for Christmas and Easter. So a prompt response would be ideal."

"If this educational opportunity is acceptable to you all, we can work out the details of transportation. Sydney is sure he can chaperone the girls to and from your lovely paradise. We hope for a positive answer. Yours cordially, Lisle Higgins, Registrar."

It was the topic of every conversation for three days before everyone was in agreement. Susanne had said "yes!" immediately upon hearing that she was invited to a school of music. Rebecca, however, was less than enthusiastic about becoming a teacher. Finally her mom pointed out that she had to have the knowledge before she could teach. "How about making up your mind when you know what it entails," her mom asked. "Maybe it will just be a great way to get very smart". That tipped the scale. Becca nodded that she understood the need for information, lots of it. They answered Lisle's gracious invitation with a positive reply.

Ten days before the start of the sugar cane harvest began, Sydney arrived to transport the girls to Tallahassee. Regardless of the hours of conversation about the subject, neither Evan nor Clarice were prepared to bid farewell to their beloved daughters, even with the promise that they would return for Christmas. Miss Clare told Dory she knew now how painful her heart ached when Molly left for school.

As it turned out, only Becca came home for Christmas. Suzanne was given a singing role in a professional presentation of the nativity at the Bella Mora Hall. Her clear soprano voice became a regional sensation. When Becca came home for their summer break, Suzanne remained in Tallahassee, with a singing contract for the dedication of the Territorial Capitol rotunda. It was a three day celebration featuring her singing and reading patriotic and spiritual selections. Her acclaim spread further. By the time Becca had finished her second year schooling schedule, Suzanne was singing in Washington at Bellamy Hall. Meg was her chaperone and booking manager, as they stayed in Mr. Higgins' new home there. They were trying to decide whether to accept the New York contract, or Paris. Suzanne had taken the stage name Clare Belle, for many had called her voice clarion. Apparently she had outgrown the plantation life. Becca, on the other hand was eager to return, even though she had found romance as well as education. Two handsome suitors were eager to have her in their budding lives in Florida, if she would only remain there. She chose to return home.

Mr. Daniel understood her attraction for the Vermillion Plantation. He never missed a Christmas opportunity to return there. Each year he would arrive with a carriage filled with gifts. After the first time, he was anticipated by each one of the folks. He brought a new hat for Mr. Evan one year and a music box for Miss Clare. Becca received a diary and pen set, which she put into correspondent use; and Suzanne's wooden flute remained unopened. Jonathan received a new invention called a harmonica, with which he only made noise. Esther received a wooden brush and comb with a lovely mirror to match. Moesh and Link both received Meerschaum tobacco pipes; and Dory and Lily received bees-wax candles to light their homes.

Molly received a pale yellow velvet dress, a string of pearls and a gold comb with a flower for her hair. Adam and Noah each received wooden construction toys and a tin of peanut brittle. His generosity caused laughter, and a reciprocal spirit became contagious. Each year he tried to out-give the year before. Actually, he was there only to see Molly again.

One New year's Day there were low clouds and a bit of drizzly rain. By the afternoon the clouds began to part and winter sun tried to warm the beach. Daniel and Molly strolled hand in hand to the west boundary of the property. She had told him of her attempt to help the sugar cane harvest. "I think I was just in their way," she said with a happy smile. "If I had been stronger, they would have wanted me again next summer."

Daniel laughed out loud, "That is the same thing they said about me!" She shared his laughter. They strolled and chatted, careful to stay on the beach where they could be clearly observed. Both Moesh and Dory were aware of Molly's longing for this gentle man.

"The new property is in full production," Molly informed him. "There were twenty seven wagon loads this year. It was a test for so few to accomplish so much. Mr. Evan has told some people in Lafayette about the uncleared part of the new land. Some charred timbers were found when they were clearing the brush. Link tried to dig them out, but discovered some very old clay pots, and cooking stones, some arrow points and tools. When Mr. Evan told the Caddo Nation people about it, they became very interested. Now they are searching for more ancient treasures. Sooner or later they will be finished, and then more sugar cane will be planted, and another long row of pecan trees to mark the property boundary." They had turned around and were following their footprints back toward the house. Daniel stopped and turned Molly toward him, holding both her hands gently. "I don't know how much longer I can manage seeing you just once or twice a year." His voice was full of emotion. "I think part of my frustration is the pure gentle joy I find here, and the increasing tension and division I sense in Washington. I thought I could shed light into the dark abyss of ignorance and hostility, but I was so wrong. There are forces that seem colossal, pulling our country apart. I am now convinced that I can do nothing to bring what your father called 'correctness' to it."

Molly mirrored his concern. "What will you do, Mr. Daniel?" She had never considered the possibility of his limitations.

"Well," he began a discussion that he had no idea how it might end. "I can always work for my father's newspaper. But that is only more of the same numbing negative business I dislike now. And it still keeps me from you." He took a deep breath as though preparing for some challenge. "I have been thinking about becoming a Louisiana farmer, somewhere south of Lafayette." They both giggled. "I have heard of a new produce that is just now being imported into Florida. Large trees grow a fruit called an 'Orange' that is very sweet and juicy. Folks seem to have a real hunger for them, especially as juice in the morning. I think I will speak to Mr. Evan about the process of acquiring some land." They walked a ways in silence.

"I would rejoice in being able to see you often," she said softly.

"I was about to say those exact words," he said tenderly. "There are many reasons that could keep us from sharing our days completely." He was remembering a kiss in the darkness.

She squeezed his hand and giggled, then whispered, "but there is nothing keeping us from completely enjoying this moment. She took a deep breath before going on. "May I tell you something I am observing," she asked, changing the subject.

"I think that would be a good thing," Daniel answered, aware how much more he wanted to say to Molly.

"I believe there is something very healing in the water here at Vermillion." Daniel nodded vigorously, for he had experienced it. Molly continued, "But it is not in the pure spring water, as most believe. I have served hundreds of pitchers at the beach. I believe there is some healing quality in the sea water of Vermillion Bay. My folks drink of the spring water every day, but they have been injured and healed very slowly. They have had fever and suffered many days before it went away. They are wrinkling and their hair is turning gray, which is natural, but not for the healing water of the bay. I swim every day, but they do not. They bathe with a cloth and soap on the back steps of the house. It seems they age, but I do not." She expected some strong reaction, and when none came she finished, "I have watched some very sick or severely injured people rest in the bay water, and revive in wonderful ways, as you did. Sometimes I wonder if it is the gift of prayers, but I am pretty sure it is not the spring water."

They strolled and chatted all the way back to the beach chairs. Daniel turned toward Molly again and said softly, "I must leave in the morning, and want to say farewell before I go. I would ask you not to come into my room tonight. That is a temptation that could be uncontrollable. I do not want to cause Mr. Evan or your father any distress or distrust. We will earn their respect if we act with Christian love."

"I do not understand Christian love if it keeps me away from you," Molly said sadly. "But I will do whatever you ask, for I always want to enjoy your respect."

He embraced her warm body and kissed her as he had longed to do. "Molly, I seem to perpetually promise to return to you. I do believe the time is very soon when there will be no more parting." He kissed her again and felt her press firmly against him.

At the dinner table Daniel gave Evan a recap of the conversation he had shared with Molly about acquiring nearby property to grow the new fruit. There was unanimous enthusiasm for the prospects. Evan offered to visit the tax records office in Lafayette straightaway. They all were eager for his next visit.

After unearthing the charred timber from the upper property, the Caddo Nation search team dug for two weeks. They found enough antiquity to fill three wagons. Curiously, the carvings on the timber were not identified at first. Finally, a history professor who had extensively studied the Atakap origins and languages, determined that the carvings did not say, "Lodge of the Ancestors," as was first translated, but rather "Lodge of the Ancient." He shared the native ghost-story legend of a chief who had outlived several generations, with many wives, children, and grandchildren. No one knew how old he was, but older than their great grandfathers. He was ultimately one who was thought to live between the physical and spiritual worlds, not fully in either. He became so feared by his people that they turned on him. In an angry night they destroyed his lodge, with him in it. The unearthed antiquities, including the charred beam, were moved to the native display in Lafayette. To demonstrate the gratitude of the team for permission to retrieve the old treasures, they finished clearing brush, and planted four more rows of sugar cane. Evan put the finishing touch on the property line by planting another two hundred pecan starts. Eventually they would challenge the production of both sugar cane and Taro.

Fat Trouble

One spring afternoon a very unusual thing happened. Mr. Evan received two complaints from guests. There had only been one complaint in all the time they had welcomed guests. On this day the first complaint was from a gray haired school teacher who was hoping to find relief from a nasty case of shingles in the healing water of Vermillion Plantation. She alleged that while she was at her beach treatment one of the Hospitality staff had taken her money pouch out of her purse. She was, as you may guess, distraught and angry. Since Lily was the only staff person that would enter a guest's room, she also was upset, for the full weight of suspicion was cast upon her integrity. While all the guests were being served lunch, Link set about an investigation that would explain the missing purse and clear Lily's name.

The second complaint was raised by a very large guest who said that he was quite dissatisfied with the menu being served. "I asked for a steak, and she served me soup!" the bulbous man bellowed so all could hear. "You guaranteed my satisfaction or you would refund my money. I am most unsatisfied! This is not the grand service as advertised." He was puffing from the exertion of his complaint.

Evan was quick to approach the man, offering apologies for the menu and service. "I am terribly sorry for your inconvenience. Your satisfaction is our aim, but frankly, we are not a hotel with a large kitchen or staff. No one has ever lifted a complaint before."

"Well, I'm lifting one now, and I want my money back," he said, shaking folds of fat in anger.

Evan was fairly convinced that this incident had little to do with the quality of the food, for he could see the man's empty bowl. Something else was going on here. "Well Mr. Rustin, since you have been here three days without paying, I think there is nothing to repay. But we certainly do not want an unhappy guest to remain here against their will. Let me call one of our staff to help you with your luggage. In fact, here comes Link with your suitcase now. You can be on your way." A very angry Link strode to the table, and dropped the suitcase, open, on it. Several wallets and coin purses spilled out. The fat man's face went white with alarm.

From a nearby table the lady whose money had been stolen recognized her coin purse saying, "There it is, that's mine!" She rose and claimed her little cloth pouch. When she had counted the contents, she declared that it was all accounted for. But another guest identified his pouch, which he had not as yet missed. When he counted his he said there were two twenty dollar gold pieces missing. The fat man's face turned even more pale.

Evan had a completely different tone of voice as he said, "Link, it's too late to take Mr. Rustin to the Marshal this afternoon. Will you tie him in the barn so we can do that in the morning? Make sure he is not too comfortable. I'm not a vindictive person, but I really didn't care for his tone of voice. Perhaps we can teach him some manners during a sleepless night." Before Link led the trembling man out of the dining room, Evan asked one last question. "Whose purses are these? Where did you steal them?"

Young Jonathan, drawn by the sound of loud voices, watched as the fat man was hoisted from his chair. Link was holding the man's wrist up behind his back. With his other hand he fiercely gripped the elbow that was already in pain. The man screamed, "I'll tell you! Don't break my arm!" One other guest had been victimized on the day of Rustin's arrival; the rest of the wallets had been stolen on the train from New Orleans. Mr. Evan searched the man's pockets, removing a leather pouch with a dozen double eagle gold pieces, which would apply to his stay, and replace the two the other guest had lost. The overweight thief was violently led from the dining room.

On the way toward the barn, the fat man seemed to stumble. As he staggered forward, he jerked his arm out of Link's grasp and with surprising speed, sprang toward the brush. Link was loping just behind him, and for a moment the man thought he was going to be free. With a couple powerful strides, Link drew almost beside the man who veered to the left, maintaining his momentum. If he had thought a bit more about it, he would have realized that he was being guided into a disaster. One stride felt the ground soften below his foot. The next stride caused him to fall flat on his face into the quicksand pit. He screamed with pain as his knee hyper extended, then he began to thrash, feeling himself sinking below the liquid surface. Shocked, Jonathan stared open mouth. He had never witnessed a physical contest between two men.

"Help me, God damn it!" Rustin screamed, as his shoulders began to slide below the surface. "Help me, for God's sake!"

Moesh stepped up beside Link, holding a length of rope. "Shall we see how deep this pit is?" he asked.

"Help me!" the desperate man cried. His chin was going under.

Moesh cast the loop of the rope over the man's flailing arm. It was not going to be easy to hoist all that flab safely to solid ground. To the delight of the two slaves, Jonathan grabbed onto the end of the rope to help tug the struggling sand covered man out of the pit.

It took a while but finally he was securely snubbed with his hands behind his back and his ankles tied tightly to his wrists with his knees bent. He would not have anything close to a comfortable evening and night.

At the Marshal's office the next morning, Evan was surprised to learn that a $100 dollar reward was on the head of Theodore Rustin for robbery. Mr. Evan turned over the stolen wallets and the names of their owners as best he could. He suggested that Link should receive the reward, since it was his diligence that had discovered the thief.

"That reminds me," the Marshal said, "I just sent a young pair of darkies out to your place. Did you come by Live Oak?"

"No sir," Evan answered. "We came by Abbeville. The road is a bit smoother, and we were in a hurry."

"His name is George, I believe," as I recall, the Marshal said. "They both look like teenagers, but they have papers saying that they are freedmen. I'm afraid they will get in trouble if they stay here. For sure someone will want to put her on the block. For a colored, she's a pretty good looker. If you go back on Live Oak, I'll bet you catch up with them." He counted ten $10 dollar gold coins into Link's hand. "You did a good job on that big old boy. Thanks for your service." Link's smile was as wide as it could be.

Before they headed home, Mr. Evan stopped at the records office as a courtesy for Mr. Daniel. He was told that the auction had drawn few bidders and only a handful of small parcels nearest Lafayette had been sold. There was still ample available land for whomever wanted to pay the back taxes. Mr. Evan and Link talked about the prospects of even more land, as they headed back to Vermillion Plantation. It didn't take them long to agree that there was no practical need for them to acquire any more. They had all the work they could manage.

Sure enough, they were about three quarters of the way home when up ahead they spotted a couple trudging along. When the wagon approached them, the man and woman stepped into the weeds to let them pass. Instead Mr. Evan pulled to a stop beside them. "I'll bet your name is George," he said cheerily. Startled expressions reacted to his greeting.

"Yes sir, it is," the young man answered cautiously. "We've got papers." He drew a folded document from his shirt pocket.

Ignoring the opportunity to examine the paper, Evan said, "The Marshal told us we might catch up with you on this road." Now the pair took a step backward toward the safety of the brush. "Are you looking for Vermillion Plantation?" Evan's tone remained cheery.

"Yes sir, we are." The answer was still cautious, one even with a twinge of fear.

"I'm sorry not to introduce myself. I'm Evan Cossindale, and this is Link. We are from the plantation. Would you like a ride, or do you prefer to walk? It's only about a couple more miles or so from here."

The young man was about to say that they would prefer to walk when the woman tugged at his sleeve. "Let's ride," she said softly.

"We have to trust someone sooner or later." She tried a wan smile. They hopped on the back of the wagon and didn't say anything more for the remainder of the trip.

As Evan drove down the lane toward the house, he suggested that Link hop down to tell Dory to set an extra couple places at the table, while the horses were being unhitched.

Link responded, "I'll also tell Lily we might have a couple extra for supper. It seems to me that these two have papers, but they may still have slave souls. They don't want to have much to do with white folks. I remember what that feels like." He ran ahead to convey the news.

He was right. The new couple was not comfortable eating at the Hospitality House table, so they joined Link, Lily and the boys for the first good meal they had eaten in ten days. Then Molly took them to the beach where they enjoyed a refreshing evening swim, and the promise of clean clothes in the morning. They accepted the old tarp that made a passable tent to sleep in, and the agreement that they would all gather for a conversation after breakfast. Without knowing it, a major shift was happening in the living conditions; for those who didn't think it could get any better, a surprise was at hand.

New Help

The coolness of the morning was pleasant on the Hospitality porch. Introductions had been made; glasses of sweet tea had been shared. Jonathan had told an excited account of the capture of a wanted thief, and his assistance in saving the man from the quicksand. Now the attention was turned to Mr. Evan. "George I hope you and Joy feel welcome here this morning. It seems there is always some exciting thing happening. We know this may be a very different sort of time for you both, so why don't you tell us why you are with us."

"The easy part of the tale," the young man began, "was the Marshal told us that the only safe place for us would be here. I want to keep Joy safe, so here we came." He even cranked out a weak smile. "Thank you for your hospitality."

"The long part of the story, he continued, "is that we were both born on a tobacco plantation just near Macon, Georgia. Our grandparents and parents were slaves there. Our owner, Miss Samuelson, who had been raised by my grandmother, had cancer, and promised our mothers that before she died, she would make sure we were freed. Then when we got old enough, she said we should be married, and freed, so she did it. She made a paper that we signed, husband and wife, and she signed it too, along with our freedman paper. When she died Mr. Samuelson told us to skedaddle or he would burn those papers and sell us. We didn't have any money, but the other fellows on the plantation pitched in enough for us to ride to Florida on the train. We wanted to get as far from slavery as we could. Then we found an empty cattle car going west and hitched a ride to New Orleans. I almost lost her there to an auction. Seems like we didn't get very far from it. We don't have two pieces of paper, just one with both our names. While they were trying to sort it out, I got her loose and we ran for it. We've been walkin' for several days, just tryin' to stay out of the way." He looked at Mr. Evan as though the rest of the story was to be told.

"Well George, we're really glad you are safe today," Evan replied. "Your freedman document means that you are free to leave this place and go wherever you want. It doesn't mean you are free to stay here." Everyone took a quick breath because that was an uncharacteristically blunt thing for him to say. "But… you are in luck, because we have been having a long conversation about what would happen if all the slaves were given their freedom."

"Today, I will offer you a job working here at Vermillion Plantation as a part time laborer. I'll pay you a dollar a day for those days we have work to do, which are quite a few. You can live in one of our help houses for nine dollars a month rent, and we will be glad to serve you the meals that Dory cooks for just fifty cents a day. If I figured that correctly, that leaves you with about two dollars a month for clothes and anything else you want to buy. But you would be free."

"A second choice is this," he looked at all the listeners. I will offer you the opportunity to become part of our expanded family, living in your own house and helping with whatever you want to do. Your food could be eaten alone in your own home, or with us at the big table. Dory cooks enough for all of us. You can have a garden row, just like Moesh and Link, to grow your own vegetables, or Taro for barter at the store, where you are free to shop. Miss Clare could teach you or your children to read and write, maybe play the piano. At the end of the sugar cane harvest, and the spring and fall Taro harvests, you will receive a bonus, as do Moesh and Link. When you help our guests with their luggage or with their beach time, there is often a small gratuity, which is yours to keep. You can ask one of these others seated around you if they are free. I'll bet they will answer that they are free to remain here."

Before there was any conversation, Evan went on, "I have two other notions I need you all to consider. I would like to go into Lafayette to the lumber yard today, and order enough material to build two more help houses. I think the boys need a bedroom, as does Molly. We might get Charles to help us, although I'm not sure that is necessary."

"The last idea I want to share is that George has presented a new era for us. I have never thought of slavery in any sort of favorable way. If you will accept the documents of freedmen," his gaze went from Moesh to Dory, then Molly, from Link to Lily, it would be my privilege to write them." A deep silence held the porch. On one hand it would make little difference to them. On the other hand it would mean the world!

Moesh finally said, "For more than twenty years I have been your slave, but more importantly, you have been my friend for all that time. A document would have little meaning between us. But there may come a time when clarity needs to be expressed, and then, like George's it would be useful." Link agreed, and Molly's thoughts were on Mr. Daniel. She wondered what he would think about this conversation.

After several moments of quiet, George softly asked, "Do we get to swim again soon?" Their serious discussion would wait until another day.

Daniel pondered the entire summer how he would break the news to his father. Each day away from Molly was a wasted day as far as he was concerned. But he knew that the old south values ran through his father's veins, and an interracial marriage had no place in there. Daniel considered writing a letter, explaining his deep affection for Molly. He knew that was a coward's way around a confrontation with his father.

Grief and opportunity

At an 1836 Democratic campaign fund raiser dinner, Henry Higgins excused himself from the table, suggesting that he was not feeling well. He nearly made it to the front door before he collapsed. The Medical Examiner said that his heart simply stopped. He died instantly. Instead of talking with his father about the possibility of a problematic union, Daniel had to plan a funeral, and then deal with the legalities of inheritance. Almost lost in the details were his powerful guilt feelings for failing to talk with his father. The Will directed the Post and the Washington mansion to him, along with considerable investments. Meg had already taken her inheritance to purchase a French villa where she and Clare Belle based their European concerts. Lisle received the Tallahassee plantation to continue as a school for women. Sydney was granted a lifetime pension. The rest of the household staff were sent to Tallahassee until they would be needed in a new venture. Daniel set a goal for himself to have the Washington properties completely liquidated by the first of December. He had all his father's furniture packed into a railcar and directed to Lafayette. It might be a while before he could use it, but it would be waiting, and spectacular.

The Christmas of '38 was the happiest Molly could remember. Mr. Daniel announced that he had purchased the section just northeast of the Vermillion plantation. His property ran 1760 paces along Live Oak road, and an equal distance east of it. He was within walking distance every day! Once again his carriage had been filled with gifts for everyone, even George and Joy. Perhaps the highlight was Miss Clare's announcement that from now on Sunday services would be held in the Hospitality dining room. Molly played the piano to lead the singing of hymns and carols, and Mr. Evan led prayers and read scripture. Even the guests participated. It was wonderful!

Dory had been experimenting with a holiday dessert for the Hospitality House. With such an unlimited supply of pecans, she mixed molasses, nuts, and sugar with a bit of butter and eggs. In a pie shell it baked into such a pleasant concoction that the guests asked for extra servings. It was so simple, she expanded to a sweet snack by browning the sugar and butter into a caramel. When the nuts were stirred in and the small portions cooled, she dipped them in a chocolate sauce that hardened into a shell. Pralines became so popular she limited them to the first week of the month only.

Just before the first of the year, Daniel and Evan were sitting in front of a toasty fire in the Hospitality House. Dried Pecan husks made a warm and fragrant flame. Daniel was trying to plan the events that would begin his citrus orchard. "It seems to me," he speculated, "that I need some housing for the folks who will clear the land and plant the trees. After that is complete, I can think about a house for me. Isn't that about the way you all started here?"

"Our first few weeks here, we had a tent for Moesh, Dory, and Molly. Clarice and I slept in the bed of the wagon with a canvas top. She refused to sleep on the ground with crawling things," Evan remembered with a smile. "I had the help of Moesh when we built the first living spaces, one for us, and one for them. When Link and Lily came, the three of us built the third house. But we found a carpenter named Charlie who designed and framed the big house on the mound."

"Did you need to clear much brush for these places?" Daniel was trying to envision where there might be an ideal spot on the property he had acquired.

"Not much heavy stuff. Because we have the beach as a point of interest, and the mound, there was little brush in our way at first. We got into clearing when we put most of the property into production. I think that's a favorable option. You might think of placing your houses on an edge or corner, so everything else can be fruit trees."

Evan felt like he was speaking to a younger brother. "I'll tell you that a section of land is a lot, a mile in each direction. You will feel at first that you must scrimp to save it. Then you will see how very much space you have to work with."

Daniel was quiet for a moment, not sure how this was going to come out. "It's going to take three or four years for the citrus trees to get any sort of harvest. What would you think if I tried to start a rum distillery in the meantime? There is ample sugar cane and spring water. I think it could be a new industry."

Evan had a large grin as he replied, "I would have no exceptions, if you could manage that. Now Clarice might; she's from a completely teetotaler family. I once offered her a glass of beer, and got punched for my kindness. I suppose you would start pretty small to see how it develops."

"Yes, and maybe not so much. The Tallahassee plantation has a slave that was raised in Jamaica. He has told me that his father worked in a distillery, and has shown him the tricks to making quality beverage. He would be one of four or five I would bring with me. But that is a ways down the road from here." He squirmed a bit cranking up the next topic. "With your permission, I'd like to hire Moesh and Link to help me clear some initial room, and I need help building those first shelters. I'm also going to offer that to Mr. Cal's fellows. Do you think a dollar a day would be fair?" He studied Evan's face to see if there was any expression that might warn him.

"You won't believe how this dovetails with a discussion we had before Christmas. George and Joy are freedmen. They're staying with us as we work out some new considerations. I've offered freedmen status to Moesh and Link as well, but we are in a wait-and-see time right now. I have suggested that there might be jobs that pay them some money, on the side, so to speak. We never came to a conclusion, but I'm sure it will continue." It was a difficult subject, so he paused before adding, "Of course you can have their help. If you choose to offer them a bit of compensation, it will only add to their respect. It's a good, but slightly dangerous idea. I don't think they will abuse it."

It rained for the day they had set to begin; but the next day was perfect. Moesh, Link, and George were eager to accept the offer of a dollar a day, Evan came along, but he stressed he was only being a good neighbor. With five workers, Daniel was sure this was a great beginning. Moesh drove a stake at the corner where he calculated the opposite side of the road was from the corner of Vermillion Plantation. At this point Live Oak road ran due north. It was a perfect beginning indeed.

After that first day of pulling roots out of the sandy soil, and piling brush that would be burned when dried, Daniel paced due east for one hundred paces, feeling quite satisfied with their progress. Moesh quietly reminded him that they had another sixteen hundred and sixty paces to get to the southeast corner. He also shared that Mr. Evan liked to mark the boundary with a row of Taro. They are both visible and edible. Since it was time to take another wagon load to Mr. Lester, there would be ample crowns to begin a line, if he wanted. Daniel wondered if Moesh was being extra nice to him because he was aware of Molly's affection. By week's end, they had cleared enough land to place the barn and three help houses. The Taro row was four hundred paces due east. It was an excellent way to maintain a boundary line. It was time to get some lumber. Moesh, Link and George felt the rush and weight of five silver dollars each!

Mr. Evan asked Molly, Adam and little Noah to help him with the Taro for Mr. Lester. It took them a couple hours to dig, clean and cut the crowns off of a hundred and forty heads. He playfully asked her if she wanted to help him deliver the crowns to Mr. Daniel's. She didn't even think about the answer before giggling, "Yes, please."

By Easter Daniel had made great progress. A deep well had been dug to insure year-round water in abundance. Three help houses were complete, one with four bunk rooms for men, and another with two bunk rooms for women. Mr. Daniel had the smallest, a one room, which he stressed was only until the main house was built. He also had most of a sizable barn built. His idea was for the large structure to have stalls for four horses, aging rooms for rum barrels, and a loft to store as many sacks of pecan husks as he could buy from Evan. The distillation process would need a lot of inexpensive fuel.

Perhaps the largest surprise was the plan for the main house that he had conceived with Charles the carpenter. Since there was a slight slope to the property, he had designed an excavated partial basement that would be 60 by 100 feet, with a brick floor. The ground level one story mansion upstairs would have a tile roof in the Spanish style and be called simply, "Grove House." It took two months to clear the section of land and plant 500 three year old Orange tree grafts. With Daniel's four men, three of Cal's men some of the time, and three of Mr. Evan's, plus Adam. Noah and Jonathan, all the work was completed and all the other fields harvested. Daniel finally moved all of his father's furniture from the parked rail car. It was a colossal year! And Clarice was doubly happy because all those folks, plus Rose, her two boys and baby, and all the other women, plus beach guests, were at devotions every Sunday. There truly was an outpouring of faithful gratitude.

No longer a child

It was time for another load of Taro to go to Mr. Lester. Moesh smiled with satisfaction to see how willing Adam and Noah were to pitch in digging, cleaning and chopping the crowns off. They had a hundred and twenty in the wagon in less than two hours. Moesh told them he would challenge them to a race. If he got back before they had the crowns quartered and planted up at the Taro rows, he would enjoy a hard candy from Dory's kitchen. If the job was done by the time he got back, they could have the treat. George wanted to know if he could get in on it, but was told it was for the boys only, and Jonathan was coming along with him. The race was on.

Mr. Lester carefully counted each Taro head. "Looks like you brought a hundred and twenty to trade for merchandise". Then looking at the selection of items they were taking, he said, "That's a case of canned milk, a bag of flour, a bag of sugar, a box of salt, a box of eggs and a jar of hot sauce. That looks just even to me." He turned to care for another customer.

"'Excuse me Mr. Lester." Jonathan asked. "May I see that list? I don't think it is quite even."

"Son, can you cipher these numbers in your head?" the storekeeper asked with a sneer.

"Of course I can. I'm not a kid anymore." He looked at the grocer's list. It totaled forty three dollars. "It looks to me like you are shorting us seventeen dollars," a frustrated growl added, "again! Do you recall what my dad told you would happen if you keep trying to cheat us?" His young voice curled into a snarl. "This is the last load of Taro you get, sir. Now put another case of milk on the wagon and we will be gone…. for good!"

"Wait. It was just a mistake." The exasperated grocer tried to explain. "I didn't try to cheat you. I'm just so darned upset! Look I'll double your purchase." He looked pleadingly at Moesh as he reached for additional items. "It's happening again. With the new businesses in town we have some burglars who have us all really upset. They broke in my back door to steal a knife and some tobacco. The door cost a lot more than what they took. They got in the new hardware store, and stole a couple guns and a barrel of black powder. The hotel lost some bottles of whiskey. I'll tell you it has us pretty upset."

Moesh asked, "Do you have a deputy yet?"

"No, there is no one willing to accept the job for what we can pay.

Moesh thought for a moment, then headed for the wagon saying, "When you add up how much it is costing you to worry about it, maybe you will see the wisdom in offering more for a law man."

On the way home, Jonathan said bravely, "If I could find that burglar, I would punch him in the stomach."

Moesh snorted in correction, "Then he would cut your throat. Fighting is not a playtime thing. These men who break the law have no conscience; they have no heart. They would take a life as simply as taking a bread loaf."

Jonathan understood that he had been corrected in wisdom. It was a serious subject. "Moe, will you teach me how to fight so I can protect myself and the ones I love?"

"Mmm," he answered, "We'll see. First I must ask your father. It may not be a skill he wants you to have. Fighting changes the soul of a man. When you learn to defeat another, it is a spiritual as well as physical thing." The subject was over for now. But it would come up again.

Daniel asked if he could purchase the first and last load of sugar canes, and all the dried pecan husks. Roman, his Jamaican man, had put together the necessary elements to begin a rum still. First they would grind the canes, add water, some yeast and let it ferment for a week. Then they would fire up the distillation pot and in the wonders of modern science, out the small cooling pipe would come the first run of rum. It would be distilled a second time, to double the alcohol content, then put in aging barrels, or tanks. It depended upon the availability of good barrels. Roman said the process would be concluded by the addition of caramel for taste and color, and a bit of ground cinnamon spice. With a final filtering to make it polished, the rum could be bottled and sold. Daniel had chosen the brand name of "Grove House Rum". With the cooking pot outside the basement door, and the fermentation and aging tanks inside the barn, it was both safe and practical.

Unspeakable Sorrow

The season of grief began one autumn night when Moesh heard the barn door latch. With the house all sleeping, he was sure it was an intruder. Stepping to the door he called to Link in a voice loud enough to warn a prowler, "I think there is someone in the barn! Get your axe!" He could hear the rustling of brush as someone retreated into the shadows. A sleepy Link joined him, only to be told that the uninvited person had disappeared into the dark. "I'll try to find his tracks in the morning," Moesh said as his friend headed back to his warm bed. But the hunter in him wondered if there might be a connection to the unwanted guests in the Abbeville stores. He mentioned it to Mr. Evan in the morning and was thanked for being so attentive. Both he and Link started wearing the long knives on their belts.

The main Taro harvest was completed for the Lafayette store, but Mr. Lester still needed a small load. Jonathan said he would accompany Link for the delivery, but Esther said she would like to go instead. She wanted to see if there might be a new pink blouse for sale. When they didn't return by mid afternoon, Moesh began to worry. When they failed to return by supper, he set out on foot to find them, carrying his throwing stick and a quiver of lances. There was still plenty of light, although the sun was setting.

He had jogged about three miles when he came upon the grizzly scene. At a wide fork in the road, Miss Esther was lying dead beside the road. Her clothes had been ripped off and her body defiled; but by the bullet wound, he understood that the indignity had happened after her death. Link's body was in the middle of the road. He also had been shot twice, but neither had been fatal. The knife wounds on his chest, arms, and back spoke of a valiant battle to protect her. Neither of his knives were present, so Moesh understood that they were in at least one of the attackers. Gently he moved his friend's body off the road beside the fragile beauty of the child he had watched grow into a wonderful young woman. Tenderly he replaced her blouse, and wept furious tears. Then with deadly resolve he began to follow the wagon tracks and blood trail that led down an unfamiliar road heading east. It was quite dark when he finally came upon the frame house with the wagon still hitched to nervous horses. A dead body lay in the wagon bed, along with some groceries. Link's knife protruded from the man's chest, hilt deep.

Moesh stood stone still until he was convinced there was no one awake within the house. He then made his way to a feeding manger that had a half bale of hay. He took a large portion of the hay and a board laying nearby. He propped the board under the back doorknob securing the door tightly. He took a deep breath and released it slowly, then he struck a match, lighting the hay that was now resting against the dry wood. He took the rest of the hay, lighting one side of it from the growing flame at the back, and hurried around to the front of the house. He broke a window, and threw in a cascade of flame. Voices were shouting inside. Moesh stepped back and prepared his throwing lances.

The first man to open the front door had a serious limp. He was dragging his leg with a groin injury. Moesh thought that was certainly a wound from Link. He hit him squarely in the chest, with a lance. The dead man crumpled right in the doorway. Now other voices were shouting, and a woman screamed. Moesh was sorry for her. She had probably not been part of the assault but would suffer the judgment. Another man leaped through the broken window and as he stood up to run, he was struck with another lance. He managed to take two steps before he died. Another face looked out the window space, surrounded by flames, then darted toward the door. A tremendous explosion, like a canister of ignited black power exploding, filled the night sky with a pillar of sparks and embers. In the echoing reverberations, the only sound coming from the house was the hiss of hungry fire consuming the wood. The silence of death filled the shadows around the burning house.

Moesh pulled the lance out of the man lying outside the house and carried him as near to the open door as he could stand the heat. With a violent shove, he drove the body beyond the one lying in the doorway. Then going to the wagon, he pulled Link's knife from the dead man's chest and did the same thing, casting the body over the other two. The smell of burning flesh was nauseous and filled the night, not with justice, but acrid judgment. He waited until the roof collapsed and the walls fell in on the incinerated scene. Then he knew he had to take the wagon, and the bodies home. Once again hot tears streamed down his face. He was sure that this night had changed his life forever, and certainly not for the better.

When Moesh reached the top of the Vermillion lane, he was prepared to stand a vigil until he saw stirring in the morning. The candlelight in the big house, and also in Link's, however, signaled that he had to break the unwelcomed news to them tonight . He proceeded to the big house where he called Mr. Evan's name. Within a heartbeat he was surrounded by the entire group, all in uncontrolled weeping. Sobbing, Miss Clare knelt beside the wagon asking God's compassion on this darkest night of her life. Her broken heart didn't know what else to ask. Mr. Evan knelt beside her, cradling her shoulders, and weeping openly with her.

After painful moments watching these parents in tragic grief, Moesh was finally as honest as he thought necessary. "The signs showed that Link tried to protect her. He was shot twice, and set upon the attackers with his knives. I know for sure that he got at least two before receiving his fatal wounds. Miss Esther may have been shot by accident, or by some panicked kid. She was only assaulted after they were both dead." He wasn't certain how accurate or comforting that information might have been, but it was the signs he had read.

"I would like you not to ask me about the terrible people who did this terrible thing. I am sure that your God does not smile at what I did tonight. I do not regret my action. Let me tell you that judgment was swift and complete. No one who hurt Miss Esther or Link is breathing now, and no evidence of their crime is left. If hell is a place of fire, they are all there. Please don't ask me more about it." He unbridled the horses and led the weary animals into the barn. Lily brought a sheet from the house and with wracking sobs, spread it gently over Miss Esther and Link. This was all beyond her understanding or belief. The weeping sound of grief continued through the night. Mr. Evan would tell them what to do with the bodies in the morning.

In the saddest morning of his life, Evan asked Moesh to help him move the bodies up the south end of the mound, where they were again covered with the sheet. He knew that he had to go to the Marshal to report the deaths. This resting place had as much solemn dignity as he could find. Jonathan asked to ride to Lafayette with him.

When it came time to give an official account of the day, Mr. Evan told Marshal Baldwin, "My daughter and a man servant took a load of Taro into the Abbeville store. When they didn't make it home by dinner, another man servant went to see what the problem might be. He found my daughter naked and dead by the road, and the other man servant shot and stabbed to death. He followed the wagon tracks down a new road. When he found the wagon with the horses still hitched, the house was but smoldering ashes and there was no one around."

The Marshal asked, "You say this happened south and east of Abbeville?" When Evan nodded, the Marshal continued, "That sounds like the Henry place. Luke Henry, his wife and three boys just moved there after Luke got out of prison. They are a rough bunch for sure, and crooked as a snake. It sounds to me like they lit out after committing such a terrible crime. I'll put out wanted posters on all of them." Evan chose not to tell him that would be a waste of time, The family was dead already.

Then thinking of another question, the Marshal asked, "Are you going to bury them at the plantation, or bring her up here to the cemetery?" It was obvious that the cemetery had restrictions about accepting people of color.

Evan avoided the obvious remark by saying simply, "Our place has been a burial ground for centuries. I think we will make it our place of memories too."

Jonathan couldn't hold back his question any longer. "How can I become a deputy? Abbeville hasn't had any law man as long as I've lived. If someone had been after that pack of dogs, maybe my sister would be alive today." He hadn't raised his voice, but there was an obvious intensity of emotion.

The Marshal understood that this young man had just lost a loved one. He responded quietly, "You're right son. Most of our cities are fairly civilized, but there is a lot of wild country outside of them. We need peacemakers, law men who can and will enforce the rule of order. I'll tell you what, I can give you a book of French Civil Obedience, which is what Louisiana practices. You read this, and come back in a reasonable time for a test, and I will make you my deputy in Abbeville. It doesn't pay much, and occasionally it is dirty work. Have you got a gun you can learn to shoot?"

Jonathan nodded and said quietly, "A couple old ones I think."

"It would please me a lot to see you pass the test, and wear a star for Abbeville." Little did they know the distinguished path of bravery and service that was beginning this sad morning.

While they were gone, Moesh dug two graves on the mound and, using scrap lumber, crafted frames that would keep the sandy soil from crumbling into the honored vaults. Gently he placed the bodies into their final resting place. When it was time for the heartbroken family and friends to gather, Mr. Evan knew that he had to do a very difficult task. As patriarch he had to give leadership to this sad farewell.

"Friends," he softly began, "we are gathered here to worship God who gives every perfect gift, and to witness to our faith even as we mourn the death of these loved ones, Esther and Link. We come together as neighbors in grief, acknowledging our human loss. May God in divine mercy search our hearts, that in pain we may find comfort, in sorrow hope, and in death, resurrection. Now we lay them to rest, remembering how Jesus said, 'The one who lives and believes in me will never die.' This we faithfully do in Jesus' wonderful name. Amen." Together they said the words of the Lord's Prayer. Then with deliberate care, he reached down and gathered a handful of dirt, sprinkling it onto the still form within the frame. He repeated a handful of dirt to the other.

In a soft soprano voice, Molly began to sing. "God be with you till we meet again," Clarice, Becca, and Rose joined her, "by his counsels guide, uphold you, with his sheep securely fold you," Evan, Cal and Daniel joined the song, "God be with you till we meet again." The top of the mound was bathed in sunlight and a communal spirit of tender love. The song grew in volume. "God be with you till we meet again; keep love's banner floating o'er you, smite death's threatening wave before you; God be with you till we meet again." Lily sobbed while Dory embraced her.

Once again Evan cleared his throat and said, "Words cannot express how much our family values your support today. You truly are great friends. You are invited to share a bit of lunch with us before you make your way home. There is coffee or sweet tea. Dory and Molly have made a delightful Shrimp and Ham Taro chowder. There are also pieces of that Pecan pie she makes. Please join us in the dining room. Jonathan and Moesh will help ease you down the steep steps." As several of the folks turned to leave, they paused to admire the serenity of the bay. This truly was a vista worth appreciating.

The volume of voices in conversation filled the Hospitality dining room, aiding in understanding the community strength that was building. While the households were still more or less clustered, it gave George and Joy, the youngest, an opportunity to get to know where each person lived. The conversations of the men focused on the prospects of next season's crops. The women were more interested in Miss Clare and Becca's offer to teach reading and writing classes. The subject of Sunday devotions was also a highlight of discussion.

Mr. Cal was organizing his folks in preparation to leave when he noticed Evan and Jonathan lifting buckets of ash up the mound. He realized they were filling the graves, and could use some help. It only took a word to recruit a line of strong men passing the buckets, now filled with sandy soil, up the mound, where they were used to carefully fill the frames. Evan had said, "Ashes to ashes, and dust to dust." Now the burial was completed.

Two questions of destiny

As the men stood quietly looking out at the tranquil scene, Jonathan took advantage of the moment to ask Mr. Cal an important request. "Mr. Cal," he began, "as a military man, I suppose you have a lot of knowledge about guns."

Cal answered with a grin, "Sometimes I wish I could forget what I know about them."

"But my dad knows almost nothing about them," Jonathan went on. "I can't ask him to teach me how to handle a sidearm, so I am turning to you as a friend. I think I would like to become the deputy for Abbeville, and that would entail at least a bit of gun knowledge." When Mr. Perry looked at him with a raised eyebrow, Jonathan said, "Oh no. It is not only because of what happened to Esther and Link. I think we need law and order to become a healthy town. It is something I believe I can do to help us grow. But first I need to know about the hardware."

"That is a noble attitude, Jonathan. I believe I can help you with the basics. Come by any time and we'll go make some noise together." He wrapped his arm around the shoulder of the young man he had watched grow up. Cal felt like a favorite uncle."

Another life changing conversation occurred just moments later. Evan was standing in the dining room with Daniel. They had recapped the events of the tragic deaths. Now pensive, they were quiet until Evan asked, "Daniel, may I ask you a very personal question?" When his friend nodded, he raised a question that had been a source of several conversations. "Are you in love with Molly?"

The smile that bloomed on Daniel's face was not one of embarrassment, but true joy. "I am," the young man answered. "You can't imagine how much consternation I have felt over that." Before Evan could ask for clarification, Daniel went on, "I wanted to ask my father's permission to wed Molly. He was such a conservative man in that area, that I was afraid to bring it up with him. Then he died, and I have been wrestling with the guilt of failing myself, and Molly." His eyes searched Evan's.

"Let me understand this," Evan said playfully. You love her and want to marry her. She loves you, and would probably say 'yes,' before you finish asking, but you are doing nothing about it because of an imagined conflict with your dead father? Is that the problem?"

"When you put it like that, I sound a bit deranged, don't I?" he asked sheepishly. He pondered just a bit before saying, "But we both agreed to honor you all, and conduct ourselves only with righteousness."

"And you have been a perfect gentleman, Daniel. However, you are what, thirty, and she is twenty seven? Will you remain righteously chaste until you eventually receive your father's blessing?" Evan knew he was well beyond his appropriate point, but he continued bravely. "If you are seeking someone's permission, let me give it to you. Moesh and Dory have long been aware of her affection for you, but they are slaves. How can they give you a blessing? Clarice and I have always believed your fervor for the cause of abolition is based upon your love for Molly. We are all in complete support of a union between the two of you, even understanding the obvious challenges. For goodness sake, marry the woman!" He gave Daniel an embrace that took the place of a dead father's blessing. "Our only wish is for both of you to be happy."

"But what would people think?" Daniel asked painfully.

"What does that matter?" Evan mused. "For sure there will be critics. They have nothing to do with your happiness. The ones who love you are offering encouragement and support. That should be your consideration."

Daniel embraced him again, saying, "Thank you. That's all the boost I need." He turned and sought Molly.

At supper Evan introduced the topic with Moesh and Dory. Molly listened in uneasy silence. It was such a huge subject, and there were many parts to it. Finally, her father said to her, "It is beyond our imagination that you would be married to Mr. Daniel. Do you suppose you can stand beside him, not as a slave, but as a wife?" His eyes were steady, but not unkind.

Molly said softly, "I will always desire to serve him as mother has served you. Is she your slave? I think it would be an honor to give my life to this man as I have given my soul to Jesus, to love and follow him always." She was still for a moment, then added, "I'll try not to let the color of his skin keep me from being a good wife." They all burst into giggles.

When the laughter subsided, a nod from Dory urged Moesh to say, "Then our blessing is happily upon you both. We will be your truest support." He gave his daughter an uncharacteristic embrace, and Evan gave them each a hearty handshake.

For three days a heavy rain kept everyone inside. The plantation was quiet except for the chores in the barn. Evan ran through the puddles to get back into the house. At Grove house, Daniel was nervously pacing, praying for an end to the storm. He was positive there had been many conversations that would have been of interest to him. His house was large, but without her, it was very empty. He looked again at the clouds, hoping to see a hint of blue sky.

It was Sunday morning when the sun finally returned, warm and inviting. Clarice was adamant that they must observe the Sabbath. After their devotions, however, Moesh was quick to get the row boat out onto the bay to replenish the shrimp supply. Daniel wanted nothing more than a long conversation with Molly, then Evan, and finally an open conversation with anyone who was interested in their matrimonial union. Jonathan, on the other hand was eager to follow Mr. Cal home so they could share an introduction to the use of a pistol.

"You say this has been in the barn for a couple years?" Cal was examining the .44 that Jonathan had brought. "Would you trust your life to this gun?" he asked, looking at the accumulated dust and dirt.

"I suspect that neither the gun nor I am in any condition to be ideal," the student answered wisely.

"Well let's get to know the easy part first," the teacher said with a grin. "Always assume the gun is loaded, so point it down in the general direction where you are intending to shoot. Think safety and you won't be accidently sorry. Here's how the gun works," he cocked the hammer back. "The hammer is connected to the trigger with a strong spring. If you pull the trigger, the hammer strikes the cap on this little nipple." He carefully showed Jonathan each part. "A spark is driven into the cylinder where it ignites the powder, which blasts the ball out the barrel. If you make sure your gun is regularly cleaned and oiled it will work every time." He pulled the trigger, and Jonathan gave a startled jerk as there was only a small pop of the cap, with no explosion. "I'm assuming this is full of dirt," he pointed to the cap opening. It took a few minutes for Cal to lift off the caps and insert a needle to clean the small channels.

"Now there should at least be some reaction from the powder," he said with satisfaction. A board was standing in the tobacco row a short distance away. "Remember, a gun can be dangerous up to a three hundred paces." He lifted the pistol to shoulder level and pulled the trigger. The hammer struck the cap, which ignited the powder inside the cylinder. The detonation once again made Jonathan jump; he saw the board fall over from a direct hit. "Yup, it works just like that. Now you try it," he handed the weapon to an eager student.

Jonathan remembered the instructions, so he kept the muzzle pointed at the ground while Cal reset the target. The instructions paraded through his head; he hoped he could remember them all. When he hesitated before pulling the hammer back, his instructor said quietly, "Just think about it as an extension of your finger. You can point your finger right at that board; it's that easy."

The recoil was amplified by the loud detonation. Dirt in front of the target was kicked up. Cal observed, "You jerked the trigger," he demonstrated a sudden motion, "just squeeze it."

Jonathan thumbed the hammer back again, still remembering the rush of the powerful detonation. He lifted the revolver, and keeping both eyes on the target, then carefully squeezed. Once again the gun bucked in his palm, but this time the board fell from a direct hit.

"That's all there is to it!" Cal hooted. "You made that look easy. Let me set it up so you can do it again!" They went through three reloads before Jonathan began thumbing the hammer for a quick second shot at the falling board. It would become a signature move on the part of a determined deputy. For this day, he was convinced that the ache in his hand was a clear message that this lesson was complete.

"Thank you, Cal," he said sincerely. "If dad will trust me to do a refresher before I go into the Marshal's office for the test, I think I will pass it all just fine." He shook his hand trying to get some of the feeling back in it, then he shook Cal's saying, "I'll remember this day always.

Lawman!

Seventeen year old Jonathan Cossindale was the youngest deputy Marshal of Lafayette district to wear a circle star. He was assigned to keep the peace in Abbeville, which meant that he was on duty every Saturday evening, and had one monthly meeting with the Marshal to turn in his reports. For that noble service he received $7.50 a month. He faithfully made his rounds, determined to make his presence known to the merchants, and any possible trouble maker who might respect the star he wore. The first two months were uneventful.

As he approached Abbeville, Jonathan's thoughts were on Esther. Each time he approached the fork in the road where she died, he breathed a silent prayer. In the distance he heard the unmistakable report of gunshots. "Boom, Boom, Boom," it rumbled. He kicked his horse into a lope, "Boom!" It was louder as he slid past the first of the scattered homes on the main street. Ahead of him he saw a rider pushing his mount, and firing into the air, "Boom, Boom!" Jonathan stopped his horse in the middle of the road, and drew his pistol.

The approaching rider pulled hard on the reins, skidding to a stop. "Wooee, lookey here," he said happily in a drunken slur. "Here's our new deputy!" His gun was pointed at the ground.

"Get off your horse!" Jonathan shouted.

It took a few seconds before the inebriated rider responded. "O.K. but I'm a little tipsy. I could fall down." His gun was still in his hand, but he managed to drag his leg over the saddle and slide to the ground.

"Drop the gun!" Jonathan commanded.

"Why? Do you think I'm gonna shoot you?" he slurred. "Are you gonna shoot me?"

"No, you dumb head. I'm going to shoot your horse if you don't follow my instructions, and then I'm going to eat him." There was a pathetic sort of humor beginning.

The man started to sniffle, "Nah, please don't shoot the Colonel. He didn't do anything bad." Wet eyes turned toward Jonathan. "Maybe I should shoot you instead."

"I'm going to assume the liquor is doing the talking, because your gun is empty. But if you point it at me, I'm going to shoot your horse dead on the spot. The man's gun dropped into the dust of the street. "Good, now take off the gun belt and hang it over the saddle horn." When the man obediently responded, Jonathan stepped off to retrieve the gun and catch the horse's reins. "Hold on to the saddle while we walk up to the hotel." It was a sight that all who saw it would retell often. The new Deputy was leading a horse who was leading a bawling drunk to lock-up. No one was hurt, and a lasting friendship was beginning. No one really believed he would eat the horse.

At the hotel, Jonathan explained that he needed to use the storage space under the stairs for the night. The manager found a mattress and a bed-pan, then agreed that a dollar for the night was a fair price. He said it with a wide smile. Abbeville now had a useable jail, until a real one could be built.

The next morning Jonathan was there to open the door for an embarrassed young man who apologized for getting so carried away with liquor. He promised it would never happen again. "I've learned my lesson for truth," he said.

Jonathan believed him.

"Now, if you will empty the bed-pan," the deputy directed, "then pay the hotel a dollar for your room, you'll be done here. Pay a dollar to the livery stable for putting up the Colonel, then you can go home. The toughest part might be in makin' peace with whoever is angry with you for getting drunk. I really don't want this to ever happen again." He shook the young man's hand. "What's your name?"

"Lowell Stanley, sir. I want to thank you for not shooting my horse." Both men chuckled. "It will never happen again," he repeated. After a brief silence, he added, "Are you here every Saturday? I'd like to see you again, to show you that I am a fairly rational man when I'm sober. Maybe you'd like to have supper with us some quiet evening." Once again he offered to shake Jonathan's hand.

For the next three years something like that would happen again and again. Jonathan found a lost child; guided a wandering flock of sheep back into their grazing field; settled boundary disputes, and even collected some delinquent taxes. He was a committed peace keeper, upholding the law while respecting the people, and working toward a positive conclusion to any problem. Even the people he arrested wound up thanking him and wanting to become his friend. During that time Abbeville would enjoy a building boom; a new bank, a church and another saloon would make it a fair town. Then it would finally build a jail with a Marshal's office.

Time for a Wedding!

Molly floated leisurely in the shallow water of Vermillion Bay. There had been several conversations about the marriage with Mr. Daniel. Everyone had advice to assure her that the difficulties could be manageable, if she was convinced it was the right thing to do. Here in the gentle water, she was positive it would be wonderful to be Mrs. Higgins. She smiled at the thought; she had never had a family name.

She gave a couple gentle kicks to guide herself toward the shore. While she could remain swimming longer, she was sure there were chores waiting her attention. But for one more lazy moment, she recalled Miss Clare's advice. She had told Molly to think of each month in three parts, Four days of blood flow could be followed by two weeks of intimacy. The two weeks after that was the fertile time of conception. Molly daydreamed about a light skinned child, then realized she had to hurry in to dry off and dress for the work of the day.

A week later, Hospitality House was filled with eager folks. A letter, inviting Lisle to attend this special service, had brought her and Sydney from Tallahassee. The Sunday devotions were concluded with the announcement that Mr. Daniel and Molly's nuptials would follow the closing prayer. Miss Clare was softly playing Peer Gynt's "Afternoon of the Fawn" as Molly walked in with her soft yellow velvet dress. Daniel was dressed in a light tan suit. Lisle smiled warmly, remembering when she had last seen them in just those same clothes.

Together they were a very handsome couple. Mr. Evan prayed a blessing prayer on the formation of a new home. Then he directed a question to Daniel.

"Daniel Higgins, do you love Molly, and intend, to the extent of your ability, to dearly receive her as your wife, and with her, build a Christian home?"

"Yes I do, sir, God being my helper," the nervous groom answered

Turning to Molly he asked, "Molly Moesh, do you love Daniel, and intend, to the extent of your ability, to dearly receive him as your husband, and with him build a Christian home?"

Her voice was as soft as a prayer as she replied, "Yes I do, sir, God being my helper." Daniel slid a gold band on her finger.

"Then we, assembled in your honor, collectively declare this 8th day of May of the year 1839, that God has joined you both in holy matrimony. May all glory and honor be unto His Holy Name. Amen.." Without invitation, Daniel kissed Molly. The gathering broke into happy applause.

Oh my, there was so much delightful food! As usual the Hospitality kitchen had produced a shrimp and ham Taro gumbo; there were also several pecan pies. From the Grove House kitchen, Mary and Martha, the cooks, had made a platter of crispy Taro fingers, with salt and seasoning; they also brought a fluffy lime pie that just dared you not to eat another slice, and a lime cake that was every bit as good. Lydia, Mr. Cal's cook had baked a huge serving of ribs with sauce. The folks who enjoyed the feast marked it as the very best they had ever known. Finally, when the men were standing near the mound smoking, Molly asked Daniel if he would enjoy a swim with her. This night she especially wanted her body cleansed as a precious gift. He promised to join her directly. He felt an obligation to thank the hosts.

Molly was already wading into the water when he reached the bungalow to change. There was a tiny bit of relief, for he had been anxious about disrobing completely in her presence. Moments later she welcomed him with a warm kiss, pressing herself against him.

"Does this seem like a dream to you Mr. Daniel?" she asked softly. "I can scarcely believe the wonder of this day." Her arms were comfortably wrapped around his shoulders.

"It is like a dream," he answered, moving them in a slow circle. The movement caused her body to rub against him in a most pleasant way.

"Do you think Mary and Martha will welcome me to Grove House? I am bringing a new condition to it."

"They have known about my affection for you for a long while. They love me and want my happiness. Of course they will welcome you." He turned them in another circle; this time kissing her slowly.

They leisurely watched the sun setting over Vermillion Bay, two lovers becoming more and more aroused. The heightened endorphin glow was not only the gift of the Seerier, but they certainly did add a bit to it. Finally he suggested that they dry off and dress so they could go to the Grove House. He added that he might be a bit nervous about this first night together.

"Mr. Daniel, my mother has given me good counsel about this night. I will help us if you need me to." They both enjoyed the relaxing chuckle.

"Please, Molly, it is not necessary for you to call me 'Mr.'

"But I only want to honor and serve you, my husband. It is a respectable way for me to remind you that I love you," Molly said, just above a whisper. She pressed against him once more.

"Then I will refer to you as 'Mrs. Molly', for the same reason." They waded ashore toward the bungalow and dry towels.

Sydney was waiting for them in the carriage, He said it was too dark to walk home on their wedding night. The smile that blossomed on his face was another of the many affirmations they received that day. And as they arrived at the Grove House, lanterns lined the walk up the steps of the big door. Inside the soft light of lanterns warmed their way to the bedroom.

Dory had smiled when she had said, "Don't be shy about your nervousness. He will feel the same way; and perhaps making love will be over more suddenly than you want. That is also due to the nervousness. Just hold him, and say what is in your heart." True to the mother's counsel, it was too soon over, and Molly held Daniel firmly against her. Time stood still in the wonder of their union, until she felt a spreading warmth that grew to a shuddering breathlessness. She whispered, "For all my life I will love you."

Daniel whispered, "I love you for all my life as well." Then after a very long silent moment he asked, "Do you think we can return to the beach again tomorrow afternoon?" They both giggled into the covers.

An important invitation

The following Saturday Jonathan was making his security round at Abbeville. Slowly he had walked his horse down one side of the street, examining doors and windows, looking for anything that might seem unusual. Then he turned back and gave the stores on the other side the same scrutiny. He reminded himself that while it seemed boring, he was the representation of the law in town. What he was doing was building confidence in a small town that needed it.

When he was just finishing his inspection, a horseman joined him. It was Lowell Stanley. "Evening Deputy. It seems pretty quiet tonight," he said formally. They rode on for a couple minutes. "Pa butchered a beef, and Ma has been cookin' it for a couple days. I think it's a roast tonight with trimmin's. Could I invite you to join us for supper. You haven't eaten, have you?"

The invitation was a surprise to be sure, but Jonathan could tell that it was also a very sincere one. "You know, I've never tasted beef," he answered. "That would be a very kind offer; I'd be glad to have a place at your table. You're sure it's not the Colonel that you're serving?" Both men chuckled.

"You wait and see what a good cook Ma is, and I'm sittin' on the Colonel."

Jonathan kept the banter going by asking, "By any chance do you have a sister?"

"Whooee," Lowell laughed. "You're in luck, I got one! She's not spoke for, 'cause she is only sixteen. But that's not why I invited you to dinner. I want you to see that I'm not a drunk, just a guy who can get carried away."

"And I hope you understand," Jonathan replied with a happy grin, "that I'm not the sort of guy who would shoot and eat your horse." There was more laughter, as Jonathan realized that he was following Lowell's direction to turn down a lane headed for a plantation house surrounded by sugar cane. "It looks like we have a lot more than sisters in common."

During the supper, which Jonathan declared repeatedly was the best he had ever enjoyed, there were several surprises. Since he was at least a head taller than anyone else at the table, they were shocked to learn that he was only seventeen. Lowell's sister, Elizabeth, called Betsy, was just a year younger than the deputy.

Jonathan smiled saying, "That's a coincident, 'cause your about the same age as my sister Becca. By the way, do you folks carry sugar canes to the mill for a place down on Vermillion Bay? I thought I recognized the wagon." They had a lot in common. Perhaps the most urgent discovery however, was the fact that Mrs. Stanley wasn't eating, due to a bleeding ulcer, the doctor had diagnosed. The frail woman looked pale even though she tried to maintain a cheery attitude.

"Ma'am, I know this is going to sound like one of those travelling hucksters selling vitality serum. I'd like to invite you to Vermillion Plantation tomorrow. Hospitality House is a place where dozens of people have come to find relief from illness or injuries. The stories would sound unbelievable to someone who hasn't tried it. I don't know if it is the pure spring water, as some declare, or the healing salt water, as others claim, or a combination of both. I just know that incredible healing has happened to folks who give it a try. As a way of thanking you for this wonderful dinner, will you come and spend an hour at our beach? If you feel some better, come back for another session there. At worst, you will have a pleasant swim, and a fine lunch." Jonathan's gaze was inviting, and winning.

"I have been feeling poorly for so long, I've forgotten what good feels like," the slight woman said with a weak smile. "I've eaten chalk and drank nasty concoctions that didn't help a bit. I'm desperate enough to try anything if it has a chance of making me feel better.

The next morning when Jonathan saw the carriage turn into the lane, he was delighted to see Lowell and Betsy along with Mr. and Mrs. Stanley. Fortunately he had told his dad about the evening meal and conversation, so it was no surprise that extra bathing robes and towels were ready in the bungalow.

The water was delightfully refreshing to the four as they waded in. For Lowell and Betsy it was a unique opportunity to try to swim a bit. Mostly they frolicked and splashed. Their folks were taking this as a serious opportunity to experience new health. Mr. Stanley, Irving, attended his wife, Lois, into the shallow water and helped her to be seated in water not quite chest deep on her; he sat beside her, bracing her with his arm. The smile that warmed her face, however, was reward enough for their short trip. Unseen by them the Seerier were busy. One host in particular needed urgent attention; it was near death from internal damage! So each administration was accompanied with a cell replacement boost and an immunity stimulant. The endorphin signal was repeated several times to all four. It was the best they could do to repair their host. Lily brought a pitcher of pure spring water and four glasses for their refreshment, When at last they agreed it was time to get out and dry off, she brought a couple more pitchers for them to rinse the salt water away.

When they were dried and dressed, Jonathan guided them into the Hospitality dining room where four bowls of Ham Taro gumbo awaited them, with tall glasses of spring water, or sweet tea if they wished. Evan brought Clarice to be introduced as well as Becca, who was an instant interest to Lowell. There were so very many possibilities to the day. All the while Lois fairly blushed with her buoyant feelings. She even dared eat some of her gumbo, declaring it the most flavorful she could recall.

Before the Stanleys left, Irving negotiated with Evan, "If we can return a couple more times to bathe Lois, I'll transport your sugar cane in exchange."

"That is a bit one-sided in our favor," Evan replied with a smile. "Let's see how she feels by the end of the week. Perhaps you folks would like to join us for Sunday devotions here in Hospitality

House? We could talk more then." Yes indeed, there were many possibilities in the day.

As it turned out, Irving hauled the sugar cane again, then agreed to transport two loads of Taro to Lafayette for a fair price. He also hauled the first picking of three hundred boxes of Oranges for Daniel.

After her third visit to the beach, Lois declared her stomach to be fully healed, no more vomiting, cramps or complications. Her appetite was back and her rosy cheeks affirmed her statement. Perhaps Lowell was the most pleased, because it gave him another reason to stop by and thank Evan….and Becca, of course.

Daniel and Molly swam every day, usually after supper. Folks smiled believing that the honeymoon couple were still preparing their bodies for intimacy. It was a very happy time. Becca may have been a tiny bit envious of Molly's joy. She welcomed, and coyly encouraged Lowell's interest in her romantically. They were married at Hospitality House just before Christmas. How does the poet say it? "So be not sad if times seem long and slow, too often man is urgent, forgetting light and hope, while the Master does not halt nor grope, but builds, and builds, and subtly builds again in ways unrecognized, unknown."

Trial by Fire

Twenty year old Jonathan was doing his first round on Saturday afternoon. He was a bit bored with a job that had started with a bang and had become more of a whimper. He knew every board in every building front on this street. Steadily he rode past the general store, then the hardware store. Maybe he should stop and get... The thought never finished for just in front of him a man ran into the street shouting, "They're robbing the bank!"

Jonathan pulled hard on the right rein, turning his horse away. As he dismounted, he pulled his pistol. Perhaps he had taken three or four strides toward the bank when three men burst out of the door. Instantly Jonathan recognized the gun in the center man's fist. The deputy recalled how easily he had hit the board in the tobacco field. He squeezed and felt his pistol recoil. He had shot high, about a foot high. Instead of hitting the man's chest, he saw a dark void bloom in the center of his forehead and his hat flew off the back. Without thinking about it Jonathan fired twice at the man on the left carrying the money bag. This time his aim was accurate and both rounds hit the center of the man's shirt. He also crumpled, lifeless. The third man was just clearing his gun from its holster when Jonathan fired again, twice. The shocked look of mortality grimaced across the robber's face, as he joined his comrades in death. The entire skirmish had taken no more than three or four seconds. Jonathan stood statue still and took a deep breath, then he hurried to the bank door. Peering in he asked in a loud voice, "Are there any more in here?"

The banker's shaky voice answered, "No sir, there were only three. Did you get them?" A wave of nausea swept over Jonathan.

"You might want to come out and retrieve your money," the deputy said with a tight voice. A circle of town's folks were gathering around. A couple of the men had rifles. Jonathan finally holstered his gun and stepped back out to the three bodies. He rolled them over onto their backs, checking for any sign of life, even though it was obvious there would be none. He searched their pockets and found sparse coins and a folding knife.

"Anyone recognize these fellas?" he asked. Folks shook their heads. They were not locals. There was quiet talk about this horrible event; nothing like this had ever happened in Abbeville. Heads were shaking in disbelief, and in new confidence in their law man. Finally Jonathan said, "This is new ground for me too, so here's how I see this working out. We need to get these guys in the ground before they start to smell bad. The Marshal is going to claim the big bay with the Sharps Rolling Block rifle." He pointed to the red horse at the hitching rail. "The holsters and guns also are now Marshal Baldwin's. The other two horses will be taken to the livery stable for sale, $25 dollars apiece to pay for burial. Is there anyone who will bury these boys for fifty dollars? Three hands were raised. Jonathan pointed to the first one. "Do you want money, or would you rather have the horses and saddles?"

"Shoot fire, deputy, I'd sure like to have those horses." The man said as though he was receiving a gift.

"That makes it pretty easy. If you'll get a wagon, we'll help you load these bodies on it to move them to the cemetery. Drop them on the ground off to the side. If Marshal Baldwin from Lafayette wants to try to identify them he'll come out on Monday. Then any time on Tuesday you can put them in the ground. Their hats, belts and boots are yours too if you want them." Jonathan noticed a gold ring with a shiny red stone on one of the little fingers. He bent and twisted the ring loose. "I'll take this to the Marshal, too. It might help in identifying these men."

Jonathan left Vermillion while it was still dead dark. He was convinced the Bay could make excellent time, but he was hoping to be home before supper, and that only gave him a couple hours in Lafayette.

The Marshal reread his report, then asked, "This sounds like you fired five shots while they were running down five steps from the bank porch. Is that correct?"

"Yes sir, Jonathan quietly replied. "I was not aiming for his head. The first round was high. They were only about twelve or fourteen feet from me. Then I fired twice at the one on my left, and twice at the one on my right, who was just clearing his pistol. It was only as I examined their dead bodies that I determined that those four shots were heart shots, center mass." The deputy took a deep breath. "The bodies are lying in the Abbeville cemetery, if you would like to inspect, or identify them."

"I'll do that this afternoon, and interview some folks who may have witnessed the shootings. Do you have anything else to tell me?"

"I believe Jim Kirby is the name of a witness who first reported the robbery in progress. Only one more thing, the one who was carrying the money was wearing this ring on his little finger. I thought that might be something you would recognize. I also commandeered the dark Bay with a Sharps in a saddle scabbard. It will be a more reliable horse than the old fellow I've been straddling all my life. The other two horses are covering the cost of burying the three bodies tomorrow."

"Did you also confiscate the guns and holsters?"

"Yes sir. They are in the lock box at the jail in Abbeville."

"Jonathan, it can't be done better than that. You are completely within our instructions. I'm thinking there are a couple full-time positions if you would like a promotion."

"I'm glad I haven't let you down, sir. I'll think about it, but Abbeville is my home, and this job lets me work the plantation most of the week. Thank you for your confidence in me." Jonathan held out his hand to shake the Marshal's.

He had ridden the Bay only a couple blocks when a voice right behind him barked, "Hey you on the Bay. Where'd you get my brother's horse?"

Jonathan spun around in the saddle, clearly revealing the circle star on his chest. No one met his gaze, or seemed in any way interested in him or his horse.

At supper, Jonathan was recapping the events of the day, and reflecting on the change the weekend had made upon him. He told them about the red ring he had taken from the robber's hand. Surprisingly, Moesh rose from the table and was gone for a couple minutes. When he returned, he offered Jonathan a gold ring with a shiny red stone. "Was it like this one," he asked.

"Yes," Jonathan responded with a questioning voice. "It was exactly like this. Moesh, where did you get this one?"

"Do you recall when Mr. Daniel and I were on an errand to purchase more sugar canes? The robber with an empty gun took the money. He lost his life and his horse that day, and this ring that I thought was of no value. Do you suppose the Marshal should see it?"

"You are sure the man that was wearing this ring is dead?" Jonathan asked for more information.

"He was so busy looking at the gold coins he didn't hear me approaching his campsite. I finally had to make a sound to get his attention. He thought he could club me with the empty shotgun before my lance could reach him. He was wrong. Yes, I'm quite sure he is dead." Moesh had no outward sign of emotion as he relayed the story.

"I'm sure Marshal Baldwin would like to see this ring too," Jonathan answered. "When he learns all it has to say, he will return it to you. Thank you for remembering it."

In fact, the Marshal had learned all he needed from the first ring. It directed him to a Basque family named Livonia that had settled in New Iberia, about ten miles southeast of Lafayette. Three brothers had brought their wives and children to make a new start in the New World. Regrettably they were following the same criminal path that had caused them to leave Spain; they had been a constant source of complaints. In fact, they had become such a public menace the Marshal called for all deputies to form a posse to control the situation. Jonathan answered the call.

Seven deputies followed the Marshal into New Iberia. The deputy there told them he knew of the families, of course, and would guide them to their home. Jonathan noticed that he wore no holster or side arm, but carried a double barrel shotgun. After about fifteen minutes they turned into a side road that climbed a low hill. Deep ditches were on both sides of the road, making them form an awkward double line as they approached a handful of ill-kempt buildings. Before the Marshal could call to the house, a hail of bullets greeted them. Jonathan could hear shuffling and cursing behind him as he spurred the Bay to jump the ditch and find shelter behind a shed. He dismounted and drew his pistol. There was plenty of gunfire coming both from the house and the lawmen who were seeking cover in the ditches.

A scurrying form came from behind the house and headed for the same shed Jonathan was using as a shield. If the situation had not been so deadly, the surprise would have been comical. The young man darted around the corner of the shed, only to be bashed by an available fencepost. He didn't even see it coming. Jonathan took the rifle he had been carrying.

A second runner emerged from the back of the house. He also ran nearly to the shed before he was shot with the rifle. Jonathan crawled out to him and pulled the wounded man out of sight from the house, and took his pistol. The gunfire was not lessening. With no clear orders on how to conduct the battle, or how to proceed, Jonathan took a deep breath, let it out slowly and ran for the house. He knew there was a back door, and if the fight was in front he might be able to get inside their defenses.

Jonathan scarcely got in the door when a very angry man roared at him, brandishing a very big knife. Without thinking about it, his pistol barked twice. The shocked man simply collapsed like a rag doll. Another man across the room looked up, but before he could turn his gun toward Jonathan, once again two quick shots found their mark. A young man lurched at him and died at his feet. Now attention all around the room focused on him. He dropped the empty gun and quickly pulled his own saying, "I would rather not kill you. If you do not drop your weapons though, I have no other choice." An older man started to raise his weapon and was dropped on the spot by two quick shots. "Give me a reason, and I will kill more of you." The front door burst open and two more deputies joined him. It was obvious that they were eager to fight on.

"Hold your fire," Jonathan shouted. "But kill the next one that raises a weapon." He was convinced the battle was over. Guns, most of them empty, were being dropped to the floor. Two older women came from the back of the house with cloths to bind up several wounds. Jonathan allowed them to assist, but warned them that they would die as surely as the ones who had not heeded his warning. The deputies did not holster their weapons. Finally, the wounded and mobile that could make it outside were taken out, one by one, and shackled to a long rope. The dead were piled on a wagon for burial in New Iberia; many of them wore red rings.

Only then did Jonathan become aware of the drama that was still unfolding beside the road down the hill. Marshal Baldwin lay pinned under his dead horse. Apparently, that initial barrage of bullets had killed the animal, which fell on top of the Marshal in the ditch. The pale face of the law man and his clenched teeth indicated his pain and possible injuries. The challenge was in trying to lift a twelve hundred pound dead weight off of him without further injury.

"Rather than trying to lift it," Jonathan suggested, "why don't we pass a rope under the mount and see if a couple of the stronger horses could pull from this side, and simply roll him until the Marshal is free enough to be lifted out. By the looks of his boot, his leg is busted pretty badly." A rope was passed under the head of the horse, but they couldn't find a way under the animal's shoulders. "Just get it under the girth," Jonathan suggested, "that should be stout enough."

With no small effort the two horses gave a steady pull that finally, with the help of several strong hands pushing, rolled the big animal off the Marshal, who seemed to have lost consciousness sometime during the maneuver. Eager deputies lifted him carefully. A carriage was found in a shed and rolled out so they could lay him flat. It had become obvious to Jonathan that there was no leadership in this posse now. Willing men looked to him for instruction. Maybe it was because he had found access through the back door, or his contribution to the body count. At any rate he decided to make a suggestion. It came out as a command.

"You men take the dead into New Iberia, where they can be buried. Take the Marshal's saddle too. These others can be hauled to Lafayette, and jailed until we can get the Marshal from Baton Rouge to deal the legalities with them. I've got to get the Marshal to Vermillion Plantation. He is hurt badly and I think it's his only chance of making it through this day." As he was harnessing the Bay to the carriage, he added, "If I head straight west I'll cross Live Oak road at Delcambre. I can get him there in a couple hours." Jonathan was unaware of the career path he had just carved for himself.

It was mid afternoon when he entered the lane to Vermillion Plantation. He could see Moesh run for the big house as soon as he recognized the big Bay. Evan was there to greet Jonathan and learn what needed to be done.

"I didn't know what else to do, dad. I think he is busted up in several places. He's been out cold since we put him in here. I know his leg is broken, and something seems way wrong with his hips." The Marshal moaned as the three men lifted him out of the carriage and placed him on a wooden beach chair. They carried him to the beach, where Evan asked Jonathan to ease off the injured man's boots. Then they slipped his pants off. "As long as he is unconscious, let's see if we can set and straighten that leg," Evan guided them. Jonathan held the thigh while the other two gave a tug and felt the bone snap back in place. Moesh brought a small board that was carefully bound to the damaged leg with a soft cloth strip, from the ankle to his hip.

"Now, let's get him into the water for a bit," Evan suggested. "Perhaps the cool temperature will help wake him." They lifted the seated man carefully. "Jonathan, would you like to stay with him? I'll have Lily bring down some gumbo for both of you. If he wakes up in a strange place, he may need some information to help him relax, if that's possible." Before he returned to the big house, he added, "I especially want to hear your account of this day's challenge as well."

Less than an hour later the Marshal opened his eyes. He shifted and moaned in pain. Jonathan was beside him in the water to explain, "You were pinned under your horse. We've tried to set your leg and think there may be some damage to your hip. Are you in much pain?"

The Marshal looked around in confusion. "What the hell am I doing in the water?"

"Sir, I felt the cool water might ease the swelling in your leg, and reduce the internal bleeding in your pelvis." Jonathan held his steady gaze.

"Broke my leg, you say? And my horse is dead?" He was trying to put together scraps of memory of the battle. "What happened with the Livonia folks? I just remember a shit load of gunfire." He shook his head as if to clear the memories it contained.

"We had no casualties, sir, except your horse, of course." Perhaps they both became aware of the incongruity of Jonathan giving a battle report to a Marshal who was naked from the waist down. "They had six killed, and four wounded. The seven survivors are being locked in the Lafayette jail. Since he lives in Henderson, Deputy Gerald Weeks is on his way to get the Baton Rouge Marshal to come and press charges."

"How many of those slain men were your doing?" Now the Marshal's eyes seemed clear and probing.

"Four sir, and one of the wounded; then there was the one I disabled with a fencepost." Finally Jonathan managed a weak smile.

"You never cease to amaze me, son. Was it also your idea to bring me here for medical help?"

"Yes sir. I have no idea how severe your internal injuries might be, but the leg looked real bad, but its set now, and splinted. My dad and Moesh, our man servant, are pretty experienced at helping folks get better. Captain Perry was near death when he was brought here. Now he is a true friend, the one who taught me what to do with a pistol."

"I hope I get a chance to thank him," the Marshal said as he closed his eyes.

"I do too," the deputy answered. "Here comes Lily with a pitcher of spring water. That will speed up the healing. She'll bring some gumbo for us directly." He looked at the Marshal's closed eyes not knowing if he was sleeping or once more unconscious. Actually the law man was thinking how he was about to write his letter of resignation, and how directly he could urge the Territorial U.S. Marshal to appoint Jonathan to the vacancy.

For three days the Marshal was moved into the bay for some water time, and then helped into the bungalow bed to continue the healing that, encouraged by the Seerier, was happening more quickly than expected. He felt little pain in his leg, but could put no weight at all on his pelvis. On the sixth day, however, when his wife brought the carriage to take him home, the Marshal was able, with Moesh's help and a crutch, to slide into the passenger's seat. "I promise to return here," he said, "and find some way to thank you for your mercy." Looking at Jonathan, he added, "It's not necessary for you to put all this in your report." The next time Evan visited the bank, to his surprise a voucher for $500 was added to his account from the Marshal's Service for "medical treatments."

When Jonathan went to Lafayette to turn in his monthly report, he was given a letter from the Territorial U.S. Marshal in Baton Rouge. He was being considered as a replacement for the retiring Marshal Augustine Baldwin. His interview appointment time was set for Tuesday fortnight, ample time to brush up on the law book, and talk with Betsy about what this might mean for their future.

The tests and interview were sterling, surpassed only by the unanimous affirmation of every deputy the U.S. Marshal asked for a reference. Twenty four year old Jonathan Cossindale was named Lafayette Marshal. With his father's help, he purchased a nice home where a family could be raised. Betsy was proud to become his bride.

It must have been an exceptionally warm summer in Vermillion Plantation, or as they say, it was something in the water. Molly finally became pregnant, as did Becca, and Joy for the second time. There was about to be a nursery full of babies by Easter. Clarice may have been a bit happier than Evan, but it was a close race.

Changing Political Climate

D aniel received an urgent letter saying that he was needed as a lobbyist in Washington. It triggered an unusual response within him. Perhaps because the issue of his mixed race wedding had never been resolved with his father, or perhaps he simply hungered for the recognition and respect the political platform offered to him, Daniel chose to answer the distant call. It was a decision that would take him far away from Molly. Rational leadership was in short supply as the Free states versus slavery states tension was growing daily. A tall presidential candidate from Illinois had made the argument that if the western states seeking statehood could be forced to remain slave free, the entire slavery system would eventually die out. Those slavery states considered that tactic unconstitutional, for it disrupted the equilibrium of balance in both the house and senate. The invention of the cotton gin, or engine as some called it, was making the cotton growing states incredibly wealthy. One third of the world's cotton supply was coming out of four slave states. The opposing forces of commerce and politics spelled an inevitable conflict of monumental proportions. Daniel promised that he would be gone no longer than one month, but knew in his heart that these issues were far too large to be simply or quickly solved.

Molly missed him, of course. It helped that each day she could walk to the Hospitality house and become involved in whatever plans that day may hold. They were all glad for her presence. But at night she returned to the Grove House, and slept in her large empty pillowy bed.

Daniel had been gone a week when Molly heard her bedroom door open as she was preparing for bed. She spun about, clutching her unbuttoned dress tight to her. Eli, the youngest of the men servants came into the room as silent as a shadow. He walked straight toward her, wearing a wide smile and his pants, no shirt and no shoes. "The man's gone," he said quietly, "and I'm thinking the night girl is lonesome. I can fix that for you."

"Eli, you get out of here," Molly shouted. But it had no effect on the grinning young man who drew closer to her. "Eli, get out!" she screamed.

His hands touched her shoulders and tugged at the cloth dress.

"Eli, go, get away!" He voice echoed through the halls as she struggled to keep the dress around her. He pulled harder on one side and the dress slipped off her shoulder, exposing her breast.

"There we go, Beauty," he grinned. "I'll be very nice to you." He pulled the loose dress further down her body.

"Roman, help me!" she screamed loud enough to be heard beyond the walls. Suddenly there was the sound of running feet, and the expression changed on Eli's face. For a tiny moment he was angry, but as Roman barged into the room he was terribly afraid. The older man grasped his hand free from Molly's dress. Then with the other hand he clubbed the young man's face. Eli was trying to say something, but it was far beyond the time for words. Another powerful blow struck the side of his face and the young man collapsed unconscious. Mary and Martha hurried in holding lanterns. They immediately helped a weeping Molly rearrange her dress.

When everyone had caught their breath, Roman made sure Molly was unhurt. Eli moaned into consciousness. Roman asked if she wanted him hung for his crime, or castrated.

"Please don't," a whispered voice spoke from the floor. "I didn't know. I thought she was one of us, a slave, a night woman."

Roman's foot kicked him in the side hard enough to drive out the breath from the now terrified man. "You fool! Mrs. Molly is Mr. Daniel's wife." He raised his voice, "She owns your worthless life."

"Thank you for rescuing me, Roman," Molly said softly. "Mr. Daniel will want to express his thanks when he comes home. I don't want you to hang Eli, but I'm afraid I don't want to see him around my home again. Please take him outside and securely bind him. In the morning I will ask Mr. Evan or Jonathan to take him to the auction block in Lafayette."

The now weeping man on the floor whimpered, "I am so sorry Mrs. Molly. I really didn't know. I'm sorry." Roman grasped a fistful of curly hair and pulled the young man to his feet. He led and dragged the sobbing man out of the room, then out of the house. Moments later the women heard a cry of pain come from the front. Then all was quiet.

Through the night Molly had restless thoughts about the incident. She had been insulted, but not assaulted. Her wrath had been witnessed by members of the household, and their loyalty demonstrated. They were well aware of the power of her authority. "But am I?" she asked herself. "What do I want them to see in me?" With the dawn, she was awake and reading her Bible. She had marked a special page, Colossians 4, which begins, "Masters, treat your slaves justly and fairly, knowing that you also have a Master in heaven."

Her eyes went up the page and read the preceding words, "Put on then, as God's chosen ones, holy and beloved, compassion, kindness, lowliness, meekness, and patience, forbearing one another and, if one has a complaint against another, forgiving each other; as the Lord has forgiven you, so you also must forgive. And above all these put on love, which binds everything together in perfect harmony." Molly reread the words. She became convinced of what she must do.

As soon as she was dressed, she found Roman and asked him to unbind Eli. "God's Word has shown me that I must forgive Eli for his actions last night. I am still uncomfortable in his presence, so I am restricting him from the main house, and am asking you to assign his work duties elsewhere. Mr. Daniel will deal with this when he gets home."

"That is very gracious of you, Mrs. Molly. He is a good worker, and I believe a good man, just a young ignorant one. I'm glad he is not going to the auction block today. I did give him an ear notch to remember that terrible mistake." Roman promised to keep a closer eye on the main house, and her safety as well.

The entire incident demonstrated to Molly her unique new status, and how much more clearly she could witness to her faith in Jesus. Yes, she could play songs of faith. Yes, she could read pages of scripture, and pray with the best of them. But she needed to revisit her conduct and be a completely loving person, who could "bind everything together in perfect harmony," instead of sending a young man, who had frightened her, to the auction block. There was a new life in Molly, and she was convinced she could make it an even better life than she had known.

As it turned out, Eli was allowed to attend the Sunday devotions, and proved to be an alert student. He also demonstrated a rich baritone voice that others loved to hear. Perhaps the most surprising change was his devotion to Mrs. Molly, who had shown him the depths of forgiveness. He followed her like a puppy. She assumed it was his attempt at atonement, but she didn't ask him to stop it. The bright red scar on his ear was a reminder to them all of an avoidable mistake.

By the first of November, Daniel had not returned; he had been gone three months. Roman decided the third season fruit could wait no longer without going to waste. He asked Mr. Evan, who relayed the request to Mr. Cal, for all the help they could spare. The twelve men managed to pick over thirteen hundred boxes of Oranges. Mr. Stanley transported them to Lafayette. All in all it was a heroic effort made possible only by the fabric of community that the neighbors all brought together.

When Daniel finally returned two weeks after the harvest was complete, he was deeply apologetic, and grateful for Roman's initiative. When he held Molly in his arms, now, very aware of her enlarged tummy, he tried to explain the absence. "I missed you every day, and was ashamed that I broke my promise. I felt it my duty to try to head off a violent collision that is developing in Washington. It would have been a terrible waste if the fruit had not been picked," he said, "but there is an even greater waste building in the nation's capitol. I, and several others, tried to mediate the growing schism. We finally had to admit the mounting pressure must be allowed to run its course. Words seemed empty to the opposing sides. Sadly there is no longer room for compromise between stubborn people."

Molly wanted to believe his words, but wondered if they were reasons for his absence or simply excuses. By Christmas those words were given new perspective.

Mr. Meredith Perry, Cap'n Cal's father, came from Hattiesburg for a visit. He said he wanted to see for himself this tobacco plantation that his son had so colorfully described. He also wanted to experience the beach at Vermillion Plantation, and share Sunday devotions with the community. He had a large agenda, which he revealed only after satisfying all those other introductions. The senior Perry had also brought six heavy crates with him. They were clearly marked with the words, "Fragile Piano." A moving wagon had hauled the crates to the tobacco plantation, where he explained. "Trouble is on the way, son. Thirty years ago my voice was important to Mississippi's development as a state of the Union. People listened. Today they only hear the voice of King Cotton; and I'm concerned where that voice is leading."

Cal asked his father, "You sound like trouble is eminent with the state. Do you actually believe that might be the case?' It was a concept nearly too large to grasp.

"It's a lot bigger than a regional squabble, Calvin. There are more than a few angry voices calling for the retraction of our state's constitution from the Republic. While they are not in the majority, I am distressed to say they are growing in popularity. In the face of that, I think prudence on our part is simple wisdom. I have been pulling my money out of our bank little by little. I don't want to remove it all, or contribute to the problem by causing a panic. Still, I'm concerned that the banks may lack sufficient securities, or be subject to nationalization if the worst happens. Your plantation is a more secure place than mine, so I have brought your inheritance for safe keeping, not in the form of a paper account, but gold coins. The crates can be made into a security box. I made ours into an attractive bed frame. Each bag has 500 double eagles, and there are 20 bags in each crate. The six crates filled our bed frame about half full. I'm assuming you will have some of your own income to make secure. It has given me sounder sleep than I can recall, like a mattress of gold." He chuckled at his own humor.

"Dad, I don't know what to say, Cal said softly. "Part of me wants to tell you to keep the inheritance. But I can see it is an important strategy for you. Do you actually believe the situation is this dire in Washington?"

"Maybe not in Washington yet, but surely in Mississippi," his dad answered. "I know we are in for a terrible conflict." The father rested his hand on his son's shoulder. "I'm glad you won't be in this one. For what it's worth, I've already delivered a like load to your sister in Florida. I think it's going to be bad there, too."

"It's just that this place, these people, seem so peaceful I can't fathom the sort of conflict you are implying." Cal shook his head with doubt.

"If I wasn't so invested in Hattiesburg, I would be very tempted to become your neighbor too. This is a wonderful place. I can see why you feel so strong about it." He smiled as only a grandfather can. "And how many grandchildren are you and Rosie planning?" He actually hugged his son uncharacteristically.

Cal passed the warning and advice on to Evan, who shared it with Daniel. There was no urgency, but an importance that could not be ignored. All three men began slowly withdrawing the bulk of their bank accounts in the form of gold coins, which were secretly secured in the privacy of their homes.

Gracie

In the middle of an unusual winter storm, Molly went into labor. When she was certain that this was the time for the delivery of her child, she begged Daniel to fetch her mom and Lily. Eli volunteered to make the soggy journey, and in only a few minutes, returned with the soaked but very excited women. With four mid-wives, Molly had all the help she needed. The healthy cream colored baby girl with curly hair was given the name Grace. Lowell and Becca also welcomed a baby girl, whom they named Angelina.

But six weeks later, Molly had fears that her baby daughter's health may be challenged. A fever that refused to let go and the loss of appetite had the infant crying non-stop. Three days of anguish caused Molly to resort to extreme measures. She took dehydrated Grace to the beach and waded in. The startled baby flinched and howled louder. Shortly, however, the shock of the cool water began to work; she relaxed her knees that had been drawn up tightly, and the crying quieted. Her mother held her carefully as Grace finally responded to the cool comfort. Molly began to rock her from side to side, gently singing a church hymn. "Now thank we all our God, with heart and hands and voices, who wondrous things hath done, in whom his world rejoices; who from our mother's arms hath blessed us on our way with countless gifts of love and still is ours today." She rocked and sang, and the Seerier joined in the comforting. They recognized an infection in the tiny host that required immediate assistance; immunity stimulants were administered again and again.

The moment was one of insight and understanding for Molly. This tiny child in her arms was evidence of God's tremendous love.

Gracie made it possible for her mom to understand the depth and breadth of freedom. There were no restrictions save for those of love, and no limits to what this tiny child might accomplish. When Molly finally toweled them both dry and changed into fresh clothes, Grace seemed to have found her appetite, nursing eagerly.

When she was four years old, Gracie developed an ear infection which caused a repeat of the beach treatment. Her fever had seemed stubborn to the worried mom, until they once again lounged in the cool water. Tears of protest gave way to the pleasure of being rocked in the refreshing water. Once again Molly sang to her, and once again Gracie was evidence of something strangely wonderful that happened there. It took several hours, but her fever subsided. This beach time, however, was dramatically different; there was a lingering desire in the child, to learn to swim on her own. Molly promised to teach her, but insisted she would always have supervision.

Time has a way of speeding by; season after season, harvest upon harvest, Lowell and Becca added two sons to their family. Grace grew into a lovely young girl, with a sweet disposition and a love of devotions, especially singing. Angelina also grew into a lovely young woman, but with a much different disposition. It could be said that it was not a nice one. When she was fourteen, her frantic parents rescued her from the Shores Hotel after the runaway had been gone for over a week. When she was returned to her home the only excuse she could give was that she was in love, and wanted to marry him. Distraught parents watched as their dreams for her were crumbled. The second time she ran away, she left a note saying that she was going to work on a riverboat. Lowell and Becca could only shudder at the thought.

The next morning he left in search of her. Becca would stay home with the two boys. The nearest riverboat was in Baton Rouge, so that became his destination. It took Lowell two days to get there and another to find his way into Port Allen, where he began asking questions about river traffic. Eventually he was sent to Poplar Grove, a landing where most of the riverboats stopped for fuel and supplies. For three days he asked anyone who would pay attention if they knew of a young woman named Angelina Stanley working on a boat. There were several women who said they would be Angelina if that's what he wanted, but sadly the saloons began to look and smell irritatingly alike to him. Then just as he was about to give up hope of success, a scruffy man said he remembered a Lena who worked as a good-time girl on the Dixie Doodle, which was over on the other side of the river in the Chippewa District. Lowell gave him an eagle, explaining that he was her father, and was very worried about her.

He made his way back to Port Allen where a ferry took him across the river into an even seamier side of Baton Rouge. There he started the same inquiries in even more disgusting saloons. Lowell learned that the Dixie Doodle had departed three days ago, so his search turned down stream. He was a day late in St. Gabriel, and also in Bayou Goula. The folks in Lucher Landing hadn't seen the Dixie Doodle; perhaps it had gone on into New Orleans. Finally after being on the search for a month, out of money and hope, overwhelmed by the thought of searching further into the myriad of delta towns, Lowell returned to Abbeville, empty-handed. He accepted the fact that Angelina was out of his reach.

The rattle of sabers

Suddenly it was the election of 1860. The Republican candidate, Abraham Lincoln, won the presidential election even though his name did not appear on the ballot in seven states. By his inauguration on March 4, 1861 the secessions had begun; South Carolina, Georgia, Florida, Alabama, Mississippi, Louisiana and Texas withdrew their constitutions from the United States and became the Confederate States of America. The dream of a democratic new government was shattered over the issue of slavery! On April 12th, 1861 Fort Sumter was fired upon and the greatest conflagration our nation had ever seen began. An estimated 750,000 soldiers would lose their lives, half of those by disease, and perhaps twice that many were severely wounded. Uncounted civilians, who were collateral damage, were also part of the war's expense. One in ten of the northern young men from 20 to 45 years of age would lose their life; and one of every three southern men from 18 to 40 would not return home. The infrastructure and way of life of the old south would be destroyed over the issue of slavery. King Cotton came at a very high price.

The popularity of Vermillion Plantation, however, and its serene setting far from the clamor and strife of the nation, had steadily grown over its forty years. Clarice was busy keeping reservations and schedules; they were at capacity most days. She and Evan had been wrestling with a question of the Plantation's future. Their health was remaining surprisingly strong, she at age 66 and he at 69, but for how long they wondered. Becca was a constant help, and Lowell helped during the cane harvest. But they were clearly more concerned about their own plantation. Jonathan was a successful Marshal, and had time to bring his growing family only occasionally to the Plantation. White haired Moesh was an unheard of 75, and still strong enough to do chores. Dory was 72, and while she seemed more frail, was still in the kitchen every day. Thank goodness 37 year old Adam had a love for the harvests and had assumed management of the entire Taro production. Thirty five year old Noah was in charge of the pecan gathering and husk sales, which had become surprisingly lucrative. George had convinced Mr. Evan to purchase a sugar cane wagon, which was pretty busy all summer long. Joy had assumed the task of serving the guests in the dining room. Lily continued to launder the linens and swimming robes. The team was still efficient although aging rapidly. The exception was Molly. While she was fifty two years old, she had the appearance of a twenty year old. Her skin was smooth; her hair was dark and her body was very trim. She was the object of much conversation, and envy by those who had become too distracted to visit the beach regularly.

The War

The Army of the Confederacy was well funded and motivated. On several fronts they began to press northward. President Lincoln, on the other hand, did not want to wage a full scale assault against his own people, and took a more defensive attitude. He sent the naval warships to blockade all southern ports. Tons of stranded cotton rotted on the docks. When the ironclad Union warships sailed up the Mississippi, they had a fierce cannon battle with shore batteries, but managed to push through to New Orleans, where they captured the port facilities, in effect cutting off the food and war material supply source to the southern forces. It also meant that Louisiana was spared the violence of battle that other states were about to experience.

Finally, on September 17th of '62, General Robert E. Lee, along with his commanders James Longstreet and Stonewall Jackson, pushed across the Potomac into Maryland, in a northern invasion. With 45,000 confederate troops, and a larger Union defense, the Battle at Antietam, near Sharpsburg, became a turning point in the war. It became the bloodiest single day in United States military history. The Union victory became the opportunity for President Lincoln, as Commander in Chief, to make the Emancipation Proclamation, making slavery illegal in the seven seceding states as a war tactic. Border states, West Virginia, Maryland, Delaware, and Kentucky, where slavery was still legal were not mentioned, for they had not left the Union. The President's objective was an effort to maintain the integrity of the nation. Making slavery illegal, he believed, would help end the war and preserve the nation.

Mr. Daniel received the news first. A packet of newspapers was mailed to him, giving details of the war, and the proclamation that affected millions. He read it first to his folks, and then to Evan's; soon Cap'n Cal and Lowell Stanley heard it as well. There were those who speculated that mass exodus from the plantations would occur. Others, however, held a much more optimistic view, believing there would be a large available new work force who would seek stable and fair working conditions. Mr. Evan was in the latter.

In the spring of '63, General Robert E. Lee, after success at Chancellorsville, shifted his army's target from war-torn Virginia up the Shenandoah Valley toward Harris Pennsylvania, or Philadelphia, in the hopes of changing the Union's anti-slavery stance. On May first, a call was delivered to all U.S. Marshals that they were needed in their country's defense. Jonathan Cossindale answered the call, boarding a northbound train. His instructions were to report to Major General Joseph Hooker's command at Gettysburg. He would be assigned to the Union Cavalry under the command of Brigadier General John Buford. For almost a month he was in skirmishes, proving his skill and courage. Then on July 1st, the Confederate Army arrived, sending wave after wave, testing the Union strength. On July 3rd, over twelve thousand Confederate soldiers addressed Cemetery Ridge with what would come to be known as Pickett's Charge. The newly appointed Major General George Meade sent his best to meet the charge, and repulse it. By day's end, the confederate army was in full retreat, and over fifty thousand young men, who once had bright futures, lay dead. The vulgarity of war had spat its obscenity of savage death upon sons and fathers. One of which was Jonathan Cossindale. It took nearly a month for the War Department to get a letter to his survivors, informing them of his valiant sacrifice.

The war was winding down after that perilous day. To be sure there were battles for another year, all significant to the moment, but increasingly the confederate troops were in retreat, or deserting to the west rather than face the inevitable. It was also a bad time for banks that had accepted the Confederate money as secured. Cap'n Cal was grateful for his father's foresight. Many had to close, including the

Bank of Abbeville and two in Lafayette. They promised to reopen after reconstruction.

William T. Sherman led an assault on Atlanta that fairly destroyed Georgia. His assault torched every town and plantation from the city to the Atlantic shores, destroying fully a quarter of the wealth of the once powerful state. Finally when the southern capitol of Richmond fell, General Robert E. Lee knew it was tactically and logistically impossible to fight on. At the town hall at Appomattox, on April 9, 1865 he surrendered. In an act of dignity, he was allowed to keep his sword, and Traveler, his horse. The Civil War was over at last, but its reverberations would rattle the next hundred years.

When the Gettysburg National Cemetery had been dedicated on November 19, 1863, a two hour speech was made by Edward Everett, which very few have remembered. President Abraham Lincoln gave a two minute speech that has burned brightly in the memories of a nation grateful for a Union. He said,"Four score and seven years ago our fathers brought forth on this continent a new nation, conceived in liberty, and dedicated to the proposition that all men are created equal.

"Now we are engaged in a great civil war, testing whether that nation or any nation so conceived and so dedicated, can long endure. We are met on a great battlefield of that war. We have come to dedicate a portion of that field, as a final resting place for those who here gave their lives that that nation might live. It is altogether fitting and proper that we should do this.

"But, in a larger sense, we cannot dedicate, we cannot consecrate, we cannot hallow this ground. The brave men, living and dead, who struggled here, have consecrated it, far above our poor power to add or detract. The world will little note, nor long remember what we say here, but it can never forget what they did here. It is for us the living, rather, to be dedicated here to the unfinished work which they who fought here have thus far so nobly advanced. It is rather for us to be here dedicated to the great task remaining before us—that from these honored dead we take increased devotion to that cause for which they gave the last full measure of devotion—that we here highly resolve that these dead shall not have died in vain—that this nation, under God, shall have a new birth of freedom—and that government of the people, by the people, for the people, shall not perish from the earth."

While watching a play at Ford Theater on April 14, 1865, John Wilkes Booth, a southern sympathizer, shot President Lincoln, who died the following day. What a high price King Cotton demanded.

More Staff Again

With the emancipation, there were many new faces on the road, seeking employment. Usually, they came by groups, on foot. First they would ask about the possibility of work, then it was a food handout they sought. It finally occurred to Evan that the news was being shared with the freedmen that if there was no work at Vermillion, there was at least a bit of a meal. Folks were walking for hours, just for something to eat.

Late one Saturday afternoon, a group of five job-hunters entered the lane. They paused about halfway to the big house, sending one spokesperson to ask the important questions. He was clean-shaven with light tan skin, and his white shirt was recently laundered. Evan walked out to meet him and was impressed with the man's polite demeanor and speech.

"Sir, we have walked a long way for the privilege of asking for work. We have heard that you treat your workers fairly, and allow them to learn to read the scriptures. The older women are fine cooks, as is my wife. My name is Thomas, sir, and his is Martin," he pointed toward another eager man. "We were born on a sugar cane plantation, near Eunice, just west of Opelousas, and love the work of it. All we ask is a chance to earn your trust and appreciation." His brown eyes were steady as he gazed at Evan, hoping he had said enough.

"Thomas, there have been many folks asking for work and food, recently," Evan began a response. The polite man sagged a bit, anticipating a rejection. "But none have been as polite or well spoken as you have been," Evan continued. "My folks are getting pretty well along in age, and need some fresh strength. Invite your folks in so I can meet them. You are invited to eat with us tonight, and I think we can find some place for you to find a night's rest. If you want to share devotions with us tomorrow morning, you are welcomed. Then we can all sit on the front porch with some sweet tea, and decide if your journey has been worthwhile. I will have an idea that might work well for us all."

The delighted young man waved for the others to join him. Moesh, Dory and Lily came from the house to greet the group, as did Miss Clare. With a wide smile Thomas introduced Sharon, his wife. "She has been house maid since she was a child. Her gifts are setting a proper table and preparing special dinners." Then he said, "This strong man is Martin, who can chop canes like no one I ever saw before, and this is Beulah and her sister Anita. They are both dandy cooks and hard workers. We're all from Eunice." They were surrounded by welcoming handshakes and happy greetings.

As expected, the group chose not to eat in the Hospitality dining room, but eagerly accepted Lily's offer to eat in her home, even if it meant simply sitting on the floor with a bowl of gumbo. It was a far cry better than what they had endured for the past two weeks. Adam and Noah were happy to be sources of information for the new folks; especially for the ladies. The bungalow was offered to the women as a place to sleep, and the men found the barn quite adequate. At least it was an opportunity for the group to hear about life on the Vermillion Plantation.

The morning sun warmed the porch as the folks gathered. There was a sense of celebration following devotions that was quite alien to the new group. The five sat together toward the end of the porch. They were puzzled by the friendly banter between the owners and workers. Even Molly and Mr. Daniel joined in on the conversation. When the pitcher had refilled the sweet tea glasses, Evan began. "We have chatted about this for quite a while now, and with the possibility of new folks joining us, I think it is time for me to make a proposal. Save for the terrible loss of Jonathan, the war has left us unscathed. In fact, our sugar cane prices have been higher than ever before. The Hospitality House is at capacity most days, so once again I find myself wanting more help here."

"We will work out specific duties, but to you all, I am offering this. I will offer food and lodging to each person on the porch this morning." Quickly looking at Daniel and Molly, he corrected himself, "With two obvious exceptions." Everyone smiled. "Plus food and lodging, there will be a $10 per month wage paid in addition to any gratuities or bonuses. For those who work on sugar cane, Taro, or pecan production there will be a bonus based on the production, but approximately 1%, $10 for every thousand we earn. Finally, a Christmas gift of $10 per person will be paid with our thanks for your faithful year's work. I believe that we have a sufficient team here to allow those of us who have been at it a long while to rest a bit, and the others to have the confidence of a job and regular income. One last thing, each family may have a Taro row to harvest for Mr. Lester's Store. We will miss the original grocer, but his son has asked that we continue with regular deliveries in exchange for goods or groceries, and he promises to check his figures twice. Do you all understand this offering?" He waited for any discussion.

When there was none, he clarified, "As I see it, this plan means that each of you, along with food and lodging, would receive $120 per year, plus gratuities, and a $10 Christmas gift. We made ten thousand dollars in sugar cane, nine thousand dollars in Taro, eight thousand dollars in pecans, and seven thousand dollars in pecan husks. Good job Noah! That's $34 per worker, on top of everything else." He waited for several moments for any discussion. When none came, he continued, "I don't expect anyone to get wealthy with this plan, but I do know you will quickly have much more than you do this morning." When no one spoke up again, he added, "Anyone can leave to work elsewhere if you wish."

That spurred almost everyone to speak at the same time. "It is more than fair," "I have never dreamed of receiving more money than my room and board." "You have been a loving father, and now prove to be more generous still," Moesh said with tears in his eyes." Thomas finally spoke, "Mr. Evan, sir, "I have two sisters in Eunice who are faithful workers. If you will allow me to go get them to be included, I will forgo a year's pay." Now there were tears in several eyes.

"We have an old carriage and an equally old horse that you can use. If my geography is correct, you can be there in a day, and a day back. It would be much quicker and more convenient than walking. Will that be enough time?"

Before he could answer, Mr. Daniel added, "And I have four single men and Cap'n Cal has a like number, so more ladies would be welcomed here, if they are interested in working, as well as finding a man. We also have three or four large rooms in the basement that folks can use for sleeping cots." Plans were taking shape.

"I'll be back in three days," Thomas declared. "I am sure there will be good people with me." Mr. Evan knew it was time to get more lumber for a larger help house. An influx of new folks was about to begin.

Prodigal returns

On the road there was even a familiar face. She had walked from Lafayette and now stood waiting at the top of the lane leading to the Stanley plantation. She had heard about her father's search for her. The life she thought she had wanted tarnished in sordid shame. The only thing that gave her any hope was that in port after port she was told about the efforts he had made to find her. A father's love had called her home. Lowell recognized her first, and called to Becca. He hurried out to meet Angelina, who slumped into his welcoming embrace.

"Dad, I'm so sorry. I've made a mess of my life." Becca joined in the hug, whispering words of happy gratitude to see her daughter again. "Mom, I was so stupid. I'm coming back with a body damaged and diseased. I don't expect you to let me stay, but maybe I can just rest here a while." Their daughter looked worn, haggard, and desperate.

Speaking to Lowell, Becca said, "Let's get the carriage so we can get a hospitality beach treatment to clean her up, and some tasty food to feed this girl." Then looking into her eyes with only the affection a mom can share, she said, "This is your home. We'll help you get strong again. Today is a fresh beginning for us."

Also on the road were other new faces, but these were angry and evil, not looking for work or a meal, but hidden behind white masks, robes, and conical hats, these sought vengeance. They originated near New Orleans, confronting a plantation home demanding "compensation" for the freed slaves. Their ghostly appearance at night with torches was terrifying, for they actually set fire to outbuildings, and threatened more violence. They called themselves, "Kuklos," or "Circle." Most folks determined that they were a group of former confederate soldiers, so the name for them became the "Hooded Order," or "Circle of Brothers." Their appearances spread north, then both east and west. Those who had nurtured sympathies for the confederate south came to refer to them as the Ku Klux Klan, or simply, "The Klan." Most land owners saw them as ominous hoodlums who were little more than robbers. But they also saw them as practically inevitable.

There were accounts of The Order sightings near Lafayette, and then a gathering of The Order appeared at Cap'n Cal's plantation. They demanded payment or they would burn down his barn with the animals in it. When their demands were denied they moved to torch the building and were met by a hail of bullets. Several were wounded as they fled. The only damage was a bit of fire on the barn's siding, which was quickly extinguished. But their presence made all the nearby owners uneasy.

Yet more staff

True to his word, Thomas returned with a carriage full of new help. Hospitality House was pleasantly filled with Sunday devotion folks who had just finished their service when the buggy turned down the lane, so there was a happy welcoming crowd. Thomas helped three ladies step out of the carriage. He said happily, "I'd like to introduce my sisters Celia, and Erma." The two women beside him smiled shyly. "And this lovely lady," he placed his hand on the shoulder of a young woman with skin even lighter than his, "is Daphne, who took care of the dining room of the Robison Plantation next to ours. When I had told her this place is right beside the ocean, she became very excited. She has never been off the Robison place." The welcoming folks closed in a bit more so they could shake hands and genuinely welcome these new friends. Eli especially was smiling at Daphne, who was the most lovely woman he had ever seen. The new folks came to understand that Grove House, where they were comfortably staying was something of an extension of Vermillion Plantation, and Mrs. Molly had been a slave just as they had. Truly a new day with countless possibilities was dawning. Miss Grace invited anyone who wanted to take a little swim, to follow her to the beach. Oh for sure, there were countless opportunities!

Dory prepared her special Shrimp and Ham creamy gumbo for the large crowd. Both Thomas and Martin, who enjoyed it for the first time, were fascinated by Moesh's account that wild hogs were fairly attainable in the brush not far away. They were also eager to see a demonstration of his throwing stick and short lance. Moesh had skill with it, even at his age, and soon generated a contest between the students. Their target was a bag of pecan husks that didn't stand a chance. Moesh promised a hunt soon, happy to have strong backs who could carry a heavy hog.

Before the day was complete, Thomas found a moment to speak with Mr. Evan alone. "I can hardly believe how fortunate we are to have been welcomed like this," he began. "From the depths of my heart, I thank you. For allowing me to stay with my family, I even thank you more." Then, when Evan placed his hand on Thomas' shoulder the young man said, "I know I have no right to ask for more, so this is only a simple question. Since this is more than a sugar cane plantation, and you deal with mostly white folks in the Hospitality House, would you like to have three more workers who are more milk than coffee? There are still three in the Robison place that would work for you gladly. I think they are grandson and granddaughters of the old owner. They are even more light skinned than Daphne."

Mr. Evan thanked him for his polite suggestion, and said that it was a very delicate offer. He would talk with Miss Clare and give him an answer in the morning. Silently he wondered if this might already be too much staff, or, on the other hand, if he was equipping the Vermillion Plantation to have an efficient work force well beyond his time into the future, maybe three more would be just right.

In the morning when the staff came to breakfast, Mr. Evan had a sheet of paper with assignments. Celia and Erma were going to be cooks in the Grove House, helping Mary and Martha. Beulah and Sharon were assigned to the Hospitality House kitchen to help Dory. Anita was to help Lily with the laundry. Each day sheets, tablecloths and swimming robes had to be washed, dried and ironed. Daphne and Joy were assigned to Miss Clare to learn reservations and guest room assignments. Their task was also to serve the guests in the dining room. George would be in charge of the horses and wagon, hauling to the sugar mill and Lafayette warehouse. All the men were assigned to harvesting, helping Adam who was in charge of Taro, Thomas who was in charge of Sugar Cane, and Noah who was in charge of Pecans and husks. The bottom line of the sheet of paper informed them that all were expected to attend reading and writing classes first thing each morning.

When he had finished reading the list, Mr. Evan asked, "Do any of you have questions about this?" No one answered. "Then I think we need a day to get accustomed to living pleasantly; all except Thomas." The startled listeners looked up to see if this might be a joke. Mr. Evan explained, "He's going to harness the carriage to make another trip to Eunice. It seems there are three more folks there who are hoping to join you here." Smiles and happy laughter greeted that news.

Miss Grace announced that after breakfast, she was going to the beach for a swim. "Would anyone like to join me?" It was obvious to everyone that getting used to living pleasantly had begun for them all.

Lowell brought Angelina to the beach seven evenings before she could affirm that her body was recovering from the brutal abuse she had inflicted upon it. Then with a few more, her infection seemed to be gone as well. To the joy of her parents, there was also a major shift in her attitude. Perhaps it was the endorphin applications, or perhaps it was the growing understanding of her rare affirmation and redemptive opportunity offered by her family. Her mom had told her in reply to her confession of ruining her life that it wasn't the only one she was to get. "There is still a bright future for you," the mom said softly, "if you will only claim it." It was wonderful; it was miraculous.

Moesh's voice was clear enough for everyone to hear. "Mr. Evan, the carriage is back, and Thomas has folks with him." From several directions and duties folks came to greet them.

"Mr. Evan, sir, let me introduce David, the tallest young man I know." The curly brown hair made him look even taller, although he was half a head taller than Evan, who until just now had been the tallest man on the plantation. "He claims to be twenty five years old, but I've been told he is only nineteen.

"It is a pleasure to meet you, sir," the warm voice said, "and an honor to be considered for employment."

Thomas chuckled, "He is a smooth talker, and a hard worker." Thomas let his arm rest on David's shoulder, even if he had to reach up to get there. "And this young lady is Gwen, who was a housemaid. Finally, let me introduce May, who loves the Lord and has been working in the kitchen. Like all of us, we are grateful that you will consider us for the plantation. I have explained the conditions of staying here, and they are very pleased to accept, if you will accept them." It was the longest speech he could remember muttering.

"You are welcome here. We are in a lazy time, when only the Hospitality House is busy. Next week we will begin the first Taro harvest, which means work for the fellows. For today, there is a pot of chowder in the kitchen for anyone who might be a bit hungry. Mr. Daniel has told me there is still plenty of room in his basement until we get the new residence finished, so you can find a cot and get situated. You might want to visit the beach to freshen up a bit first. I assure you we will get all our tasks figured out and running smoothly with your help. I am so very glad you are here." Without exception, each person, those who were new or those who had been with Mr. Evan for a long while, felt the sincerity of the welcome. They were all filled with anticipation.

When the first heaping load of Taro left for the Lafayette warehouse, Moesh approached Evan with a suggestion. "Mr. Evan, I have been thinking about our property line." Evan smiled at the word "our." "It seems to me that we have misplaced the corner marker. Don't you think it would be a good idea to have David re-measure from the pecan tree? His 850 paces would be more reliable than mine." There was no hint of deception, but Evan did detect a deeper part of the question.

"How do you think we made a mistake so many years ago," he asked his elderly friend.

"It has come to my attention," Moesh said softly, "that the Taro starts have been pushing the boundary of the plantation. At first it was only a few inches, but now at least a full row, all the way around. That's an extra thirty five hundred heads at least. Perhaps if David, who has a more natural stride than my little short legs, were to pace off the distance, we might include that questionable row. Then you might speak to Adam about respecting our property limits. It would be understandable that even another row might have been added to our harvest, purely by mistake of course." Now a bit of a smile bloomed on the wrinkled face.

Before Evan said anything to Adam, he took the suggestion to heart. He invited David to help him pace off the boundary. Since he owned the property on both sides of the road he decided to make it narrower and as straight as possible, which would facilitate an additional mile long row of sugar canes. Using stakes with white flags, they began moving toward the western side. To his surprise and joy, Moesh had been right. David's re-measure gave them not only the clandestine row of Taro, but enough room for another as well. The western corner marker was moved, as was the eastern. Adam was given a go-ahead to add another row, or perhaps two if he was careful. He was also given strict instructions to respect the line and not violate it. Mr. Evan told him, "If our property is not large enough to support us, we will need to pray about our greed."

The Taro harvest had become easy for Moesh. The other men dug the heads, knocked the sandy dirt off of them and brought them to the wagon. There Moesh cut the crowns off, and divided the leafy crowns into quarters. These he gave to the women to replant. While they had worried that the store's new crop, potatoes, would cut into their demand, just the opposite had happened. Taro was held as the reliable and durable crop. The Lafayette warehouse asked if they could have an additional two thousand this year.

The new help house was finished. The two story building offered four bedrooms downstairs, plus a kitchen and dining room. Upstairs there were six comfortable bedrooms. While folks chose appropriate rooms and settled in, the old houses were torn down, and the lumber used for three more new beachside bungalows.

Unwanted Visitors

The Order made its appearance at the Vermillion Plantation the night of the full moon. Moesh heard their voices while they were still on Live Oak Road. He awoke the other men, and told them to get ready to defend their home.

An angry voice called from the darkness, "Cossindale, it is your turn to pay the Order." One of the masked and hooded men shouted, "Pay us a thousand dollars or we'll burn your new building with the animals in it." The voice was angry and loud. "Cossindale, are you going to pay us, or do we burn it all down?" There were six of them standing, near the big house stairway. "Cossindale, damn it, do you hear us. Pay up, or we burn you out." The voice was louder and more desperate. The six held torches, but no weapons were evident.

Unseen by the Order, who were blinded by the torches in front of them, six shadowy figures were making their way around the mound, three on each side. They all held throwing sticks with lances at the ready.

Evan stepped out onto the stairs holding his shotgun. "There is no need for this," he said quietly. "Haven't you had enough of war and bloodshed? Leave this place in peace."

"We're going to leave it in ashes unless you give us a thousand dollars, now!" The voice was rough and more urgent. "We'll burn this to the ground."

"Gentlemen, if there is a scrap of decency in you, you will leave before someone is seriously hurt." Evan pulled back the hammers of the double barreled shotgun.

The hooded man shouted, "You called this down on yourself! In the name of the Order"…, his hand went back to hurl the burning torch, but was stopped midway by a lance that skewered him through the chest. Instantly five more lances came out of the shadows. Five of the men died instantly. The wounded sixth turned to flee, but was impaled through the back by yet another lance. The incident had been silent, swift, and incredibly lethal. The burning torches fell beside the lifeless hooded men.

Evan started to descend the rest of the stairs, but Moesh came out of the shadows, suggesting that he go back to bed. "We will take care of these fellows before the women see them. This would be very frightening for them," he said. He asked George if he could quietly get the wagon and harness a horse to it.

"I remember a story from my childhood," Moesh told them in a hushed voice. "Another tribe came at our village to steal women." He spoke quietly to the shaking listeners. "They were intercepted before they got to us, and our warriors killed them all. Then they carried their bodies back toward their own village. They placed the naked men in a circle, cross legged and bowing forward. When their people found the bodies all folded over, the next day, they assumed an evil spirit had done this terrible thing, and we had no further trouble from them."

"Perhaps you can do the same thing. Leave their masks and hood on, but remove the lances and their clothes. Take them up to the Henry junction where Miss Esther was slain. Someone will find them and draw their own conclusions. It is far enough from our plantation to draw suspicion away. Perhaps you can keep their guns, if they have any, but place their clothes in the brush away from them. Thomas, would you go look for their horses? They must be fairly nearby. These dogs are too lazy to walk very far. If you find them, just put them in the barn. It's not the first time we've had a hungry stray wander in." Moesh seemed to sag as though under a heavy burden. As the other five went about the task outlined, he shuffled back to Dory's side, where he admitted feeling a strange weakness.

Thomas found the horses easy enough. They were simply enjoying a meal on the fresh sugar cane leaves on the upper property.

He led them in a line, tethered to the saddle in front of them, all the way into the barn. Six new horses crowded the barn, but there were no complaints.

The idea of staging six bodies was a grizzly one. It took all the fortitude they had to disrobe the corpses, and pose them in a circle. Martin suggested that they build a small fire in the center as though they were attacked there by surprise. They found a few coins in their pockets, and three of the six pistols were the new metal cartridge army issue, probably from deserters. They all tried on the boots, four pair fit and were claimed, then using some branches off a nearby bush, they swept away all of their tracks. It took two hours before they could make their way back to a sleepless bed, and try to make sense out of the occurrences of the night. They had agreed to tell no one about it.

Lowell and Becca were on their way to the Vermillion Plantation to meet the new folks when they came upon the horrific sight. He confirmed that they were all quite dead, so they turned around and sped back to the Abbeville deputy's office. A large group of curious men accompanied them back to the death circle. The deputy pointed out that there were no tracks of any sort that would suggest who, or what, might be responsible for this carnage. He also noted that these were not bullet holes, which would have a small entrance wound, and a large exit wound.

The young deputy said, "I heard a story from about fifty years ago where two old boys were killed on this same road. The law found their clothes, but never their bodies, He said it was the Ojibwa Cherokee Chief's ghost on a full moon ride. Wasn't it a full mom last night?" Some of the listeners nodded in belief, but the rest shook their heads, wondering how such a numb-skull could be a law enforcement officer. The six bodies were buried in the Potter's Corner of the cemetery, and while there were various forms of the account circulated for a while, nothing more came of it.

Another time of sadness

The breakfast dishes were still being washed when Dory came to Mr. Evan. "If you have a moment, Mr. Evan, could you look in on Moesh?" Her demeanor was serious, her voice soft. "He is feeling weak this morning and has trouble getting up." The request was answered immediately.

"Good morning my old friend, are you in discomfort this morning?" Evan could tell by the ashen color of his friend's face that this was serious.

"Yes sir. Last night when I sent the first shaft, I felt like it hit me. I had a terrible pain, and haven't been able to catch my breath. I tried to walk to the out-house, and couldn't make it. I believe this is my time to say 'good bye.'" His weak hand reached for Evan's. "I want to tell you something. It is important to me. You have been a father and brother to me. Thank you." His words were coming more slowly. "You have provided a safe and wonderful home for my family." He pointed to a cigar box nearby. "I have been saving my mon…..ey." The words were difficult for him to get out. "There is four hundred….and twenty five… dollars… .. That is what you paid for us, and I want to pay you ba….. Pay you back. You saved us." His eyes closed, and the room was quiet. Evan watched his chest breathe short shallow breaths.

He went back to the kitchen and told Dory to remain with Moesh. "Give him some spring water if he'll drink a bit. I'm afraid he is very weak." Evan asked Thomas if he would go up to the Grove House and tell Molly. She would want to be with her mother. Lily and Adam joined her in what became a short sad vigil. The sun was just overhead when Adam returned to Mr. Evan with tears in his eyes. Moesh had simply stopped breathing. He was dead. Even though the sun was brightly shining, a cold poll spread over the plantation. One of the pioneers was gone.

Thomas found Mr. Evan sitting on the Hospitality porch, weeping. Evan wiped his eyes, saying, "I knew he was frail, but it feels so sad." His gaze took in the quiet afternoon on the bay.

Thomas placed his hand on Evan's shoulder and said, "This is what makes you and this place so special. You care deeply for your people. That is unique, nearly unheard of. How can I help you through this day?" There were tears in his eyes as well.

"Thomas, I think you already have helped." Wistfully he looked at the young man and finished his thought. "I think I knew from our first conversation that you were going to be the new supervisor of the plantation. I know I have a few more years, but I also know I have a solid replacement.' He took a deep breath, as though clearing his thoughts. "I suppose we must remove Moesh's body to the top of the mound. He taught me so much. Let me show you some of the lessons. It begins with a chair from the beach."

Saying "Goodbye"

The crowd was aware of the reverent stillness of the mound after all the proper words had been spoken. After several moments, Evan said, "Once again I thank you for your love and support to Dory and Molly and Gracie. This will be a different place without him. You are cordially invited to a lunch, however. Beulah and Sharon have produced a Fresh Corn and Ham chowder, with crispy Taro sticks, Celia and Erma have provided us with Pecan pie and Orange Coffee cake. Gracie is trying out a new concoction called Divinity. I've had a sample and can assure you that it is divine." Folks were making their way off the mound, but only after a lingering appreciation for the bay vista.

Evan wondered if there might even be a possibility of truth in the words he had shared. He had depended on Moesh each and every day. What might the future hold?

The soundness of Mr. Evan's plan was put to the test at the end of the sugar cane harvest. The best harvest ever, produced eleven thousand dollars from the sugar mill. When Miss Clare distributed the monthly pay, she carried a cigar box filled with coins and a long list. The men and women each received a $10 gold eagle for the month of September. The men, six from Vermillion, four from Grove Hose, four from Cap'n Cal, and three from the Stanley plantation, were paid eleven dollars each as a crop bonus on top of the monthly pay. It may have been more money than George had ever possessed.

During the night he saddled a horse, and helped himself to one of the clandestine pistols with metal cartridges in the belt. He walked the horse out the lane and rode into the night. His story was learned only in bits and pieces in the following days. He did arrive at the Lafayette saloon by afternoon. He drank two glasses of whiskey before asking if he could join the card game at the back. Later it was assumed that two of the card players were former confederate soldiers, who recognized the gun belt. It didn't take George long before his money was gone. He offered the side arm as collateral for one more hand, which he also lost.

They were waiting for him as he left the saloon. He really didn't have a chance. Brutally beaten, and stomped, George lay in the street until the deputy found him. In the morning, there was no doctor who would see him so the young man with a pregnant wife and secure job, died of internal injuries for lack of medical attention. The doctor found an old document in his shirt pocket that identified him as George Booker, a freedman. A scribble at the bottom of the page identified Vermillion Plantation as his home.

Because the memory of Jonathan Cossindale was still in the Marshal's mind, a letter was sent via the Abbeville deputy informing them of George Booker's death and burial in the slave's lot cemetery. Joy received the news of George's death with a stoic shrug. It had not been a very caring marriage, as evidenced by his sneaking away. She had not expected his return. But his death and her pregnancy were a lot for a young woman to manage alone. She was grateful that she was not alone, but part of a supportive, even loving, staff that would see her through this dark time.

A brave casualty of war

Since Clarice was responsible for reservation at the Hospitality House, she began reserving Sundays as a Sabbath day of rest and devotion. There were so many requests, the staff needed the holy rest. In the beginning there had only been a trickle, but now it was a torrent of requests, many of which were not accepted for lack of space. The stories were heartwarming of people who had found healing and new hope, a continual source of inspiration. One such was Camille Bridges, a widow from Vicksburg Mississippi.

Major General Ulysses S. Grant had determined that the Vicksburg garrison was a prime target in the war effort. If it fell, the Union army had control of the entire western flank of the Confederacy. On May 25th '63, with nearly fifty thousand troops, he attacked the garrison, only to be repulsed with a heavy loss of lives. He attempted a second assault on the garrison with the same outcome. Finally he decided to besiege the city. The business district was targeted by cannon fire, nearly leveling it. Fires devastated stores, churches and schools. Mrs. Bridges' lovely white schoolhouse was an exception. Filled with over a hundred children, she would not permit harm to come to her students, or school. Bravely Camille stood on the steps with her arms crossed, defying the Union threats. Finally an impatient young man marched up and asked her what she thought she was doing with her arms crossed so angrily. "You cain't do anything with them crossed arms," he said with a growl.

"I can surely show you which side I'm on", she answered bravely.

He strode up the stairs and knocked her unconscious with his rifle butt. General Grant bellowed from his vantage that even in war there is no call for brutality of the innocent. The school and children were spared. Mrs. Bridges was sent to his field hospital with a severe head trauma. When medical help proved unable to revive her, she was handed from one doctor to another, then another. Finally in desperation, when she arrived in Lafayette, someone thought of a way to get her off their hands. A semi-conscious woman was delivered to Vermillion Plantation.

It took three days of double beach treatments before she could understand where she was, or understand what was happening to her. Each time her yielding body was seated in the comfortable water, she was surrounded by Seerier. Their administrations of cell replacement to a damaged host were abundant, and eventually effective. It was five days before her speech was fairly normal, and ten days before she was fully mobile. Since she had arrived helpless and penniless, Evan paid for her train ticket back to Vicksburg. Along with her profound gratitude, she promised to make sure he was paid in full. She was true to her word.

Her husband, who had been a Captain in the Confederate Cavalry, had made sure that their investments were turned into secure gold before he lost his life in the northern invasion. Her home was not destroyed, and no other family member was injured. On this her third visit to the Vermillion beach, she brought hope that the reoccurring headaches would be moderated by the healing water. She also brought unique news.

The train that had brought her to Opelousas was called the "Orphan Train." For the past nine years it had been bringing abandoned, unwanted, or orphaned children from the north to be secured in rural family opportunities. Thousands were being sent by the Children's Aid Society, founded by Charles Loring Brace, or by the Roman Catholic sponsored New York Foundling Hospital. On the third Thursday of each month, the children were off loaded, taken to a warehouse and displayed for interested humanitarians. Some said it was inhumane to display children four to nine years of age like so many farm animals; others argued it was the best way to bring one set of people in need into contact with people of solutions. Some said it was just another form of slavery, of indentured servitude; others answered it was a way out of an institutional tomb into a hope for employment and livelihood. The truth of it was that until a better plan came along, this was the only way it worked.

When Gracie heard about the orphans she was moved to petition her dad. "We've got so much room, and lots of food. Why can't we help them?" When Daniel proved unresponsive, she turned to her mom. "Just remember when you were little and Mr. Evan came to your rescue. Think what a difference that made for you. Some little girl is in trouble, and we can help save her."

The first week of her campaign was sort of entertaining, seeing their daughter so moved to compassion. By the second week it began to be irritating, and even their requests for peace and quiet were ignored. Finally by the third week Molly began to be swayed, and joined the petition for mercy. On the third Thursday of October, Daniel and Molly agreed to at least investigate the availability of a child in need of a home. It was mid afternoon when they arrived at the Opelousas Armory warehouse.

They had expected a crowd of people and there was only one other wagon in front of the building, and not a soul in sight. They went in the quiet building, wondering if they were in the right place.

A congenial voice finally assured them, "Well come on in folks," He couldn't have been over sixteen. "I suspect you are lookin' for the little orphans, ain't you?" Without waiting for an answer, he continued, "There was about nine of them this morning. Folks were interested in the older boys, and a couple of the girls. But it's been pretty quiet this afternoon." Then realizing they needed more information, he quickly added, "'Scuse me. You are interested in who's here now, not who was here. There are two five year old boys. They're twins, but wheezers. Nobody wanted two, let alone sick ones. And the little girl cried like the dickens until I put her on the blanket with the boys. She must be four, and scared, sure enough. The boys talk a little, but the only sounds she's made is cryin'." He was guiding them toward a blanket spread on the floor.

Molly's breath caught in her throat. It would be terribly frightening to be a defenseless child in a strange world. But to be unable to breathe, fighting for enough strength to go on would be so much worse. And a tiny defenseless girl in a strange cold place would have only plaintive tears for comfort. Molly looked down at the fragile huddle of sleeping children. Without a parent's protection, they were finding shelter from one another. "Do you know their names?" Molly asked quietly.

"Yes ma'am," the young man answered. "The boys are Timothy and Tobias. I don't know which is which. The girl child is called Annie, but I think her baptized name is Angeline." He looked at the sleeping huddle and added, "They look pretty helpless, don't they?"

"They are helpless," Molly said more directly. "Is there paperwork to be completed before we take them home with us?"

"All three of them, ma'am? Golly, that is very Christian of you." He seemed completely caught off-guard. "Not much paperwork. You just need to sign and give your location."

Daniel wrote their names; for location he wrote, "Grove House, south of Lafayette."

The young man asked, "Is that anywhere near the Vermillion Plantation?"

"They are our next door neighbors."

"Golly, I have some friends who just went to work there. It must be big and nice."

Molly smiled, and answered him, "It is, and it's almost as nice as Grove House, where these children will call home."

"Golly!"

The Twins

When they were awakened there was the usual confusion as the boys stood up. They both were gasping a bit, trying to catch a full breath, When they were told they were about to take a carriage ride to their new home, however, no further motivation was needed. They clasp onto Daniel's hands like good boys would. Annie was folding the blanket into a bundle which she held onto with both arms. Apparently it was her only possession and she was holding on to it, like a good girl would. Molly smiled as the innocent face turned toward her, and bright blue eyes searched hers for instructions.

Their first stop was a department store where they could find new clothes for the children. The three disoriented additions to their family were a bit overwhelmed with the idea that they could choose three shirts each. Timmy found a display of red ones and declared that red was his favorite color. When Molly advised that they should be bigger boy size, so he could grow into them, the happy lad clutched the shirts to his chest. Tobias selected three blue shirts.

Molly asked Annie about her favorite color, but received no answer. It was only when she startled the little girl by touching her shoulder that they learned she couldn't hear. Frightened eyes tried to explain the silence that she was in. Finally, yellow play shirts and pants were selected for her, and she was the topic of conversation all the way home.

"Would you have taken her if you had known she was deaf?" Daniel asked Molly.

"Perhaps not," she answered. "But the truth is we intend to help children who are in distress, and Annie is definitely in need."

After a silent moment or two, she concluded, "I'm glad she is ours, and I am convinced that her story will be a happy one." Tears formed in Molly's eyes as she said, "I wish my father could help me communicate with her. He would know how to help her." It was after dark by the time they were home. Fortunately the horses knew the way, and the children were once again sleeping in a cluster under the blanket.

Gracie heard them come in and raced to learn the details of the day. When she saw three children, she squealed and embraced Daniel. "Oh thank you!" she declared. "This is so much better than I even hoped. Thank you for having an open heart." Then she was told about the challenges the children brought with them. "That only means they needed you even more, and you could accept them when other people looked away. Thank you!" She had prepared a cot in her room, just in the event a child would need a place to sleep. The sleepy boys were directed there, and Annie was placed in Gracie's bed with her. Better arrangements would be made in the morning. The grateful girl kissed both her mom and dad goodnight, thanking them again for being so gracious.

In the morning Molly found Annie holding onto Gracie's hand, following her like a shadow. The boys were both wearing blue shirts.

A chuckling Molly said, "I can't tell you fellows apart. Who is Toby?"

A cautious hand was raised. "In a wheezy voice the lad answered, "My name is Tobias. Nobody has called me Toby before." A shy grin captured his face. "But I like it. I like it a lot."

Turning to the other blue shirt, Molly said, "Well Mr. Timothy, it seems that red is not your favorite color after all." Embarrassed eyes studied the floor. "I know that you have had a tough few days, but we must start on the right foot. You must learn as of this morning to always tell me the truth, and to respect other people, and their things. I can tell just with a glance if you are fibbing, and when you are, it makes me very sad. Now please go take off Toby's shirt, and put on a red one. Celia has made us pancakes this morning with pecan syrup. It's going to be very good. Hurry, get your own shirt on."

"But I asked him to," Toby said quietly in his wheezy voice. "I asked him to wear the blue shirt. We always look just alike." There was an uncomfortable silence. "I didn't think he would get in trouble." He struggled a bit to catch his breath.

Now in understanding, Molly knelt down and drew the boys to her in a warm embrace. "Oh Sweetheart, you are not in trouble. It was my mistake for thinking Timmy was taking something that was not his. I understand now, and wish I was lucky enough to have a twin so we could dress alike. I'll work very hard to recognize which of you is Timmy and which is Toby. But you must promise me you will help with that and not try to confuse me. It would be a funny joke, but only to you." She kissed them both on the cheek. "Let's go see about those pancakes."

Gracie and Annie were already seated at the table when they entered the dining room. Gracie got up to hug the boys, but Annie continued to eat, with enthusiasm. Gracie said in a quiet voice, "That's her third serving. I hope she doesn't make herself sick."

Molly explained that she was pretty sure the little girl was deaf. "She hasn't made a sound since we picked them up yesterday, and doesn't seem to notice if we are speaking around her. Obviously she is affectionate, and wants to be with someone, but not a sound. It's going to be a challenge." The boys started on their pancakes with the same vigor. "These children were hungry."

When the platter of cakes was finally emptied, Molly asked, "Well guys, what shall we do today? Would you like to walk over to our neighbors and meet some of my friends?" When there was no response, she added, "How about seeing some horses and visiting the beach. Perhaps we could wade in the water?"

Timmy said with some effort, "We've never seen a beach or waded." He struggled to catch his breath before adding, "and we've never pet a horse." A fragile smile indicated it was as much a question as a suggestion.

"Well then, let's see if Gracie will go with us and we can do both. What do you say?"

Toby started to say, "Yes, that soun…." A hacking cough cut off his words. Breathing was a constant labor for these boys.

Evan watched the procession come down the lane, Molly and Gracie, with three children holding their hands. He immediately called Clarice to come and see this strange thing. By the time Molly arrived there was a crowd of folks happily greeting them all.

Molly said, "The orphan train is real, just like Mrs. Bridges told you. These wonderful children were unwanted in New York, and unclaimed in Opelousas. They have some problems that I am hoping we can help them overcome. The boys don't manage to get enough air, and Annie," she looked at the small figure holding firmly onto Gracie's fingers, "can't hear a lick. But we are going to give them a home and a fighting chance at a better life. I'm hoping we can show them the beach, for the first time."

"Of course," Evan said happily, "Our guests have used the bungalow and have gone home. No one else is scheduled until this evening. Will they need swimming robes?"

Molly answered with a chuckle, "I don't think we have any miniature ones. Their underwear will work just fine for this time. Maybe something later will make them more comfortable. I think they'll just wade a bit today."

The first cautious steps were taken at the water's edge. Annie was whimpering again, until she saw the delight in the boys. They began to run and jump, still in the very shallow water of course. But bit by bit they followed Molly and Gracie until they were nearly knee deep. Molly sat down, giving them a tiny playful splash. That was all the boys needed to abandon their fears and frolic, their frail white bodies dancing in the sunshine. Timmy stumbled and fell down, getting his face wet. Instantly Toby jumped to his rescue. Then they realized there was no danger, their wheezy voices laughing as much as they could. Both of them wound up sitting in water up to their chests.

Molly moved to the wooden chair, which would seem more like a safe place for Annie. Gracie helped the frightened child climb up on Molly's lap, holding on fiercely. She could see the boys playing, and the warm water was very comforting, but she was still terrified.

Molly began to rock back and forth as she softly sang a favorite song. "How firm a foundation, ye saints of the Lord, is laid for your faith in His excellent Word! What more can He say, than to you

He hath said, to you who for refuge to Jesus have fled." She was aware that Annie's grip was relaxing, and her hand was feeling the vibrations of the singing in Molly's neck. Molly continued, "When through the deep waters I call thee to go, the rivers of sorrow shall not thee overflow; for I will be with thee, thy troubles to bless, and sanctify to thee thy deepest distress." Annie looked steadily into Molly's brown eyes as she relaxed her little fist from the robe, and something like a smile bloomed on her face for the first time.

Unseen, the Seerier had found the chair to be a favorite resting place for their hosts, and were, therefore, very available to administer their healing, endorphin rich stimulants. These immature hosts needed cell replacement and immunity boosters, and were receiving them in full measure.

They would have stayed at the beach much longer, but Molly warned them that a sunburn would prevent them from coming back tomorrow. There was no enthusiasm for leaving, but very much for returning.

Evan and Clarice sat on the Hospitality House veranda, watching the children playing in the shallow water. He asked, "Do you remember those happy times when our kids were that age?"

"I do," she replied wistfully. "That sound of laughter is unforgettable. Those were very happy days." She was still for just a bit before adding, "And these are too, with so many people coming here for a chance of getting stronger."

"I've been thinking about something that Daniel shared with me," Evan said, changing the subject a bit. "A man by the name of Thomas Twyford has designed a most unusual accommodation for the house. It's a device called a 'plunger closet' that is used as a bed pan. But this has the feature of pouring in flushing water to cause a pipe to remove the waste to an underground tank, where it is made harmless and released into the ground. There is no unpleasant odor and what's much better, no sickening contact with the waste."

"Daniel is going to have some installed at the Grove House. He said it is possible to have a water pump installed in the kitchen, and a waste pipe taking the used water away too. Wouldn't that be a labor-saver? No more lugging in water to cook or clean would be wonderful. All of which causes me to ask a serious question." He looked intently at her until she said "Please go ahead."

"I've been wondering about our future. I've got another ten years or so, and you have more, hopefully. What do you think we should do with that time? We might be able to sell Vermillion Plantation and retire in ease someplace. Perhaps we could return to Acadia." The idea was rejected with a small shake of her head. "Then what would you have us do?" Her answer would surprise him, and take them on a new success path.

"No, I would never return to Acadia," Clarice said clearly. "All our folks are dead, and the ones we love are here. Why would we ever dream of going somewhere else?" He could still see the young Clarice in her eyes. "So," she said it decisively like a conclusion had already been reached, "since we are going to stay here, there are some changes we could make." Her smile was playfully happy. "I cannot welcome all the folks who would come to use our beach. I think we should build another wing on the Hospitality House, perhaps with plunger closets and a pump in the kitchen, if you like. I don't think we should take down the big house; I love it too much. Perhaps we could share the spare rooms with the staff. There are six rooms in Hospitality House now. If we could add ten or twelve more rooms, and fill them most of the time, our income would triple or more. We have the money under our bed to do it, and the large staff to run it, and a half mile of unvisited beach. Why would we choose not to do the final part of the Plantation?" Her warm voice exuded confidence, and Evan knew she was, as usual, correct.

On the sixth day at Grove House, the boys arose and dressed as usual, this time in red shirts. Toby ran into Molly's room, since the door was open. "Mom, listen!" He took a large breath. "My wheezing is gone. I can breathe just fine!" He triumphantly took another large, quiet, breath, and then embraced her. Timmy padded in to declare the same thing. Tears were in Molly's eyes as she joined him into the hug. She was convinced that the miracle of the water had occurred again. Just how it worked she had no clue, but these two grinning boys were testaments that it had worked indeed. She went looking for Gracie and Annie.

"There you are," she said as they entered the dining room. Celia had prepared another large platter of pancakes with pecan syrup. Gracie looked up with a happy greeting, while Annie's attention was only on the stack of cakes. Molly shared the wonderful news of the boys' improved breathing. "Their breathing seems clear and strong this morning!"

In the exclamation of victory, Gracie said, "And listen!" Everyone was quiet.

"I don't hear anything," Molly whispered.

"Get a little closer to Annie, and listen," Gracie suggested with glee.

Molly heard it! Annie was gobbling her breakfast, and humming! She had felt the sound of Molly's song, and was humming a tune to herself. It was the first sound, apart from crying, that she had made since her arrival. Maybe the miracle of the water was working for her as well. "Let's eat our breakfast, and after we straighten up our rooms, what would you like to do?" Molly was pretty sure what the answer would be.

Toby said excitedly, but in a soft voice, "Can we see the horses again?"

Timmy was less reserved. "Can we please go to the beach today? I want to swim some more! Do you think I could swim like you?"

Molly was happy to see the exuberance in the boys. They had been through a pretty traumatic transition. "We met Mr. Evan's horses, but we have some in our own barn too. Shall we meet them first, and then go to the beach?" It was almost more than a lad could hope for.

It took a full dozen more trips to the beach before Annie began to hear sounds. She had felt Molly's singing, but the heavy blockage restricting her auditory nerves was stubborn to allow actual hearing. At first the silence gave way for occasional sounds. She heard random popping and hissing sounds, then muffled voices. Finally, the sounds began to take on meaning, and Annie began to learn and speak. Oh my, didn't she become a chatterbox. When Gracie became weary of the constant conversation, she would pass Annie off to Molly, who seemed to have infinite patience. The delightful little girl had four years of experience to catch up, but she was making phenomenal progress.

Romance was also in a phenomenal progress at Vermillion Plantation. With the addition of the new help there was increased attendance at the Sunday devotions, and a totally different expression of freedom. Men and woman had the opportunity of mate selection. Curiously there were eight single men and nine single women who were regular attendees, all of whom were delightfully aware of emancipation. Their selection process was expressed by standing beside one another for the songs and prayers. Eli was perhaps the first to stand by Daphne, but the following Sunday, she stood beside David. To everyone's surprise, Joy found a convenient place beside Eli, and the decision seemed to be acceptable by both of them. Martin seemed complacent when Mary stood on one side of him, and Martha eased in on the other side. The sisters even each held a hand at the conclusion of the devotions, with three happy smiles. Adam and Beulah seemed like teenagers in their happiness, while Anita seemed as delighted with Noah. Roman and Erma had already established a fond friendship at the Grove House, so they stood together from the very start. Willie, who was in charge of Mr. Daniel's Orange Grove, had the same sort of connection with Erma's sister, Celia. One of Mr. Stanley's men, Jed, was most delighted standing beside Gwen. Felix, one of Cap'n Perry's men fell head over heels in love with May, even though her skin was unusually light. All in all, the romancing amounted to standing together, and maybe some hand holding with an occasional kiss. Then Eli asked Mr. Evan if it would be possible for him to marry Joy. Suddenly the concept of dormitory living seemed inadequate.

Eli had become aware of the death of George, her husband, and the distant relationship they had brought with them. Her quiet sorrow and appreciation for the kindnesses of the Plantation staff indicated a woman with a tender heart. His first kindnesses were accepted graciously. He even explained the significance of his scarred ear. When she went out of her way to serve him a bowl of chowder or a slice of pecan pie with a sweet smile, he knew she had not judged him critically. Then it was important for him to be extra thoughtful right back. One thing does lead to another.

When Miss Clare heard about the proposed wedding, she giggled, "Perhaps this might become Vermillion Chapel. We can offer weddings for the folks who have found new strength and vitality as our guests, and are now well." She was not serious about the suggestion, but on the other hand she was not completely joking either.

Mr. Daniel heard the news of another possible wedding with another interpretation. He brought an idea to Mr. Evan that would blossom into good news for several families. "I've been thinking about all these new folks. It feels like we have shifted the focus of our places from production to providing housing for the help. What would you think if I tried to purchase the property adjacent to your north boundary line, and make a cluster of small homes that these folks could purchase as their own. With all the newly freed folks who want to become families, we might even found a village, with a store."

Evan's smile was genuine. "You've given this some thought, it sounds like. I'll bet this is a wonderful opportunity to get available land, and labor that might become helpful to us all."

Daniel added, "And this is the best opportunity to control what happens to the land around us." With a handshake that turned into a hug, he asked, "Then I gather you think the idea has merit?"

Evan nearly laughed as he said, "Clarice has a very large expansion planned for us. I wish your new village was already established because we will need to hire some laborers. How can I help move this along with you?"

"Oh I think that was all the help I need. I'll stop by the tax office and see what's available. Perhaps that will be the clearest affirmation to proceed."

"You think just as Clarice and I do. If opportunity presents itself, we look closely, knowing that so often that is how God has guided us." He chuckled, then finished the thought. "So far it has worked amazingly well."

Daniel found a very affordable quarter section of land just north of Evan's, which ran along Live oak Road. It was large enough to eventually offer forty home sites. Roman was an enthusiastic helper in marking the placement of a couple pathways that would be lined on both sides with an opportunity previously unthinkable. Laborers could have their own property with a house and a garden. He sincerely hoped that one of those might be his, and Erma's. They might still have a family of their own.

Molly volunteered to be the oversight of placing people with property and arranging to collect payments. She remembered to include a dollar a month for taxes. It would be an exercise in bookkeeping, but an enjoyable one. The whole notion of a community of former slaves whose status was so changed that now they could be land owners, neighbors, was a pure delight to her. She promised herself to make a special effort to help this along.

Evan found a carpenter in Lafayette named Henry Pearce, who could build the new wing right after the sugar cane harvest. He would bring a tent for himself and the two men who would install the new plunger closets. The construction plan included using as many as six local laborers The new wing would create twelve new guest rooms, plus a lobby It even included making one of the existing rooms in the Hospitality House into a new kitchen with indoor plumbing as well. While they were at it they would also install plumbing in the big house.

The building was coming along well until the weather turned unseasonably chilly and wet in October. Daniel offered a bonus for the men who would work extra hours to get the largest Orange crop picked before the fruit was damaged. Henry decided to wait until it warmed up before trying to paint the exterior. Then the storms marched in the first part of November and guest registration fell off drastically. Only the most desperate were willing to go into the water at the beach. There was even a frost warning, which was unheard of in the area. The carpenter said he would return after the first of the year to finish the trim and outside of the addition. It was complete enough to use if necessary, but conditions were less than ideal to work outside. Then the rigid fingers of grief grasped the heart of Vermillion Plantation.

The sorrow side of love

Dory was washing her face before breakfast when the stroke struck. She collapsed, unable to call out for help, or even move toward the door. Lily waited a few minutes for her friend to appear before she looked in and found her on the floor. Her call for help brought Thomas and Martin on the run. They helped place Dory onto her bed. Her frightened eyes tried to convey a message, but when Miss Clare arrived just moments later, those eyes were closed, and there was no breath. Dory had died in the presence of caring people; she had suffered very little.

Mr. Evan and Thomas crafted the coffin frame, and working in a steady rain, dug a place on the mound next to Moesh. Because the heavy rain was uncomfortably cold, they decided to put her body in its resting place and fill the frame with ashes and dirt. Dory's service would be after the devotions service in the morning, in the shelter of Hospitality House. Molly played the piano and sang her mom's favorite songs as a tribute. They didn't know they were setting a precedence.

The weather remained horrid most of December. For two weeks not one guest came to the Plantation. Mr. Evan said lightly that God was granting them a time of refreshment and prayer. But three days before Christmas, Lily came down with a hacking cough that would not let her rest. Her breathing became more ragged, and she developed a high fever. The day after Christmas, Noah went into her room to check on her and found her still cold body. She had been unable to fight off the infection. Once again Mr. Evan and Thomas made the coffin frame and prepared a place beside Dory's grave.

On the final Sunday of 1868 Lily's service was held in Hospitality House, following the devotions service. Even in the presence of sorrow, the community of affection shone in the shared food and fellowship that made this more than a plantation.

There were some superstitious folks, who believed that bad news always comes in threes, but when the weather finally returned to blue sunny skies and balmy warm breezes, their thoughts were more about business as usual. Adam said he was far behind on the Taro load for the Abbeville store, and Beulah had given him a sizable list of groceries to replenish. The five men went out to begin digging the Taro heads while Mr. Evan hitched the horses to the wagon. He grimaced in pain as his arms protested the activity. Fortunately, Clarice came out to add a couple more items to the shopping list and noted how pale her husband appeared.

Evan, are you feeling well?" she asked.

"I have strange cramps in my arms. I think I got soft during this long rest." But his face grimaced again as the pains rippled across his chest. "I think I will sit down and rest a bit." Unsteadily he walked to the veranda with her holding his arm. Once seated, he sighed deeply, "Maybe I could have a glass of…" His head lay back on the chair, and he was very still.

"Evan, Sweetheart" she cried out in fear. "Evan, are you alright?" There was no answer. His heart had beaten bravely as long as it could. They were side by side when he died. Sometimes bad news does come in threes.

For several panicky moments Clarice sat beside the still form of her husband trying to formulate some plan of action. Actually, she expected his breath to return or his eyes to open. Those reactions were impossible. She needed help, but was still unclear what to do first. She hurried into the kitchen where she found Noah talking with Sharon. When she told him of the crisis, he ran to the porch to confirm that indeed there was no life sign in Mr. Evan; then he ran for Thomas. Within minutes a crowd had gathered, the women comforting Miss Clare, and the men organizing the process of moving Mr. Evan's body up to the top of the mound. Noah also saddled a horse for the short trip to the Grove House, certain that

Miss Molly would need to be told the sad news. Then he went to the Stanley Plantation to deliver the same message to Miss Becca. Thomas, with Martin's help, set about crafting a coffin frame as he had been shown. The mood of the day was total disbelief. How could this be?

Eventually, the top of the mound was filled with neighbors and Plantation folks. Becca and Molly stood beside Clarice as she opened Evan's well-worn Bible. "These are the words of Jesus," she tried to be strong, but her spirit was trembling. "Do not let your hearts be troubled. Believe in God, believe also in me." Her voice broke as a sob tried to escape. "In my Father's house there are many mansions. If it were not so, would I have told you that I go to prepare a place for you? And if I go and prepare a place for you, I will come again and will take you to myself, so that where I am, there you may be also." She was afraid her legs would fail her, so she let her eyes trail down the page…. "Peace I leave with you; my peace I give to you. I do not give to you as the world gives. Do not let your hearts be troubled, and do not let them be afraid." Tears traced their way down her cheeks.

"Thank you for gathering to say 'goodbye' to Evan, my darling husband." Again her voice broke, but she continued bravely. "He would want me to welcome you and say again how much your friendship meant to him. When I think that 53 years ago we arrived on this undeveloped piece of shoreline, which today is a productive plantation that welcomes visitors from far and wide, I know we could not have accomplished it without your help." Once again a sob failed to be stifled, and she allowed the tears to flow unchecked. "I have asked David to read from the Book of Prayers, knowing that my sorrow would distract us."

David continued speaking from his heart. "I have known Mr. Evan for less time than most of you, but the day I met him, he made me feel like we were long-time friends. I have come to believe that was how he treated everyone he met. It was the light of Christ Jesus that shone through him. When I first thought about coming here it was to get something for myself. After just this short time with Mr. Evan, I want to stay here for what I can give to others, as he did. I am sad that I didn't have more time with him, but praise God for the time I did have! He has made a deep and lasting impression upon me."

Adam took the opportunity to add, "When my dad was killed, I was pretty sure our world was going to spin off into ruination. But Mr. Evan showed me that same sort of love. He was our security. I have come to love and respect him as a father. I agree, David, he made this place into something unbelievable.

Thomas said quietly, "Some men try to control others with power and threats. Mr. Evan did it better with kindness. I never heard him raise his voice except in song." Several chuckled with the humor.

Mr. Cal spoke up, saying, "When I first came here I was in a coma with war wounds. Mr. Evan and the gracious people here brought me back to life. I so fell in love with this place, which means with you all, that I couldn't stay away. I became a neighbor in the truest sense. I know I owe it all to him." He looked down into the depth of emotion.

When no one else added their words of praise, David spoke again, lifting the silence. "These are the words of the prophet Isaiah, 'Say to those who are of a fearful heart, 'Be strong, fear not! Behold your God will come and save you.' Will you pray with me, once again?"

"Forasmuch as the spirit of Mr. Evan has entered into the life immortal," he read from the Book of Common Prayers, "we therefore commit his body to its resting place, but his spirit we commend to God, remembering how Jesus said upon the cross, 'Father into thy hands I commend my spirit.'" Then David lead them in the Lord's Prayer, and after placing a handful of dirt on the still form within the frame, gave this benediction, "Now as we take our leave, merciful God, may we receive that blessing which thy well-beloved son shall pronounce to all that love and fear thee, saying. 'Come, ye blessed of my Father, receive the kingdom prepared for you from the foundation of the world'. Grant this, we beseech thee, O Merciful Father, through Jesus Christ our Redeemer. Amen." The top of the mound was bathed in reverent silence.

Becca broke the silence by saying, "We are invited into the Hospitality House for the goodness from the kitchens. Once again I thank you for this tender tribute to dad and all of us from Vermillion. You are our blessings." Folks began slowly making their way to the steps, assisted by Adam and Noah. There had been a changing of the guard.

Land Owners

Sunday, as the Vermillion devotion service was finished, Molly announced a rare opportunity that she believed would be of great interest to everyone. "A large plot of land is available to anyone who wants to have their own home," she said confidently. "There are thirty lots for sale, along with the material to build a home with two bedrooms. The cost is only $8 dollars each month for eight years. You will have the help of one another to construct the houses. There is a double lot and material to build a store for $10 per month for the first year and then $20 dollars per month for ten years. The new town will be called 'Bethel,' which means 'House of God.' If you have any questions, be sure to talk with me. I don't think these will be available forever."

Before she could get a glass of sweet tea, she had promises from eleven men. By the next Sunday there were ten more, one of those also wanted to own the store. All the new owners were former slaves. Daniel was beaming brightly at the success of this new idea. Two days later a letter from Lisle announced a change that was not as welcome.

Toby was very serious when he asked, "Miss Grace, will you please ask Mom Molly if we can go into town too? We both need new shoes and she doesn't like us padding around barefooted." It was the third time the subject had come up this morning.

"Most times, I'm sure she would say 'yes, of course you can,'" Grace answered with a patient smile. "But this is a very important trip to a lawyer's office to sign very special papers. There won't be any time to go to a shoe store." She hoped the answer would be accepted, finally. It hadn't worked the other two times she had said the exact thing.

"But who will take care of us if she is gone?" His voice sounded weak, and a little whiny.

"What are you saying?" she had a playfully sad voice. "You are eight years old and Mr. Eli needs your help digging Taro for the store today. Besides, I'm your sister and will always take care of you."

"Huh-uh," he shook his head. "Annie is our sister. And she needs someone to take care of her too." Now his voice was almost convincing.

"Now you have hurt my feelings," Gracie said still in that playful hurt mode. "Who is your Mom Molly? She is my Mom Molly too! That makes you my brother and I'm your sister. So I get to take care of you." That should have taken care of the issue.

"But we need new shoes," he said plaintively. They were back at the beginning, again.

"Toby," Grace began again, but less playfully. "Daddy Daniel had to go on a big trip with Aunt Becca. His sister in Florida is very sick, in a hospital, and Aunt Becca is going to be asked to run the school for her."

"What kind of school is it," the semi-interested boy asked.

"It's for teachers. Mom Molly went there and was taught many helpful lessons. I think I will get to go next year." Grace hoped the subject had been changed,

Toby said, "I could probably go too, if I had new shoes." Obviously, he had not forgotten what they were talking about.

Thomas sat in the waiting room outside the Lafayette attorney's office of Clarence LaDoux. Inside, Clarice and Molly sat across from a wrinkled gentleman in an equally wrinkled suit. Before them was a sheath of papers which he was explaining as they signed.

"And this page names, in the event of your passing, Molly Higgins as the sole executrix of your estate, Mrs. Cossindale, in the event Mrs. Rebecca Stanley precedes her in death. This document must be presented to the bank to authenticate her signature." All three signed the document.

His raspy voice continued as another sheet of paper was slid across to them. "This final page is an addendum to your last will and testament. It stipulates that Molly Higgins shall be the sole heir of all property and investments, in the event that all the other people named herein have deceased." He gave Clarice a long stare, indicating that he was less than supportive of the idea of bestowing all this authority on a woman of color. It was a new era following the emancipation. Regardless of his personal feelings or social attitudes, they all signed the document. Copies were placed in an envelope for Clarice's records, and the attorney placed another set in his file. There were several major changes at hand.

In the Tallahassee Hospital, Daniel and Becca listened to the doctor's grim assessment. "We managed to stem the Cholera. This outbreak was not as widespread as the epidemic of '58 and '59. We believe it began with tainted food at a hotel fundraiser. I believe it is over. The challenge for Miss Higgins now is the cascade of organ failure that has resulted from the disease. We can do little about the liver and kidney failure, but try to make her comfortable." They looked behind him at the still form of Lisle, her jaundice color distinctive.

Daniel asked, "How long do you suppose it will be before we can take her home to recuperate?

The doctor shifted his feet nervously. "I'm afraid I didn't say it clearly enough. Miss Higgins' organs are failing. Her body is shutting down. I believe she is in the final days of her life, and there is nothing more we can do for her." The anguish on his face told the story more clearly than his words. Becca's flowing tears were a testament to the grief she was feeling for the woman who had long ago opened the door of learning for her. "I suggest you get her house in order for the inevitable. Her time is close. I'm so very sorry." He turned and slowly walked away.

For a while they hovered near her bed, holding Lisle's hand and quietly talking to her. There was no response, either to their touch or encouraging words. Finally, Daniel said a prayer and invited Becca to return to the plantation with him. He had a proposal to make to her.

Unforeseen opportunity

As the carriage turned into the tree-lined lane, Daniel said, "You probably remember the big house that was near the town center before the fire. This was Monticello Plantation until that fire, and is now called Monticello Normal School. It has grown significantly in twenty years, but nothing like the surge since the end of the war. Enrollment now is over two hundred; there are two semesters and a summer session. Lisle has received so much support from northern donors that a dormitory was built for residential students. With seventeen instructors, there is a wide variety of subjects being offered. My favorite is the downtown bakery supplied by the domestic culinary department ovens. The school has a wonderful wide reputation, and a pretty large staff to keep it running smoothly." They pulled up before an impressive two story building with white columns and balconies that would please any architect.

As she stepped from the carriage, Becca said, "Daniel, I'm delighted to see all this." She had spoken with a soft voice. "But why are you showing this to me, and not Molly, or Gracie?" She looked carefully at him. "I have been wondering why you asked me to accompany you since we left Lafayette."

Instead of answering her, Daniel drew a folded piece of paper from his jacket pocket. "This is a letter from Lisle I received a few days ago. It seemed urgent enough for me to take immediate action. Let me read it to you."

"'Dearest Brother Daniel. These are dire times. I'm writing to you in desperation. I am very ill, and fear that health may never be mine again. I love this school, and I am troubled that it may not survive if I don't. I have instructed my barrister to contact you as my only heir in the event of my death. But even before that, I am pleading with you to assume directorship of Monticello. This is the fulfillment of all my dreams and I cannot accept the idea of it passing into public hands. Please respond with haste, for I fear my time here is quite limited. I love you, and am delighted in your success and happiness at Grove House with Molly. I know you will do what is right for Monticello. Yours in eternal affection, Lisle.'"

He took a deep breath to steady his emotions. "Becca, I would probably sell Grove House and assume responsibility for this school, except for Molly's attachment to the Vermillion Plantation. She is being groomed to become director of it. I'm not sure if Lowell feels the same way about your sugar plantation, but I have no one else to ask. Would you consider taking control of this school as its Director? The living quarters are lavish enough for your family, and Tallahassee is a marvelous city. You would be well compensated, and instantly welcomed as a community leader." They walked through the hall to a large office.

"You only spent three years with Lisle," he continued as they admired the awards on the wall. "That was not much time, but it is more than anyone else I can ask. You know her and how she feels about education. You also feel kindly to people of color, as does she. You probably have ample reasons to turn down this opportunity. I hope I have given you a few reasons to favorably consider it. Let's see a bit more of the school then catch the westbound afternoon train home."

Becca had a counter suggestion. "I think you should remain here with Lisle. Let me fetch Lowell, the kids, and your family. We can be back in just three or four days. Then we can talk about big responsibilities." She was thinking about the impact this positive situation might have for Angelina and the boys.

It was a gracious idea that Daniel could add onto. "I'll ask Simon, who replaced Sydney quite some time ago, to have the family coach hooked onto the train. He will accompany you. There will be more comfort and safety, regardless of how many you bring back with you."

They returned on the fourth day, and Lisle was buried on the fifth day. Her grave site was near her father's, in a family plot. Daniel thanked Becca repeatedly for making it possible for him to be with Lisle until the end. She had never been completely awake, but he was convinced that she was aware of his presence and his tender care.

They were all seated around the dining room table at Monticello. The dessert dishes had been cleared and the children whisked off by Gracie and Angelina, with a student eager to apply teaching skills. Lowell leaned closer to Daniel and asked, "Do I understand that the use of this four bedroom facility goes with the job? How much land does to the school have?"

"Yes, the living quarters and all the rest. I think it's about three quarters of a section, a mile east and west, and three quarters of a mile north and south," Daniel answered. "The previous owner raised thoroughbred horses, so there is a fantastic barn and grazing meadow. But these days there are only a handful of horses and carriages in there. The pasture is pretty much overgrown."

"Could a fellow plant some bearing crops?" Lowell asked.

"It's great land, flat and rich. It would surely be a fine spot for Orange trees. But they would take five or six years to become profitable. Sugar cane or tobacco would be quicker. Then there is Taro, which I haven't seen around here. You could have a crop by next year. The good thing about Taro is you could ask Thomas for all the crowns he would just throw away this year. I'll bet that would plant as much as you could get plowed." It was a playful conversation.

"Who would I have to talk to about that?" Lowell still was not grasping the magnitude of Becca's opportunity.

"Well Buddy," Daniel smiled, "if Becca agrees to become the Director, she's in charge of the entire place. If she doesn't, I'm going to recruit a handful of Trustees, who will become the guiding principle of this school for a long while. With continued donations and funding, it could be a model enterprise into the future. Goodness knows, education is standing on the cusp of our nation's finest era." He didn't want to say more, sounding like he was pressuring Becca.

But he had said enough to convince her that this was a once in a lifetime opportunity.

By breakfast time, the decision had been made. It really wasn't that difficult. Lowell would return to Abbeville and begin the process of selling the sugar cane plantation. Both sugar cane mills had "For Sale" boards. It would be an easy way to begin. Becca and the children would remain to get used to city living. She would begin immediately learning the scope of the Director's responsibilities and applying her own organizational and entrepreneurial skills. Daniel also invited her into Lisle's closet to see if any of her business dresses would fit. They were a tiny bit large, which made Becca smile with satisfaction. She had passed the first test!

A busy month followed for them all. Becca met with each faculty member individually. The house staff was eager to get to know a daughter who was hoping to attend classes, and two energetic boys who wanted to live in the spacious barn. Daniel wrote personal letters to the major donors, announcing the sad demise of the Director, and introducing her replacement, an early graduate and protégé of Miss Higgins, Rebecca Stanley. He stressed the smooth transition to the new leadership, and announced that with a successful funding campaign, a school of nursing would be added to the curriculum. The twins were regular visitors to the teaching classes where they demonstrated an accelerated level of reading skills. Annie was a star with the teachers in the kindergarten class. She told stories, richly adorned in fantasy, of her adventures at Grove House and the magical beasts who live in the basement there. Gracie also visited classrooms as a future student. And Molly looked after her busy family, keeping track of their work and play. They most enjoyed the daytrips to St. Mark, a small port just south of the school. There they saw many colorful birds and water fowl. But most fascinating were the Manatees, Sea Cows! All the time she was missing her daily swim in Vermillion Bay.

Perhaps Lowell was the busiest. As soon as the for sale notices went up at the sugar mills, he had interested folks stopping by. The easy access to the road and close proximity to the mills made it prime real estate. Their offers, however, were far below what Lowell was asking. He told them he would keep the plantation and share-crop it before he would just give it away.

Three days later, Dr. Terrance Winston, a retiring physician from the Lafayette Hospital drove his carriage down the lane. He said it was just the perfect time and place for his retirement. He offered Lowell full price, and to hurry the sale along, he threw in three Cleveland Bay broodmares, and a yearling filly. Their characteristic deep red color with black legs, mane and tail would be a welcomed sight in the big barn and pasture at Tallahassee. Dr. Winston also agreed to keep the present staff, complimenting Lowell on his transition from a slave owner to an employer. On Sunday, after the devotion service, Lowell announced that everything in his plantation house was offered as a moving sale. It would be more practical to replace whatever they might need than move it. That was of special interest to those who had dreams of their own home, now with furnishings. Yes, it was a very busy month.

The harvest season of '68 was more abundant than ever. The first Taro harvest caused Thomas to seek another wagon driver, That was followed by sugar canes that seemed endless. Then more loads of Taro, followed by a bumper Orange crop. Roman had to hire more pickers, and another distillery worker because the Commodore Hotel in Lafayette had placed a large annual order of rich dark rum. He also asked Thomas for any Taro crowns that were unused. Molly had suggested that the space between the Orange trees would make a lucrative extra crop, with nearly unlimited space. It was clear that the development of Bethel was just in time. The cluster of plain houses was filled completely with families that found adequate income from the plantations. Almost lost in the agricultural abundance was the dynamic growth of the Hospitality House. With the new wing finished and the former rooms refurbished, there were seventeen rooms available for guests, and three beach bungalows. Miss Clarice kept the staff busy with a near capacity schedule that allowed each guest at least one hour of beach therapy daily. She was diligent to also respect the Sabbath for devotions, and no guests. It was meant to be a day of rest.

The second Monday of August, Stanley arrived to escort Gracie to Tallahassee for the Monticello school opportunity. In the weeks preceding this leave-taking, she had spoken consistently of the inviting challenge of learning, meeting new friends, expanding her talents. She was eager to be reunited with Becca. Even though she was the Director of the school, Gracie thought of her as an aunt of sorts. But now that the time for parting had arrived, she wanted one more beach visit, one more Hospitality lunch, one more ride around the plantation. It was far too important to pretend that she could casually leave.

Gracie's arrival in Tallahassee was no less significant. Rebecca Stanley had leaked the news to the Herald that the daughter of Daniel Higgins, noted Washington lobbyist, and Granddaughter of J. Henry Higgins, revered former owner editor, was beginning her academic education at Monticello. A lecture series featuring Lucy Stone, outspoken advocate of Women's Suffrage, was a fascinating introduction to Gracie's learning experience, and would lead to a lifetime cause.

One autumn Sunday Miss Clarice asked Molly to sit with her on the veranda after the crowd had finished devotions and the meal that now always followed. They sat quietly for a bit, sipping sweet tea. "I don't understand how you stay so young," Clarice finally said. "You seem immune to age. Aren't you but fifteen years younger than me, and look at the difference." Her happy smile and wrinkled face was as dear to Molly as her mother's had been.

"I believe it has something to do with my daily swims," Molly said truthfully. "The boys and Annie join me. Timmy has become an excellent swimmer."

"I believe it has to do with trying to keep up with those twins, and darling Annie. You are a very busy lady." Clarice knew what she wanted to ask, but was anxious that Molly might not welcome the proposal. They watched the sun chase shadows on the peaceful surface of Vermillion Bay. "I have something important to ask you."

Molly looked at her with interest, but said nothing.

"I thought adding more rooms would be a good thing for the Hospitality House. It has proved to be a productive addition, but

I'm not sure I can keep up with its demands." She reached out for Molly's hand. "It has turned into a very large job." A sigh ended her sentence, and Molly understood just how weary Miss Clarice had become. "Molly, would you be willing to take over for me here at Hospitality House?" Miss Clarice's shoulders sagged a bit now that it had been said.

Molly held on to her hand, more aware of how frail it had become. "Tell me what I would be expected to do," she asked.

Now that she had asked without being turned down immediately, Miss Clarice put on a bit of a hopeful smile. "Noah gets the mail from the Abbeville store on Mondays and Thursdays. First I read the requests and divide them by how urgent they sound. I have a calendar that I can write their names and possible room numbers. I try to schedule at least three weeks ahead, so I can write back to them and agree that we have space for them. I also make sure they know about paying upon arrival. Usually I try to reserve a downstairs room for anyone who may be disabled. There are seventeen rooms, and for the past month, we have been nearly full every night."

Molly raised her eyebrows in surprise. "That is a lot," she exclaimed. "It's a lot of details, and a lot of income."

"Yes it is, Sweetheart. I am proposing that you pay the staff each month from our income, and pay yourself 10% of the Hospitality House as well." When Molly drew in a breath, Miss Clarice added, "and I think you should ask either David or May to help you with some of it. There is too much temptation for me to imagine anyone else."

Now incredulous with thoughts of that much money, Molly asked quietly, as though there might be listeners, "But how do you get the money to the bank?"

Smiling even wider now, Miss Clare answered, "Without Evan it is a bit more complicated. But he fashioned a sizable vault under the Hospitality House fireplace. When that was full, he made a vault with a trap door under our bedroom in the mound house. That's about half full of bags. Our big bed frame is also a vault which is full of bags. Once a month Adam and Noah have some errand to run into Lafayette, and the wagon carries about a dozen husk bags which are hiding our bank deposit. If there is a load of pecans or husks going into the store for barter, we feel pretty safe." Then as though sharing and after-thought, she whispered, "We never dreamed of being this rich. We just hoped we could get by. Evan had such great insight, making successful dreams come true." A radiant smile spread across her face.

Molly gave a soft squeeze to the hand still in hers. "I think you know who helped him make these wonderful plans." A soft breeze stirred the air around them. "Miss Clare," Molly used her old familiar name, "I would be honored to help you in whatever way I can, I'm thinking that May will be delighted to have a chance to earn a bit more money too, and learn to keep our books. Her man, Felix, who was Cap'n Cal's field foreman, wants to buy the Bethel double lot and build a store. New income can insure their success. There is also two lots in the front that I have been saving, thinking that a school could fit there for all the kids who are bound to be born with all this romance going on." They shared a happy chuckle. "I'll be here tomorrow when the mail comes in. You can show me how you set up the calendar, and answer the guests." For such an important step, they had accomplished a positive conclusion with relative ease.

From the very beginning, Molly had the opinion that Hospitality House would function best if she filled only most of the rooms, and not all. That meant the dining room would be comfortably filled, the beach chairs too. Then if a true emergency occurred, or an unscheduled guest showed up, there would be an available room, without a panic.

The guests were a constant stream of injuries and ailments. Some had been ill for a long while; others were fresh afflictions that needed special attention. Each found a compassionate welcome and an opportunity to rest in the tepid comfort of Vermillion Bay, quite unaware of the multitude of Seerier who were there to administer their assistance. By the first of November Molly was doing all of the calendar assignments and May was keeping the books in competent order. Daniel was once again summoned to Washington to give rational assistance to the nation's reconstruction process. The war had done so much damage, now the healing process needed wise guidance.

He returned a week before Christmas, but said he had to go back to the Nation's Capital by the first of the year. With Christmas Day on Monday, Miss Clarice instructed Molly to pay everyone a double Christmas bonus early to help them prepare for the holiday. The grateful joy was contagious. She also directed the kitchen staff to pass the word to the other cooks that the meal after devotions would be extra special.

Later Christmas Eve, the folks were gathered again in the Hospitality House dining room, now lit gracefully with candles. Molly led the singing of several familiar carols and David read the popular poem, "'Twas the Night Before Christmas." Eli sang "Sweet Little Jesus Boy," and folks were inspired again by his rich baritone voice. Miss Clarice ask folks to bow in prayer, remembering how Mr. Evan loved to give a Christmas blessing to all. When she had finished the prayer, she announced that as a memorial to her beloved husband, a school was going to be built in Bethel for the education of all ages. Four or five carpenters would be hired after the first of the year, weather permitting. It was a memorable Sabbath devotion.

As folks were enjoying the desserts and punch, Dr. Terrance Winston and his wife Barbara reintroduced themselves to Miss Clarice. "We attended a couple of Sunday devotions last summer," he confessed. "It has been a challenge to move our household, while still feeling responsibilities to the hospital." His gaze swept across the room with the obvious capacity for several guests. "Will you tell me about Hospitality House? Is it a hospital of some sort, or a clinic with a staff of doctors and nurses?" He could see few Caucasian faces and knew of no doctors or nurses of color.

"Oh, no sir," Clarice said with certainty. "Vermillion Plantation grows Taro, sugar canes, and Pecans. That's our purpose. On the side, we do welcome folks who are weary or injured, who find rest and invigoration in what we call a beach treatment. Some people believe there is healing in the artesian spring water that has never failed us. Others believe it has something to do with bathing in the warm salt water of the bay. There are a few people who are convinced our kitchen makes the finest shrimp gumbo around, and it is the combination of all three gifts that produces amazing accounts of invigoration. For fifty years it has been a delightful mystery to me because they do get better. If my opinion counts, I'd say it has to do with the spiritual purity of this place and the prayers of its people." Her smile was unfading.

The doctor stroked a bit of a chin whisker as he said, "I believe there is a town in eastern Belgium named Spa. It's famous for its mineral springs, which allows people to rest and be invigorated, I believe you called it. Perhaps your spring is such a mineral source."

A totally new idea had just occurred to him. "Mrs. Cossin..." She interrupted to ask him to call her Clarice. "Miss Clarice, do you believe in destiny? Do you believe in random coincidence, or is there a higher purpose to the world around us?" Before she could answer, to say that she believed in a powerful and mysterious God who was always at work in this world, he told her a secret. "Barbara, my lovely wife is in need of some healing minerals. About ten years ago she began to notice red rough itchy patches on her skin. They were small at first, mostly on elbows and knees. She could easily cover them. But they grew and spread. Now she wears heavy dresses with high necks and tries to find comfort in salves and ointments. Nothing has helped much; it has spread over most of her body, even into her hair. She refuses to go out socially for fear of embarrassing others. She calls it leprosy, which eczema is not. Ma'am, I did not imagine imposing upon your generous nature this evening. If there is any possible avenue of hope for treating Barbara's situation, I will do anything in my power to explore it." It was obvious he was feeling intense about this new idea.

"Tomorrow is Christmas Day," Clarice answered, "and we have no guests scheduled. If you will come back at about eleven o'clock, she can have some beach time, and we can share lunch together. I would love to get to know Barbara." It was such a simple thing to do, but the consequences would lead them on a bold new path.

The Winstons sat chest-deep in the warm morning sun and gentle water, wearing swimming robes and huge smiles. Barbara reminisced that she had not been swimming since she was a child.

This was an idyllic location and moment. Just as Gracie brought a pitcher of spring water and glasses, Dr. Winston agreed, saying that this moment was one of buoyant delight. "Maybe this is how retirement is supposed to feel. I feel light and ever so content." Was it the pure water they drank, or the calm water that supported them? It didn't matter which. When they concluded their visit with some rich Ham and Taro jambalaya, they were grateful for the gifts of the day.

Actually, it took three beach treatments before Barbara could be certain that her skin was truly healing. With two more after that, she could declare that eczema was no longer present anywhere on her. At first Dr. Winston wanted to take water samples to determine what medicinal properties were at work. But when the test showed nothing but pure spring and ocean water with no identifiable particulates, he accepted the conclusion that it was a mystery indeed.

After devotions one Sunday he took the opportunity to ask Miss Clarice a question. "You have mentioned that with Bethel homes housing most of your staff, you have two residential buildings that are pretty empty. Would you accept an offer that would turn them into a moneymaker?"

"Evan always welcomed questions," she answered brightly. "So often they were guides into brand new areas of thought," Clarice looked up with a reminiscent smile. "Of course I would be happy to think about those help houses, as we called them."

"The hospital frequently has patients who need more than our medical knowledge can cure. I'm thinking of burn victims, pelvic fractures, abdominal injuries, pulmonary failure, just about every cardiac challenge. We can sedate somewhat, but not bring the sort of healing that I witnessed with Barbara. I don't want to compete with you on your own property. That would be unacceptable. But what would you think if the hospital leased your help houses, painted them with a sterile white interior and brought patients that were beyond the assistance of our scientific knowledge? They could have access to pitchers of spring water, and visit the beach some distance out of the way from your current area. Nurses or orderlies would move them, feed them and wash the sheets. Perhaps some folks who have little hope, might get well."

She thought for a moment before replying, "Since we are only exploring an idea right now, what do you think these buildings would lease for?" Clarice was not very enthused about the suggestion, so far.

"I have no idea what they might agree to, so I am suggesting to you that a hundred dollars a month might be very attractive starting place." He wore a confident smile

"Forgive me, Dr. Winston, for being less than thrilled about the idea. To be quite frank with you, that's just the income of one room for one night for the Hospitality House. For a tiny bit of money, that I do not need, I am not motivated to add anything that may disrupt or detract from what is already working well as a humanitarian retreat."

His smile faded.

Then she added, "But I am motivated by the thought of assisting children or youth back to full health. Our neighbor's boys where wheezers when they were adopted. Within two weeks of beach treatments they were breathing just fine. A four year old girl was deaf until she had several beach treatments. Now she is a chatterbox with perfect hearing."

"Then you would agree to the hospital bringing some of its younger patients here if we could offer a thousand dollars a month, understanding that is still far less than you going rate?" Now the smile was budding again on Dr. Winston's face.

"For matters of negotiation, I think the hospital may have use of the large help house, which has six rooms plus a kitchen and lobby, for two months. We will provide meals for whomever is here, but the hospital must provide care and support folks completely, plus transportation. Compensation for this trial period will be the painting of the help houses inside and out, plus painting the outside of the new barn. After the two month trial period we will negotiate the lease terms. But I must warn you that we will not tolerate the hospital charging folks for more than the costs here. If you try to inflate expenses beyond Vermillion Plantation costs, our agreement will be terminated immediately."

Dr. Winston really liked this feisty lady. Her wrinkles suggested a softness, but her attitude was spunky as the dickens. "I'll have a meeting with the manager. What have we got to lose, right?"

By the first of the month, a team of five painters had completed the first part of the agreement, painting the buildings bright white. A thorough treatment of a new product called sodium hypochlorite, which had been developed to sanitize surfaces, was liberally spread on the former residences. On the following Monday morning a procession of white box wagons began delivering patients to what the hospital was calling "Bethesda South". Its translation meant "House of Flowing," and it was south of Lafayette. For those who were part of it, the understanding was clear; invigorated health, wholeness, and vitality were flowing into children in a surprising fashion.

The first patient placed upon a narrow cot, was a six year old named Patty, who had been in a coma for over a week. Scarlet Fever had raged her frail body into submission. There was still a detectable breath and heartbeat within her, but just barely. Spring water and puréed soup were introduced by a feeding tube. There was no response from her tiny body the first three times she was placed on the beach recliner in the shallow bay water. The Seerier scouts that located a new host location nearly passed her, determining that she was so near death applications would be wasted. Thankfully, they gave her ample cell regeneration and immunity boosts for a different prognosis. By the fourth morning when the nurse came in to check her temperature, blue eyes watched from the pillow, and a wan smile signaled the return of consciousness. Recovery for Patty was clearly in process.

Upstairs, a room had two young boys suffering from food poisoning. While they may not have understood the term Botulism, they knew that one had eaten poorly preserved canned beans, and the other had eaten rancid pork and beans. The tainted meat had been masked by the sweet molasses flavor. They also were at death's door when they were brought to Bethesda.

The treatment that had pulled Patty back into the realm of the living was used as the model for assisting children. The semiconscious boys were fed a thin soup mixture with plenty of pure spring water. They were then taken to the beach for a gentle opportunity to sit in the quiet bay water. Unnoticed but no less effective, they received an abundant visit of Seerier applications. On the fourth day of their stay at Bethesda, both boys were ready to be returned to their grateful parents, not completely recovered, but well enough to make room for other children in need.

On average, Bethesda welcomed twenty children or youth a week. The white box wagons from the hospital became a familiar sight on the road each day, coming from Lafayette, or returning. The lease-use agreement was welcomed by all parties, and deposits were made directly into the bank. Miss Clarice was also a daily visitor to every room, praying for the children and staff. Three of the single nurses were grateful to receive an invitation to reside in the big house on the mound with Miss Clarice. She once told Molly, "If this merciful care of children was all that we accomplished founding Vermillion Plantation, it would have been well worth the effort." In the year 1870, just a few less than a thousand children received wondrous new health there; only three were too ill to be helped.

The spring Taro harvest had been very productive. The Abbeville store had to renegotiate its barter terms. The shrimp were still abundant, but the number of wild hogs seemed scarce. Miss Clare had determined that without Moesh's hunting skills, market meat would be more reliable, and if the store could provide it through barter, they would continue to receive Taro, but at the same rate the Lafayette warehouse paid, sixty cents per head. Now, once a month a wagon load of Taro was exchanged for Smoked ham or beef roasts.

Staff Problem

One summer Sunday evening, when all the day's chores were finished, David came to Molly's office, asking if she had a moment to talk.

"I always have time for you, David," she answered cheerily. The expression on his face however was more serious.

"Miss Molly, I have a puzzle that has perplexed me. I hope I can talk to you. I don't want to bother Miss Clarice." He used her formal name.

"Of course we can handle any puzzle," Molly continued in her jovial tone.

"This is pretty serious," the tall man said with something of a shrug. "You know that Daphne has been my choice since the first time I met her. I was sure she would be my wife, and we would live happy ever after, as they say." He shifted from foot to foot nervously. "I acquired one of the lots, as you know, and with the help of Thomas and Martin, have built a nice home. She has stayed in her Grove House basement room. I assumed it was because she is a proper chaste woman, which I have applauded."

Molly could not imagine where the puzzle might be in this conversation.

David went on. "She convinced me that she was going to attend school with Miss Gracie, perhaps to become a teacher in the new school."

He was speaking so slowly that Molly interrupted him. "Do you mean that she wants to postpone your marriage?'

David shook his head. "I only wish it was that simple." He took a deep breath, which signaled Molly that indeed this was a difficult matter. Finally he let it roll out. "She asked me to help her steal your money box!" His face twisted in anguish. "She believes there are several thousand dollars in the box in the corner cupboard. It's too heavy for her to carry far. She has asked me to steal a carriage so we can go west into Texas." There, it was said!

Now Molly understood his dilemma. He had been asked to betray people he loved, for one whom he apparently did not know as well as he thought. "How does she know where the box is hidden?" Molly asked as she tried to quiet her surprise.

"She came in to clean last week, and had time to look through all the drawers and cupboards. I think she looked inside the box. It was too much temptation for her."

Molly remembered the words of Miss Clare in identifying David and May as being trustworthy in the face of all this temptation. "Do you know when she plans this theft?" Molly asked, trying to keep a normal voice.

"I think her plan is for tomorrow night, since there will be many new guests checking in. That doesn't give you much time, I know. She only hatched this plan yesterday. I'm so sorry for her betrayal." He looked sad enough to cry.

"You have done an honorable thing, David. Thank you. If we are fore-warned we are prepared to deal with the situation. I want you to go along with her wishes; help her as she wants. When you are confronted by the men who will stop her, do not try to resist them. You will not survive, I'm afraid." Molly was feeling righteous anger heating up within her, and knew she must quell that. "Now that we know, everything will be manageable." She placed her hand on his shoulder reassuringly.

Monday was an incredibly slow day, as if time was crawling by on hands and knees. The guests began to arrive midmorning. David's task as Host was to greet them, care for the check-in process, and guide them to their room. Each guest was given a schedule of meals and their beach time. If there might be some complaint about the menu at lunch or dinner, David's standard answer was, "We've been doing it this way for fifty years, and frankly we don't know which part is the miracle, food, spring water or beach time. We are afraid to change any of it for fear the healing magic won't work." If there was ever a continuing murmur, he would say, "I'll check with you later to see if it worked well for you." It always does.

Felix's task was taking the carriage and horse to the barn, situating them in an orderly and convenient way. The meals were served by Daphne and Gwen with cheerfulness, as was the pitchers of spring water at the beach. All in all, the program worked smoothly; but on this Monday it was agonizingly slow in David's opinion. He feared that something sinister was going to happen, and worried more that it wouldn't.

The last guest to be fed finally finished and the dishes were removed. Miss Molly finished her piano serenade and the Hospitality House became still. David had been instructed to go about his regular routine. He extinguished the lamps, looked around once more hoping to see Daphne, then trudged up the hill to Bethel and his neat little home.

She was waiting for him, sitting on the steps with a huge smile. "I thought you would never finish," she said playfully. "Can you believe how many guests came today? And some of them paid for three or four days. That box will be full!"

He was sad to see how blatant she had become. "Daphne, not so loud!" he cautioned. "Remember there is staff right next door."

"Why are you so tense, David?" She began slowly unbuttoning her dress. "Let's go inside. I know what will calm you down."

"Are you out of your mind? You are acting like a child, when the task of the night requires focus and a clear head. One or the other; do you want bed play or that money box? You can't have both!" His rough voice was only a disgusted whisper.

Immediately she turned toward the door, angrily saying, "We'll see how pious you are when we get to Texas. Then you'll want both, and might not get what you want." They didn't speak again until it was time to go back to Hospitality House.

It was after midnight when the two shadow figures made their way silently into the barn, where David harnessed a horse to the carriage. Then carrying the lantern inside, they found Miss Molly's office behind the kitchen. The box was in the cupboard just as she had discovered it. Daphne opened the lid and caught her breath, saying in a whisper, "It's almost full." She could almost lift the heavy treasure, but finally had to ask David to take one handle. It was more than she had dreamed. Silently they struggled their way out through the dining room.

Just before they reached the steps of the porch, a man's voice spoke from the darkness, "Daphne, put it down!" She jerked to a stop in surprise, and David lay down on his stomach, releasing the handle.

"Oh no," Daphne moaned. "No, this is not supposed to happen!" She struggled to get the other handle and carry her treasure by herself.

"Daphne, I don't want to hurt you. Stop now," the voice commanded.

She was pretty sure it was Thomas, but she was too near the carriage to obey.

Out of the darkness there was the whirring rush of a rake handle being thrown at her legs. She screamed, stumbled and collapsed all at once, landing on top of the money box. From three directions, shadows converged on her, roughly forcing her to the ground, then tying her hands behind her back and fastening her feet securely together. She wept, "No, oh no!"

From the dark dining room, Molly stepped out onto the porch. In a soft voice she spoke to no one in particular. "The most beautiful flower of the garden, the one with the most potential, is lying in the dirt in tragic shambles. What a monumental waste!" Then in a firmer voice she said, "Mr. Thomas, will you return the horse to the barn, and bring out one of ours. If Martin will join you, you can take Daphne to the Marshal first thing in the morning. Her crime is burglary, and the attempted theft of a money box with nine thousand seven hundred dollars, a carriage, and Mr. Prentiss' horse. I'm afraid she is going to be locked up for a very long time. What a waste!"

Daphne lay bound in the carriage all night, listening for approaching footsteps. She was certain David would rescue her. Someone would set her free. Finally in hopeless desperation, she simply wept.

As expected the fall Taro harvest was the largest ever. Roman brought a wagon to haul away the unwanted crowns from the Vermillion rows Grove House still had miles of empty rows that awaited planting between the Orange trees.

As expected Daniel was not present for the Grove House November Orange harvest. Roman once again issued an invitation for any able bodies who wanted to pick to come and help. His agreement was ten cents a box, which meant that a dedicated person could earn as much as three dollars a day. To his satisfaction and relief a dozen women and older children joined the men who came to earn extra money too. The bumper crop produced nearly three thousand boxes.

As expected Daniel sent Molly a heartfelt apology for missing Christmas again. His lengthy letter explained his many travels between Washington and Baltimore, Philadelphia and Pittsburg. He was once again in the fervor of serving his country in patriotic sacrifice. She missed him terribly, but perhaps not as much as the children missed their father. She often wondered whether it was something in his nature to love her less than Mr. Evan had loved Miss Clarice. Or was it something in her nature? Perhaps it was the color of her skin after all. It was a puzzle to her how he could forego this beautiful home and affectionate wife so casually.

What was not expected was the rapid decline of Miss Clarice's health. She had three or four very mild strokes. The accumulation of their effects, however, was slurred speech and her dependence on a cane to get around. The steps up to the mound house became an increasing challenge, so her appearance in the Hospitality dining room was less and less frequent.

Also unexpected was a letter from Mr. Daniel's attorney, informing Molly that Daniel had been convalescing in a Washington hospital. His pulmonary ailment, an apparent hereditary condition, was not serious, but reason for Molly to go into the Lafayette law office to review his Last Will and Testament. With the death of his sister, there was now the matter of the Tallahassee estate. It was a whole new era.

They turned over a fresh calendar with little change, except Gracie and Angelina had finished their years at Monticello. Gracie was recruited by Susan B. Anthony to be an advance associate for the National American Woman Suffrage Association, setting speaking venues and press announcements. Angelina became a hospital nurse. Sixty four year old Molly hired Sarah to be her housekeeper and watch after the twins and Annie. She also invited David to join the daily family swimming session.

"The boys need someone who can teach them to be stronger swimmers," she said. "They believe I am a fair teacher, for a girl. I think they would learn a lot from you." She smiled warmly, knowing that this was beyond a routine expectation.

With a sheepish grin, David admitted, "But Molly, I'm not much of a swimmer. More like a flounderer, I think."

Confidently she said, "I try to swim each evening after supper. If you would like to join me, perhaps I can teach you the basics first, and then you can simply pass it on to the twins." With a giggle she added, "You are tall enough to simply wade. If you use your arms, it will look like you are a fantastic swimmer."

David was at the beach four of the next five evenings, and after that almost every afternoon. He was mystified at the joyful experience of swimming. It was like being a young boy all over again. Little did he know that the Seerier were applying endorphin boosts regularly, and in abundance.

A Troubling Dream

On a rainy February morning, Molly carried a pot of tea to the mound house to share with Miss Clarice. She was prepared to see her labored movements, but not her pale skin. "Are you feeling well, ma'am," Molly spoke softly.

"It is a more comfortable day, isn't it dear?" she replied without answering Molly's question. They sat on the veranda, watching the showers march across the bay like children chasing one another. "You know," the matron said quietly, "I had the strangest dream last night. It's still clear in my thoughts this morning. My sweet Evan visited me. He held my hand between his, like he used to do when he wanted to encourage me. I could feel his warmth and strength." She sipped her tea with a gentle smile. "He told me how proud he was for the achievements we have made, and how good it was to treat the sick children." Her forehead furrowed a bit, remembering the rest of her dream. "He told me not to be concerned when the storm comes." She looked steadily into Molly's eyes. "He told me you could rebuild it bigger and better than ever." A smile of encouragement blossomed on Miss Clarice. "He told me that you shouldn't be upset, dear. It will be wonderful."

Molly took one of Miss Clarice's hands in hers, studying the fingers, gnarled now by age and labor, but a hand she could remember as graceful and slim, playing lovely piano melodies. She looked at the thinning white hair on her head that she could remember clearly as curls of golden brown. She studied the familiar face with the affection of a dear daughter. "Tell me what you think the dream meant," she finally asked.

Raising her eyebrows in surprise, Miss Clarice asked, "What dream would that be, dear?" The moment was gone, leaving not even a scrap of recollection swirling in its wake.

"Oh, we were speaking about the rain storm" Molly said casually. "But I think it will only turn out to be showers." They both focused on the bay speckled with raindrops. But the thought of the dream lingered in Molly's thoughts. She wondered about the health of both this matriarch and her Daniel. Could that be the storm? She pondered the growing number of people coming to the beach treatments, could that be the storm? Her concern about the slow incursion of the hospital into Vermillion Plantation may also be the meaning of the dream. For several days she felt uneasy about the visit with Miss Clarice, but finally the routine of work overshadowed her anxiety.

March came in like a lamb and left the same way. It seemed inconceivable that the Taro could continue to set production records. More help meant that the work was accomplished in about the same time, but with much greater reward. The staff was becoming accustomed to the feeling of financial security at last.

Thomas was agreeing with the warehouse foreman. "Yes, that's what we counted too, six thousand five hundred, at 60 cents apiece."

The burly man named Butcher, smiled and asked, "Do you want that in double eagles, or if you are going straight to the Federal Bank with it, may I give you a voucher?" It was the first time Thomas had heard about a "voucher" so he asked for more explanation. "We give you a piece of paper to take to Mr. Maurice Bandeau, and he deposits $3,900 in Vermillion's account. It's easier for us than counting out a hundred and ninety five double eagles; and it's easier and safer for you than hauling gold to the bank. Give it a try. If anything goes wrong, come back and I'll count out the coins for you." A new day of convenience was beginning.

"By the way," Butcher added. "Are we getting all of your Taro? We have a new government contract that could use a lot more."

"You're getting all we grow, except for a few that we barter with the Abbeville store. But our neighbor at Grove House, who

211

has been planting our crowns for a while, is about ready to begin digging them up. I'll tell him about bringing them here. Come to think about it, he doesn't have a wagon, so I might bring them in for him." Thomas held out his hand as though striking a new contract.

As the handshake was lingering, Butcher said, "I can use all the pecans, both nuts and husks you can bring me too."

"What do you pay for Oranges?" Thomas asked, now into the new era of possibilities.

Miss Clarice did not come to the breakfast table the Monday after Palm Sunday. The nurses who were sharing the mound house with her finally knocked on her door. When there was no answer, they went in to check on her well being, and found that during the night her sweet life had come to an end. It appeared that her death had been gentle, fitting for the one whose entire life had been devoted to her loving Lord.

The nurse hurried to tell Molly the sad news. She turned to Thomas, who found Adam and Noah. Working together with a beach chair, the three men easily moved the slight body down the back stairs to the top of the mound. Thomas and Martin set to the task of building a coffin frame, a task nearly familiar. Her gravesite would be next to that of Mr. Evan's, appropriately. Because there was a full guest list for the Hospitality House, her memorial service would be after the Easter devotions, also appropriately.

When Molly saw the folks gathering for devotions it made her heart happy. The women were dressed in their finest, and the men all had white shirts. They were showing their respect for Easter of course, but also for Miss Clare. Sadly, when Molly thought a bit longer about the gathering crowd, her heart was also aware that Capt. Perry and his family, Dr, Winston and his wife Barbara, were not in attendance, and hadn't been for several weeks. Only people of color were there, and Molly wondered if she understood the significance of that. Without Mr. Evan's leadership and Miss Clare's support the white folks felt a lack of motivation to attend. They were still making selections based on skin color. One Monday when she went with Noah to pick up the mail, Molly had heard the rumor that the Perry place was up for sale; they were returning to

Mississippi. Now Molly was more than ever grateful for the many men and women who chose to share devotions here because they found inspiration and authentic fellowship.

Somewhere between her first glass of sweet tea, and her first slice of Orange tea cake, Molly realized three strong truths, since she was now, by attrition, the matriarch of Vermillion Plantation. First, there was an abundance of great staff to do the work; secondly she had to do something with the accumulation of wealth contained in the vaults; thirdly, she no longer missed Mr. Daniel. In fact, she was more than mildly insulted by his absence. She didn't need action on the first; it would be easy to do something about the second. And, most importantly, she could quit grieving the third.

On her first venture into Miss Clare's bedroom, she felt like an intruder, but she had to discover the two vaults that Miss Clare had mentioned. The first one was easy. When the bedding was removed from the bed, she could see a well fashioned heavy base with boards that covered a large hidden space. It was filled with leather sacks, each of which contained five hundred gold double eagles! She carefully remade the bed, and looked for clues to the other secret place.

When she finally moved the easy chair by the window, under the throw-rug, she found the lid to the second vault. It was larger than the first, but it too was filled with leather bags. She didn't even peer into one, already convinced of the contents. Carefully she rearranged the concealment. It would take some thought how to transport this wealth to the bank. Perhaps David could help her form a plan.

Annie chose to stay in the kitchen with pans of fresh cookies while the boys followed Molly to the beach. As the trio of swimmers arrived at the shoreline, David was already wading waist deep. The boys saw that as a challenge to reach him first, so a ragged charge with a lot of splashing, brought them to his waiting arms. "Hey Mom," Toby called, "David's going to teach us to duck our faces! Watch!" Molly was nearly laughing, for she had to work three evenings to get the big guy to relax enough to get his head under water. Now he was boldly sharing his talent.

"He's good, isn't he?" she called, delighted in their enthusiasm.

When the boys finally satisfied their hunger for instruction, they wandered back into the shallow water where they could frolic and play with floating sticks. Molly moved closer to David so she could share the discoveries of her search. She told him of her trust in his ability to keep this secret. "They have hoarded the profits from the Hospitality House as well as the crops for the past twenty years. It's a scary big amount, and I don't know how to get it to the bank," She floated nearer to him and rolled over so she could face him.

"It would probably be more than the carriage could handle," he thought out loud. "But folks are pretty familiar with the wagon going in with either Taro or bags of pecans. Why not cover some of the bank deposit with crops. That might take several trips, but there would be the wisdom in…" He didn't finish his sentence because a small wave, or perhaps her intent, caused Molly to brush against him, warm and mysterious. He quickly pulled away, apologizing for his clumsiness.

"It was my fault," Molly said with a warm smile. "I trust you, and your insight is helpful to me. You just confirmed Miss Clare's suggestion. Suddenly I feel small before this big task." But she paddled a couple feet away to prevent more contact.

On Friday morning, in the early dawn, she supervised the placement of a hundred bags to the wagon floor. Then two hundred Taro heads were placed on top of them as a covering. With Thomas driving and Noah along as security, Molly sat in the middle. The trip to Lafayette was too tense to be enjoyable, and there was very little conversation.

The wagon was parked by the employee's entrance on the side of the bank, and the men stayed with it while Molly went in to speak with Mr. Bandeau. A security guard appeared to provide safety as the men finally carried two bags at a time in to be counted. Molly watched over the entire process until it was complete. Then they could breathe naturally again.

Maurice Bandeau, the vice president of the bank, explained to Molly that the money could be deposited to her account, or it could be converted to the new U.S. Treasury Bearer Bonds, which pay a growth interest. They could then be secured in a deposit box in the bank's basement. Since the Vermillion account was already large enough to more than meet operating needs, she agreed to the latter, after a bit more explanation. The wagon with the empty leather bags and a small load of Taro went home via the Abbeville store. It seemed like a pretty safe banking process, which was repeated seven times without incident, before the three vaults were emptied.

With the Hospitality House dining room at capacity most days, the staff began sharing their lunch at the mound house, which had a large beautiful table. Over a short while it became a time and place to share conversations about various tasks, a working conference table as it were. One afternoon Adam was trying to explain to Molly why a larger Taro wagon should be purchased. "It only stands to reason," he said with a tone of voice that Molly resented, "that each season our production is greater. We need more hauling capacity." It was not the first time Molly had heard the suggestion, only the first time it had been directed toward her, bluntly.

"You've been doing an excellent job, Adam," Molly said in soft reply. "I've wondered how you manage the two season harvest." She was quiet for just a heartbeat, then added, "and why do we only harvest twice a year?" Adam leaned a bit closer, listening to a very new thought.

Molly said in her soft voice, "I've been thinking that with the new plants growing at Grove House, we could choose twelve sections of the Taro plants. We could then dig for two days, haul, and replant the crowns for two days, every week! If we hire three more folks who only did Taro, we could be delivering all year long, at a steady easy pace. Instead of a larger wagon that we seldom use, we could use the one we have. We would just use it much more often."

Adam shook his head, "No..." But then he asked with growing interest, "Do you really think there is that much to harvest?" He looked into her eyes as though for the first time. He was very interested in her thoughts.

"Just think about it a minute," she said with growing enthusiasm that was contagious. "With all our perimeter and section rows, we've got at least six miles of Taro rows planted two or three wide. The

Grove House has already planted the south boundary, that's another mile. And the first row in the Orange grove has a good start, three wide. That's another mile and there are six more rows that are being planted. There is an available mile a month right now, twice a year! Yes, we have production right now to work this plan, and it is going to double, maybe triple. Think about monthly bonuses instead of twice a year!"

"But…." It seemed too easy and too good to Adam; there must be a reason it wouldn't work. "But what about the sugar cane harvest, and the pecans? Everybody is needed during those peak times." Yeah that must be the reason Molly's idea couldn't work.

"Did you see what Mr. Roman did with the Orange harvest? He paid seasonal folks to come in and get the job done. There's no reason that wouldn't work harvesting our sugar cane and for sure pecans just as well. Besides, that might be a great way to find new permanent workers."

There was nothing left for Adam but to agree that the plan would be a step forward. Rather than a larger wagon, they could use the adequate one they already had, more often. He began designating the harvest zones to begin next week. The more he thought on the idea, the better it became. Monthly bonuses were great!

Molly was eager to have beach time with the children, and with David. She had so much to tell him about her success as the director of two large plantations. For the moment, all areas were working smoothly. The promise of the gentle water and its revival of her spirit was a daily anticipation.

On a Sunday after devotions, Molly found herself standing near May. They exchanged cordial conversation for a bit, then Molly asked another policy changing question, "May what would you think about setting up a small table in front of the Hospitality House before lunch time, the last Friday of the month, where we could offer pay and bonuses to everyone. I could dispense and you could keep the accounts. It would be so much better than the 'hunt and go seek' delivery way we are doing it now. Folks can know that their pay is ready, and the ones who don't show up, we can look for later. Does that make sense to you?"

"It would be so easy!" the happy lady agreed. "I really like the idea. When can we start?" A time-saving practical improvement was inaugurated just that easily.

Molly was not intentionally changing her status, but with each of the policies she established, she was taking the place of the matriarch. She was the Boss, Miss Molly!

The school house was finished during the warm summer. It was even painted white so everyone could identify it. Miss Molly put an advertisement in the Lafayette newspaper seeking a teacher, and had three apply.

The first one to come in person, however, was a young woman with tan skin. She told Molly that she had been born on the Jounier plantation outside Baton Rouge, and had taken that as her last name when she attended normal school. She had not been able to find a teaching position in a white school, however. It only required that first interview for Miss Molly to see the quality and character of this wonderful applicant. June Jounier was invited to teach all grades at the Bethel School, and live in the mound house. Molly offered her a salary that was a bit more than expected. Being the Boss had its happy side.

The pile of Thursday's letters seemed larger than usual. There were more and more folks who requested a visit to Vermillion. But there was also a letter from Daniel's Washington attorney that Miss Molly opened immediately. Anxiously she read the brief message. "Good day to you, Mrs. Higgins. This letter is written to inform you that your husband, Daniel Higgins, is once again in Sacred Heart Hospital in dire physical condition. Once again his cardiac deterioration has caused critical pulmonary complications. The doctors have advised the family to gather, and last rites to be administered. This situation is critical, as I hope you can understand. Mr. Higgins has requested your immediate presence. You are in our prayers. Sincerely, Jamison Stewart, Attorney of Law.

Molly reread the letter with tears running down her cheeks. Her first impulse was to rise and immediately prepare for whatever journey might be required. Then the irony of the request caused her to pause. The husband who had been too busy to care for his home and family was asking her to drop everything and hurry to his side, if she could even make it in time. The one who had once before experienced the life saving healing mystery of Vermillion was dying in some distant hospital alone. Molly wiped the tears from her eyes. She was terribly sad, but aware that Daniel had made his own choices, poorly. She decided to go swimming, alone. But first she had to share this news with Adam, Noah, and Roman, the only people who had an opportunity to know Mr. Daniel.

Four days later in the Monday letters, Miss Molly found another letter from Mr. Stewart, Daniel's attorney. She hesitated before opening it thinking that it was either very good news, her husband was recovering, or very bad news. She took a deep breath before she started to read it. "Good day Mrs. Higgins. I'm afraid the news I have for you is heartbreaking." A tremble shook her body. "It will be doubly bad if you are currently in transit, coming to answer his request, and arrive only to find that Mr. Higgins' body has been sent to Tallahassee to be buried in the family cemetery plot. You have our deepest condolences. I can assure you that he was in very little discomfort and his suffering was only brief."

"In accordance with Mr. Higgins' instructions, his assets here in Washington are being liquidated, i.e. the home in Chevy Chase, Maryland is being sold, as are his horses. His bank account balance and investments will be forwarded to Mr. Jenkins, his attorney in Lafayette for you. The household furnishings along with personal items, will be crated and sent by rail car to Lafayette, also in care of his attorney for you." All of this was a total surprise to Molly, She had never guessed that Daniel had a home in Maryland. "Our deepest sympathy is offered to your family, and our gratitude for the honor of serving such a valiant patriot, a selfless public servant who has had a profound effect on the future of our United States. If we can serve you in any way, please do not hesitate in calling upon this office. Sincerely, Jamison Stewart, Attorney of Law."

Miss Molly read the letter again. Daniel had been gone almost three years. Now she understood what a great distance that had been. Weeping, she decided to go swimming, alone.

For the next eighteen months Miss Molly was absorbed in the plantations' management, and in the development of the twins and Annie. They attended school, and swam just about every day, with David's company. He was such a good friend, filling the void where a dad should be. He taught them how to plant Taro crowns, and then how to nurture flowers. He showed them a host of interesting birds. He introduced them to the row boat and the daily sweep of the shrimp sock. The catch was decreasing, but the trip on the bay was delightful. He taught them how to start a campfire without matches. The boys were a tiny bit upset that Annie succeeded before they did. But they quickly forgot about that when, as they sat around the campfire eating pralines in the gathering darkness, David told them the account of Betty Bat, "who lives in the rafters of the barn" he whispered confidentially. "She sleeps during the day, but just about now every night, she goes hunting for something tasty to eat." His soft baritone voice sounded ominous as six anxious eyes scanned the dusk sky to spot her flitting silhouette. But perhaps his most appreciated gift of affection was the rare times he would show them how to saddle the horses of the Grove House barn, and leisurely ride the four mile perimeter of the property. He showed them how to appreciate their marvelous home.

One afternoon at the beach, when the children had wandered back to the shoreline to look for shells, Miss Molly swam slowly toward David. He extended his arms in an invitation, which she accepted. Her hands held on to his shoulders as she pulled herself against him, and deliberately kissed his lips. It seemed the kiss lingered on and on, until he whispered, "We had best stop before the lust of this moment becomes more than we can honorably handle." He eased her away from his chest, but continued to hold her buoyant body gently. "Molly, I would gladly spend the rest of my life with you." He took a breath before finishing the thought, "as your husband, if you will let me."

Miss Molly floated an arm's length from him, looked into his warm brown eyes and said softly, "Several years ago Mr. Daniel said those same words to me, and my heart beat fast just as it is now. I want to believe you, David. I am fond enough of you that I can honestly say that I love you. I want you in my life. It may take me a while to completely believe that you will remain with me." She expected a downcast expression, but his smile only spread wider.

"That is so good to hear," he nearly giggled. "In as many ways as you will permit, I will show you what a loving husband can be."

For the rest of the year, nothing changed; Miss Molly competently ran both Grove House and Vermillion Plantation. Crops were harvested, and guests were welcomed. Yet everything changed! The staff recognized that romance was in full bloom, and was delighted that the days of sorrow were over for Miss Molly. David was a champion admirer. Whether at his job hosting guests, seeing to their needs, laboring to bring each crop to its fullness, caring for the Sunday devotions, or guiding the children to the beach, it was plain to see that he was completely smitten as a suitor. It gave a happy polish to the Hospitality House.

On one of Miss Molly's monthly bank trips, she mentioned to Mr. Bandeau her frustration in trying to get affordable teaching material for the Bethel school. "I've spoken to the Principals of three elementary schools here in Lafayette, simply asking to purchase their used, outdated, and cast off books and teaching aids. None of them have given any consideration to a request from either someone who is not a teacher, or worse, someone of color." Her frustration was evident.

"How many children are attending the Bethel school?" the banker asked.

"Only sixteen," Molly answered. "But this is only our third year with a wonderful teacher, and three of those students are orphans that we adopted from the train. I would like them to have a better chance at learning."

Nothing more was said about her irritation, but a week later Miss June came running to the Hospitality House. Breathlessly she told Miss Molly about a wagon that had stopped at the school. "A young man is unloading boxes!" she got out. David joined the group that hurried up the lane to see this unusual thing. First they found a young man grateful for the help of unloading the last of several boxes. "I didn't know books could be so heavy," he chuckled. Then, looking inside the boxes, they found story books, language, mathematics, geography and history books. There were reams of colored paper for projects, with boxes of scrap pencils and pens. There was even a brass bell to call the children in the morning, and an American flag so they could learn the new pledge of allegiance proudly, and even a mounted clock with a thermometer and a barometer, which would become a life saver in the near future.

"Where did this all come from?" Miss Molly wondered.

The lad replied, "Mr. Bandeau from the bank said you can look through these boxes, keeping what you can use and burning the rest. It's just the school's throw away scrap. They were glad to clean out a storeroom."

"Well how much do we owe for all this?" Miss Molly was not sure how this had worked out.

"No ma'am, you don't owe a thing. Like I said, it's just the school's scrap pile." But Miss Molly understood that her banker had been instrumental in it, and promised to let him know how appreciated this "scrap pile" was to them.

When the wagon was empty, she invited the young driver to have lunch at the Hospitality House, a swim at the beach if he would like, and a $10 dollar eagle for his labor. Gladly he accepted all three. On his way home there was satisfaction in doing a charitable task for a beginning school, the weight of a fresh coin in his pocket, and perhaps most importantly, an interesting meeting with an attractive school teacher. He would make this trip again if possible.

As the days and weeks passed, Miss Molly marveled at how contented she felt. Each day had its demands, of course, but there were so many more rewards! The staff was functioning smoothly, and David was attentive, thoughtful, finding an infinite number of ways to please her and show his affection. May was constantly playfully envious of the courtship.

The Storm!

Just before the sugar cane harvest, the weather became hotter than usual with stifling humidity. On Tuesday morning July 19th, before school, June ran back to the Hospitality House. She told Miss Molly that the barometer had dropped four points since last night. It was a sure sign that a bad storm was coming within twenty four hours. "It's a warning to allow us to get ready" she advised. Miss Molly told Thomas, who found Adam, Noah, and Martin. She also told David, who tactfully told the guests, one by one, offering to refund their money if they wanted to move inland to safer ground.

"Have you ever had a damaging storm here?" one of the guests asked.

"None since I have been here, and no history of any before that," David answered honestly.

Two thirds of the guests decided to heed the warning and gladly accepted credit to complete their stay at a later date. A line of carriages made their way up the lane and north toward Lafayette. Bethesda had three box wagons to move nine children and the three nurses. For the Hospitality staff, there was no clear process of preparation for a storm. It had never been suggested. By evening all doors and windows were securely closed, in spite of the muggy temperature, and all loose tools were put in the barn. June reported that during the day the barometer had fallen another two points. She was relieved to accept the invitation to take shelter in the Grove House basement for her and the families of Bethel.

The leading squall line of the storm came in about midnight. They had seen lots of thunderstorms with lightning and rain, but this one seemed to have a fury to it. After the initial storm passed, the wind grew stronger and stronger from the southwest. Gusts rattled the house and they could hear limbs breaking. Before dawn there was an eerie calm, an ominous quiet that lasted for only a little while. Then the wind returned from the east. Harder and harder it pounded the houses. In the gray dawn they could see waves crashing on the beach with limbs and clumps of debris floating in the foam.

By midmorning the storm began to lose its punch. By noon Miss Molly reported no damage at the Grove House and the children were safe with Miss June, in the basement there. The rest of the staff could get outside to assess the damage, Thankfully the barn was intact with only frightened horses inside. Bethesda had a window broken by a flying limb, and a portion of the roofing was peeled back. But nothing worse than that. The mound house had two broken windows, and the veranda had suffered some structural damage, losing the front steps and a corner support. Perhaps the greatest damage was to the stairs structure that had been twisted loose from the porch. It would be unusable until a carpenter could get to it. But, all that too seemed repairable

The Hospitality House had been protected from the west wind by the mound, and it was situated so the east wind only had the far end of the building in its path, so there seemed to be little damage other than some roofing material, which must have been gratifying to the four guests who had chosen to ride out the storm. The beach bungalows had not fared so well. All four of them were in shambles, beaten by the pounding waves, and in the debris all that was left of the row boat were splinters. It was apparent that beach time would be severely hampered for some time by the thick mass of floating trash. Still unknown and unseen, the Seerier had felt the violence coming and had moved to deeper water where they were safe along the sandy bottom as the hurricane passed overhead.

Inside the Hospitality House there was a near hysteria of relief. The storm had been so terrifying, but now it was gone. Laughter and happy voices were sharing the joy of survival, even though it seemed to be growing darker outside. Beulah and Sharon said they would whip up a quick lunch because there had been no breakfast.

Eli and Joy said they wanted to go check on their house, and Adam and Noah agreed to go along to check on Celia and Erma in the Grove House, even though Miss Molly had reported that all was well there. Without availability of the beach, the four guests had chosen to return to Lafayette after all, as quickly as they could harness their carriages.

A few minutes later, David was inspecting all the weather side of Hospitality House, when the hair on his neck stood up in alarm. The air felt dead still, but at the west end of the bay a twisting, writhing, cone shaped finger of water was hissing to life. He had never seen a water spout before, but had heard of its devastating power. A tornado might sweep a path of destruction a half mile wide or more, but a water spout was concentrated devastation by the weight it carried. Its destructive narrow path might be limited to fifty paces or less. And it was coming straight at them, not a half mile away. He ran for the dining room, shouting for the retreating carriages to hurry as fast as they could to get out of the path!

As he burst in the door his eyes searched for Miss Molly. "Everybody get under cover!" he shouted. "There's a twister coming right at us!" He had assessed the possible shelter areas in the room and continued, "Get under the stairs over there!" His voice was too powerful to ignore, and his advise too good not to obey. The clump of folks began to huddle together. "Push in as far against the wall as you can!" His body was tight against Miss Molly's, which in any other circumstance would have been pleasant.

Outside there was a growing growl. A terrifying roar of inhuman power was upon them. Then suddenly the building was struck so viciously that splinters were flying and walls were falling; a portion of the roof disappeared in an explosion of water. Amidst screams, the huddling clump was doused with a dense bath of salt water. They heard crashing and felt another violent concussion as the mound house slammed against the top of the building, which crushed into a mass of ruble, but they held fast to one another. The air was filled with flying mud and dust. Chunks of debris careened off every solid object. Boards were flying, lanterns crashing to the floor, everything seemed chaos. David heard Miss Molly pray, "Lord Jesus, save us!"

In a moment of clarity, Miss Molly remembered the conversation with Miss Clare on the veranda. She had said, "He told me not to be concerned when the storm comes." She had looked steadily into Molly's eyes and continued, "He told me you could rebuild it bigger and better than ever." A smile of encouragement had blossomed on Miss Clarice. "He told me that you shouldn't be upset." She had said. "It will be wonderful." Miss Molly closed her eyes tightly and knew what she would do, if they survived.

The nightmare may have lasted a minute. It seemed like an eternity, then everything was silent and still. David asked Miss Molly if she was injured.

"No, I'm fine," she whispered. Then in a louder voice she asked, "Is everyone all right?" Several were bleeding from small wounds left by flying debris, but were grateful to have no greater injuries.

Thomas looked for some way out of what was left of the dining room. All around them was a mass of destruction. Rafters and planks, sharp pieces of the roof were shattered and scattered all around them, three or four feet deep. All the tables and chairs were smashed. Under the stairway however, was the only clear space he could see. David had saved their lives or prevented terrible injuries. "Where is Beulah, or Sharon?" he asked. Then he loudly called their names. Now everyone was struggling to get across the mountain of debris. "Beulah, are you all right?" There was no answer. "Sharon!" the distraught husband called. Only ominous silence answered.

It took several minutes of moving debris before Thomas found the kitchen table. He pulled away floor joists from the upstairs and the corner of the roof that had collapsed. Finally he was able to peer under the table and discovered Beulah's lifeless form. The massive weight that had crushed the table had done the same to her. But there was no sign of Sharon anywhere. Franticly, Thomas searched for his beloved.

David made his way through the gaping hole where the kitchen wall used to be. Once outside the destroyed building's fate could be understood. There was no part of it that was salvageable. The roof was either missing or flattened in broken disorder. It was apparent that the force of the twister had collided with the corner of the building and then the mound house, which was swept entirely off its foundation. It too was destroyed. He turned and followed the path of destruction. Pieces of the roof and piles of assorted broken lumber marked a clear path. There was a mattress and some sheets, a chair and a nightstand. He continued another hundred paces along the path of rubble, when he saw some large kitchen pots, the signs for which he was searching. Finally he saw her body, partially clothed, lying in the sand. It would be possible to imagine her asleep, resting quietly, except for the strange twist of her head. When the wall had collapsed, she and all these pots and pans must have been sucked up into the violent vortex. A tear traced down his cheek. Summoning his courage he went back for one of the sheets he had passed, and then used it to cover her before he informed Thomas that his Sharon was way out here.

Miss Molly had been organizing an assessment of the damage to all the buildings. Once again the barn had miraculously been spared. The Bethesda House had been completely blown apart. The other help house had roof damage and was bruised a bit, but was still standing. The mound house was unbelievably destroyed. It looked like a doll house that had been smacked by a giant hand. It was completely off the mound, and the parts that hadn't been consumed by the water spout, were spread in shattered fragments onto the Hospitality roof. There were many treasures to be salvaged, and many more simply gone. She sent Noah up the hill to inspect the school and Bethel houses. She asked Martin if he could inspect the sugar canes to see how much may still be harvested. Instead of standing around in shock, the staff could see that there was work to do. They were energized to recover. The very first task, however was to get Beulah and Sharon up onto the mound, where they may be tenderly laid to rest. Martin and David set about the task of building coffin frames. Adam and Thomas were men with broken hearts who needed the comfort of a loving community.

"For a while," Miss Molly announced to the group, "we will move our address to Grove House for meals, which will be closer to Bethel. Meetings each morning for prayer, will keep us focused, and there will be a place to sleep if you have lost yours. Celia and Erma will prepare all meals for us until we are back on our feet. We have lost beautiful people. Do you remember the words David spoke to us at Miss Clare's memorial? He said, 'we give her deep thanks for the wisdom she demonstrated to see what we might become. We have the courage to begin it, the faith to continue, and the strength to complete it.' If we have courage, faith, and strength, I think how we respond to this crushing blow will prove the truth of those words. Tomorrow, after we have a service on the mound for our friends, I am going to the carpenter, to see when he can begin to rebuild us." She might have been seventy one years old, but she led as bravely as a young commander.

Reconstruction

David had driven the wagon to two previous construction companies. This office of Steven Andre was very warmed by the afternoon sun. So far, Molly had been frustrated in her attempt to find a carpenter. She said, "Yes, I know that the hurricane caused considerable damage. Everyone is busy. And that is the third time today I have been told that the woman's place is in the home. I'm grateful that you did not mention the color of my skin, too. Let me ask you Mr. Andre, do you believe that notion firmly enough to see thousands of dollars of business walk out your door, as some of your colleagues have?"

The tanned young man with curly brown hair answered, "When you put it that way, I don't guess money has a gender or a color other than gold, does it? No ma'am, I would be grateful for your business."

Molly spread a rough drawing of her idea. "We called it Hospitality House until the cyclone destroyed it. Now we think it should be a bit larger, maybe about twenty guest rooms, a dining room and kitchen. There should be eight plunger closets, four on each floor. And I'd like you to build two of these, one plain, and one elegant."

His brown eyes blinked. "How soon can I start?"

With a warm smile Molly said, "I like that attitude. Most men would have started the finance dance with me, quoting blue sky figures that would shock me into accepting an unrealistically high bid. Can you do both jobs for fifty thousand dollars?"

With a chuckle the carpenter replied, "Now who is trying the unrealistic finance dance, trying to keep the numbers down?" He became serious. "I'm just guessing right now, but a low realistic bid would be about thirty thousand for the plain building and an addition ten for the higher grade finish of the other one." He waited expecting negotiation. Finally, he added, "But I'll need to come out and see what sort of land I have to work with. Do you need help with the demolition clean up? I know six or eight guys who could be part of the whole deal." A confident smile spread across his face.

Molly said, equally satisfied, "Yes we can use help, and if this project is finished by the first of October, there will be a 10% bonus. I'll pay half now and the balance when the job is complete." She held out her hand, like a man would, to strike the agreement. "We are at the end of Live Oak Road" she added. "That's the way the hospital wagons have come. They've made the road pretty smooth; or you can get there through Abbeville. I'll pay five dollars a day per worker for demolition, and, if you want to, you can stay in a help house, which was only a little bruised by the storm."

Steven Andre had been growing more committed to the idea of the construction. This might just be the springboard into a sound business for him. "What are the hospital wagons doing at your place?" It was more of a polite question than a curious one.

"They've been bringing about twenty children a week to us for healing, she replied. "That's what the plain building is for, healing sick kids." There was not a hint of insincerity or disrespect in Molly's voice.

Raising his eyebrows, now he asked suspiciously, "Are you some kind of a nature cult?"

"Oh for goodness sake, no! The plantation grows sugar cane, Taro, and pecans. On the side, people come to Hospitality House to drink the pure spring water, enjoy some jambalaya, and bath in Vermillion Bay. It must be something about that combination; we've seen a great many mystifying recoveries. You may want to see for yourself, if you are interested." She had no way of knowing what a tender cord she had just struck.

The jovial side of Steven was lessened as he said, "I can have a wagon load of men out there by about 8:30 in the morning. Then we can see just what needs to be done, and I'll try to have a drawing to see if I understand what you need." His thoughts, however, were on his young son and the sense of hopelessness his condition had made in their home.

When it was time to return home, David drove the wagon first to the bank for three bearer bonds that would amount to a down payment. Then finally, they visited the general store to see if they might have a replacement for the row boat, and a shrimp sock. The storm may have destroyed a valued old vessel, but it may also have replenished the food source in the bay.

The demolition took ten days of sorting the destroyed buildings into four piles. The largest and most used was the fire that consumed the unusable broken boards and splintered lumber. That pile burned nonstop; sometime so hot it was difficult to get close enough to add more to it, sometimes just glowing coals in the morning. Another pile near the barn was usable scrap material. There was more than enough to rebuild the four beach bungalows later. The third pile was glass from windows and broken dishes. They were dropped into the quicksand. No one knew for sure how deep the pit might be, but it took all the fragments they could toss in with no trace. The final pile was salvageable items, like swimming robes and towels, table clothes. The kitchen stoves were hardly scratched, but the mound house mahogany table and chairs were scarcely recognizable they were in so many pieces. There were enough beds, blankets and sheets to serve the folks who needed to bunk in the help house. Clothes that looked usable were made available to anyone who could fit them. Martin found three shotguns and a cache of old pistols and holsters. It was a tiresome task with moments of heart wrenching nostalgia. In a battered dresser, Molly found her dad's cigar box that held over $500 dollars and a gold ring with a red stone. She also found the strong box from her office that had more than enough cash to pay all the demolition help. Her office desk was crushed, but still contained the calendar of folks who had to be contacted not to come to this destruction site. The upright piano from the mound house was scarred with deep scratches. It was terribly out of tune, but still playable. The grand piano from Hospitality House had a broken lid and all four legs were broken. Steven announced that he knew a woodworker in Lafayette that could probably repair it for less than a replacement would cost. It was a tiring exercise in recovery.

Martin reported that while much of the sugar canes were knocked pretty flat by the hurricane, most of it was going to be harvestable, but the pecans had fared much worse. Only the trees higher up the hill were still bearing.

Finally, everything that could be reclaimed or removed was cared for, and the site was raked and smooth. Steven walked with Miss Molly and David, planning how this new space might be best utilized. It had been her idea to move the new Bethesda house to the west side of the barn, claiming a new section of beach.

"But you have a mile of beach, don't you?" Steven asked. When Miss Molly nodded her head, he asked, "Why have the barn as the center structure with hospitalities on either side? I think it makes more sense to have the Hospitality House pretty much as it always has been. Then, if the Bethesda House could be situated on the east end of that, it would be close to the beach, and far from the barn, which would have plenty of room to be enlarged eventually." They paced off some general dimensions, and agreed that his plan was the better one.

Steven had been invited to use one of the Grove House basement rooms while the demolition was going on. The idea of having a floor level slightly below grade now came up. "I've also been thinking that while this construction is getting started, you might consider putting in a siphon system." When Miss Molly asked for more information, she admitted she had never heard of that.

"It looks to me," Steven answered. "That if the basement floor was a few feet lower, a suction pipe could be run down from a water collection tank of the spring water on the hill. A valve could allow water to flow with gravity directly to the kitchen or the plunger closets, even the ones upstairs. That would be mighty convenient." A slight smile hid the fact that he was making his construction job some larger than their agreement.

"Do you think it could be piped into both buildings?" Miss Molly asked, now quite interested in the novel idea.

"I do believe it could. The only challenge might be overuse, which could drain the tank and break the suction. But if it was a good size tank, that probably wouldn't happen. You could monitor it real easy." Steven knew he was way over the edge of being qualified to make such a prediction. But it could work.

"Let's give this some serious thought," Miss Molly sounded like the conversation was ending. "Perhaps by this evening after supper, we could know how much more all that will cost. That also brings up something I was about to suggest," She looked carefully at Steven, recalling an expression of concern she had seen on his face at the mention of his family "If you are going to be working on this for a couple months, would your family like to be here with you? We have plenty of room."

There was that dark look of concern again. "That is a very gracious offer," Steven said with a pause. "To tell you the truth, when I heard about children getting healed here, my hopes rose a bit. It's one of the reasons I took the job." Taking a deep breath for courage he went on, "You see," his voice trembled and Molly wasn't sure he was going to continue. "You see," he said with pained effort, "our six year old son is spastic. The doctor calls them seizures, which make him fall down and make terrible sounds. I guess the proper name for it is Epilepsy. They tell us it's not catching, but we can't take him anywhere because we don't know when it will happen, and it seems to happen more often these days. They also seem more violent. It alarms people who think he is either an animal or dying. I don't think Ruthy has been out of the house much for a couple years. She just takes care of Jonathan.

Miss Molly smiled reassuringly. "We knew a very brave soldier who died in the war, who had that same name." Placing her hand on Steven's shoulder, she added, "With two months to work with, I can't imagine your son not being fully restored to health."

The distraught father had a tear making its way down his cheek. "If that could happen I would do this job for free."

Miss Molly gave him a pat on the back, ignoring his magnanimous words, she said, "Now that the twins are becoming young men, Sarah, my housekeeper has very little to do. I'm sure she would welcome an opportunity to give Miss Ruth a hand with Jonathan. She has helped a number of children find restored health. We'll be glad when Jonathan is well too. The next time you go into town, bring them back with you. It will be wonderful for the whole family."

And it was! Adam fashioned a new beach chair, which served to move Jonathan from the carriage down to the beach, where he sat safely in a couple feet of water, surrounded by Seerier eager to have a new host. At first he was frightened by the water, then he relaxed, and finally he made it very clear that he wanted more and more water time. The construction of the new Hospitality House seemed symbolic to his recovery. It took a while for both, with more than a little effort, but before long all their dreams were reality. Jonathan experienced no more seizures.

One evening before supper, young Jonathan approached Miss Molly. Quietly he said, "Daddy said he didn't want to build this big house for you, but you talked him into it so we could come along. Mom says that you are an angel who helps little kids who are sick." Looking at the floor, not completely sure what to say next, finally he looked into her eyes and said simply, "Thank you, Angel Molly for making me well, just like all the other kids." He ran to his mom who was weeping.

Reopen Too

With a two month backlog of requests to catch up, Molly was grateful for the additional rooms. Steven had explained that with a dining room and kitchen downstairs there could be ten guest rooms, plus the plunger closets. The upper floor balanced out with fourteen guest rooms and four more plunger closets. A patio off the kitchen offered an outdoor eating or lounging area, while the veranda was off the second floor with a marvelous view of the bay. Railings and stair treads were finished in deep Mahogany; brass oil lamp sconces lined the hallways and dining room walls. It truly was a lovely building. Beginning with the second week of October, they would be back in business. Sarah shared with Miss Molly that she had two cousins who would very much welcome an opportunity to be cooks for Hospitality House. Job vacancies did not last long when the work atmosphere was so positive, and the pay was so generous. There were two heartbroken men who would eventually find healing interest in the presence of new help.

Now that the Hospitality House was up and running, Miss Molly entertained the idea of acquiring another quarter section of land to expand the Bethel opportunities. There was a constant need for more help around the plantation, and the best way to satisfy that was to create more homes for workers. It had worked pretty well the first time, so she decided to repeat the offer.

She wished she could be that definite with David, who was more and more finding a warm place in her heart. He had learned, for example, that as they swam together every afternoon, if he simply stood in chest deep water she would soon glide up to him to deliver a lingering kiss. He was a patient suitor, holding her gently and allowing their bodies to caress one another, She was becoming convinced of his truthfulness in promising loyalty. He would stay with her! But what would their future be?

The future with Kindred Hospital in Lafayette was also something that needed her attention. Now that the help houses were no longer available, a new agreement was necessary. She made an appointment to talk to J. J. Gibson, the hospital manager who had treated her with some distain previously. He also believed that a woman's place is somewhere other than in business. Once the stiff greeting was given to Miss Molly, she was invited to be seated for a brief meeting. "I have a very important meeting in just a few minutes," he announced proudly.

Molly smiled warmly before she replied, "You have nothing more important than the ten minutes I am going to give you. Vermillion Plantation was struck by a cyclone, as you know. The previous buildings were destroyed save for one help house. Our Hospitality House, and a twin sister to it, have been replaced. I have ample requests to fill both with guests. But out of respect for our founding owner's memory, I will consider our previous arrangement with Kindred Hospital as a first right of refusal. The sister house may become Bethesda South, although we cannot offer additional housing to resident staff. The new facility has twenty four rooms, a kitchen and lobby." She was quiet for a moment, allowing Mr. Gibson time to understand her proposal. "The previous building had six rooms," she continued, "for which your use contract paid one thousand dollars a month. My offer for this new facility which offers four times as many rooms is three thousand dollars a month, with all the same provisos we had in place there." She smiled as sweetly as she could, without laughing at his shocked expression.

"You must be joking with me, Miss Higgins. That is a prohibitive price."

"Sir, you had approximately a thousand children at Bethesda last year, which breaks down to about $12 per child. The new facility will offer you four times as much space for 25% less cost per child. If you need more time to consider the offer, please feel free to stop by Vermillion Plantation for a tour before Sunday the 21ˢᵗ, when I will understand that this offer has been rejected. Then your doctors can try to explain why their recovery rate for sick children has so dramatically declined." She stood up quickly. "I know that you have a very important meeting. Thank you for your gracious attention.

"But we haven't…" the confused man began a sentence that was never finished.

"Good day, sir," Miss Molly said as she stepped to the door. "You have important business to attend." She was pretty sure that once he talked it over with the doctors who had taken credit for the fantastic recovery rate of last year's children, they would want an even greater success account. But she also suspected that the higher rate would not be approved by short sighted management, which was the reason for her bluntness. She was torn between her awareness of what Miss Clarice would have wanted, and what opportunities the future offered. She hoped that he would choose not to continue their arrangement. As a business decision, all that new availability could be filled with guests who would pay much, much more.

The Sunday prior to their reopening, the devotions were well attended. The new cooks, Iris and Hazel, had spent extra time, making their debut. Celia and Erma of the Grove House, had agreed to work on desserts, so everyone was anticipating a feast.

When David had finished the Blessing Prayer, Miss Molly said that she had three important announcements. May called from the back of the room, "We hope one of them is the invitation to a wedding!" There was instant laughter, accept from David, who looked embarrassed.

"No wedding…yet," Miss Molly said with a happy smile. "I believe this news will be even more welcome. First, because of our success as Hospitality House, there will be a raise in pay for everyone as of next Friday."

Noah asked, "Miss Molly, did you say everyone, even field workers?"

"We are a family here," she said firmly. "When one part does exceptionally well, all of us are blessed. Yes, Noah, for everyone." Then she continued, "Secondly, we have acquired another parcel of property to make more lots and lumber available in Bethel. There will be twenty same size lots, and ten double size, big enough for other businesses or large gardens, because thirdly," she took a large breath with a happy smile, "the hospital is not going to be using Bethesda. We will be hiring and training another complete staff to operate our second Hospitality House. Let's call it Hospitality Too." She spelled it so they would know she meant "also." If you have family or friends who love the Lord, and who would like a dream job, let them know, because I am not going to wait long before we welcome more guests to our new facility. Sundays will be reserved for devotions and prayerful rest." The room was buzzing with excited conversation about the fresh possibilities.

Season of Peace

So began what Miss Molly called the "Season of Peace." The request letters kept flowing in and the guests came by the dozens; no, by the hundreds. More staff made it possible for more marvelous accounts of healing and renewed health as the Seerier continued their mysterious applications, unseen, silent and magnificent. At Christmas, Miss Molly and David exchanged their wedding vows. He happily took the name "Higgins."

When the twins were fifteen, they attended school in Tallahassee. Timmy, who had learned to play the piano, developed a deep love for classical music, and mastered the pipe organ. Tobias, perhaps because of his assistance in the inspiring healing of little Jonathan Andre, chose a path towards medical school. With the Grove House assistance, he became a pediatrician. Both the young men chose to live in New York, where they tried to find their birth mother. Two years later Annie followed them to Tallahassee, where she met the son of a Virginia Military Institute professor. She never returned to Grove House, choosing rather to become a Virginia housewife.

For over two decades, Lowell Stanley was a popular horse breeder, collecting show ribbons galore. His health declined rapidly and his death was mourned by the Tallahassee community. Ironically, his wife Rebecca, also suffered a decline, so severely that a Board of Trustees was appointed to assume her leadership responsibilities of Monticello College. She died never returning to her birthplace, nor its wonders.

In the Monday mail, Miss Molly recognized a familiar envelope from Mr. Daniel's attorney. "What in the world," she wondered.

She opened and read: " Good day, Mrs. Higgins. Once again we are meeting in grievous times." Molly wondered to herself what this might have to do with her. She read on, "The death of Mrs. Rebecca Stanley has left a void in the Monticello College Directorship." That, of course was profound news to Molly, having far-flung implications here at Vermillion too. "With the death of the owner, Lisle Higgins, the property passed to Daniel Higgins, and now with his death, the property is inherited by you, ma'am. The Board of Trustees has managed the College in the interim, but now seeks a more lasting identity. They have retained me to negotiate with you some settlement of ownership, and request your presence at their quarterly meeting. In light of the importance of this meeting it would be advisable for you to have legal representation with you. The meeting place is Monticello College, of course, at 9:00 o'clock March 4, 1898. It is our hope that resolve and new direction may come of this meeting. Sincerely, Jamison Stewart, Attorney of Law".

Miss Molly reread the letter to make sure she understood the importance of it, then read it to David. "Let's talk about this while we swim," she suggested.

For the first few minutes they swam vigorously. David had developed such a strong stroke that Molly could hardly keep up with him. Finally they turned toward the shore, and gently slowed down until he could touch the bottom. Then she could kiss him. "I had no idea this would wind up as a further settlement of Daniel's estate." She kissed him again. "I should just give it to them as a school, don't you think?" She really did want his opinion.

David was still for a bit, thinking how he could help her ponder this sudden windfall. "I think," he said slowly after another kiss, "that you could collect a dollar a day from the guests who come to Hospitality House, and you might still make money, and they might still get well. But they pay a hundred times that much because they so value their health. It sounds to me like some carpetbaggers have their eyes on Monticello, and will try to get it from you. You can give it up for a dollar, or you can decide what its value really is to you." He turned her so she came close enough to kiss, sweetly, yet again.

Playfully Molly asked, "Have you ever made love on a train?" She giggled at his surprised expression, and her willingness to joke about it at age ninety.

"You know I have never been on a train," he answered in mock anger. "And you know that is not something I would tell you even if I had." They both laughed and kissed yet again, because she knew he would tell her anything she wanted to know.

"You have helped me, as usual," Molly finally said. "We've got a couple weeks to get ready. I think we need to go into Lafayette and make arrangements for a train compartment. We can talk to Mr. LaDoux, the attorney, who might help us know what to say to the Trustees. And for sure, we must get some business clothes so we don't look like a couple of jokes from the farm. Let me see," now there was a wide smile, "we are a couple good jokes from the farm."

Tallahassee negotiations

When they finally walked into the Monticello reception lobby, they looked very business ready, David in a tan suit with a white shirt and Kelly green tie, Miss Molly in a soft green light wool dress with a green scarf and an accent of pearls. They were ushered into a conference room by Jamison Stewart, the attorney, where six stern faced men were waiting. He was concerned that they had failed to bring legal representation with them. Molly lightly said, "I remember this room as the library. But that has been many years ago.' It caught the Trustees off-guard. She had declared that she had history with this place.

The chairman introduced himself, and then the other five, all respected businessmen of Tallahassee, like himself. Then he outlined the purpose of their meeting as that of finding an equitable purchase price for this old school. He even threw in descriptions of the deterioration of the out buildings and the decline of enrollment. After about five minutes, he eventually got around to the meat of the meeting. "So Mrs. Higgins, after hearing from our appraiser, we are prepared to make an offer of nine hundred thousand dollars for this property and all that's on it." He had emphasized the "hundred thousand" for dramatic impact.

"Oh my," Molly said rather breathlessly. "I hardly know what to say." She paused for a long moment before going on. "I think…. you should be preparing to close the school if that is really your offer. I was thinking more in the neighborhood of three point five million." She didn't emphasize it at all.

"Oh for…" he didn't finish his outburst. "This place is falling apart. There is no way it's worth anything close to that." He made something like a pouting face.

"Then gentlemen. I'm sorry you wasted my time. My appraiser has advised me to break up the property into parcels, which would net me considerably more. Without a practical offer, that is precisely what I will do.

"But Mrs. Higgins, this has become a recognized school of distinction." Now the chairman was whistling a different tune. "There are hundreds of students counting on the education they will get here to prepare them for a productive and meaningful life. Surely you wouldn't want to see it broken up."

"No I wouldn't want that. So my advice to you gentlemen is that you find a piece of property that you can afford, and build them a functional school." Her tone had stayed light and friendly. "Of course we all know that there is not a three quarter section of available land left in the Tallahassee Parish. We may be at something of an impasse."

The chairman turned to David, who had remained quiet. "May I ask what you think on this matter, since you share in the ownership. Perhaps you can add some sensibility to this discussion."

"Yes sir," David said softly. "If I came into your shoe shop looking to buy boots for a noble trip, and if I tried on a pair of your very best $100 boots, but offered you $10 because of my worthwhile journey, you would turn me down flat, and either throw me out or try to get me to buy some worn second hand boots. It seems to me that's pretty much where we are here."

"Oh, that's preposterous. We have given you a reasonable…"

Miss Molly interrupted the chairman, saying, "I'll tell you what is preposterous. You have no ownership or right of entitlement here of any sort, yet you have treated us as though you have all of that. There is no contract of authority for you to even be in this room." Turning to David, she asked, "Can you remember the term you used about these folks a couple weeks ago?"

"Do you mean when I said it sounded like a bunch of carpetbaggers?" David's countenance remained humorous.

Turning to attorney Stewart, Miss Molly said, "Gentlemen you asked me here to make a proposal, which I'm sure you knew is far under the value of Monticello. I refused that offer. I made an offer, which you refused. I believe we have no other business. If you would like to finish your quarterly agenda, I recommend you take it somewhere else, Monticello College is no longer at your disposal." She stood up, signaling them to do the same.

"Listen, young lady," the chairman angrily said, remaining seated. "No woman can tell me..."

Once again Miss Molly interrupted by sternly saying, "The price is now four point five million. I am not a young lady." She smiled inwardly thinking that in no way could ninety be considered young. "I happen to own this entire place, and may dispose of it as I wish. If you doubt that, ask your attorney. Do you want to keep negotiating?" A deep silence held the room. Finally she added, "In fairness, we will spend the night here in our house, so that you may prepare a reasonable and final offer at 10:00 o'clock tomorrow morning. Please be prompt and don't waste any more of our time playing squeeze games. One offer is all you get; sine qua non." The seven men looked at her in amazement. Once again she raised her palms, signaling them to rise and depart, which they did.

The three days that followed were hectic and delightful. The Trustees chairman, Mr. Morgan James, brought Miss Molly an offer of three point three million dollars, under the provision that they could pay one million now, and four equal payments on the balance, plus two percent interest, due the final day of the next four years. He informed her that the name would be changed to Florida State College. Miss Molly accepted the offer with the proviso that they could remove personal items from the Stanley residence, and they both signed a purchase and sales agreement. Payments would be made directly to the Federal Bank of Lafayette.

Then David and Molly had a challenge crating the personal items they wanted to claim from the Stanley's residence. There were more women's clothes than men's. David was less than pleased that he couldn't fit into any of the men's, but knew there would be many happy people when the crates arrived at the Vermillion Plantation.

There were three sets of china, crystal glasses and dishes, beautiful pictures, and boxes of books. In a nightstand they found a pistol with ammunition, and a box of gold double eagles, which they carefully placed in their luggage. In a dresser they found a box of jewelry that showed them Becca's fashion side. Miss Molly gladly placed that in the luggage as well. Finally they found a moving company that took the crates to the train station.

Molly remembered the family private coach from years ago and asked about it. She was told that it was still parked in storage and could be cleaned and greased for the west bound train the next day. Finally, in the barn they found two lovely horses and a parade carriage that could also be loaded in the rail car headed to Lafayette. All in all, an unbelievably satisfying three days. Before the train left, they even had an opportunity to visit the port of St. Mark to see the Manatees again.

As Tallahassee slipped away behind them, playfully Molly asked, "Have you ever made love on a train?" She giggled at his surprised expression. It was, in fact, a season of peace.

The Future

The days and weeks blurred together in a coordinated procession of guests in and happy guests out, punctuated by abundant harvests. Devotions waxed and waned according to the staff. Miss Molly taught piano lessons to a long list of boys and girls. Months turned into years and another decade passed with David and Miss Molly swimming each day and loving the nights, but showing no signs of aging. There were new faces as the old faces went away, but the Seerier were constantly present, administering restored health and vitality to all available hosts. New talent filled the voids made by folks who chose to retire or try somewhere else. Four new distillery men were hired and carefully trained for the Grove House Rum distillery. Molly hired two new workers to direct the Taro and Orange crops at Grove House. Like a well tuned musical ensemble Vermillion Plantation and Grove House thrived, as did the more than fifty people who staffed them. By the turn of the century, Bethel's new section was completely built with more new families, a hardware store, grocery, and a second hand store. Eventually the newly created homes enjoyed the marvels of electric lights, and automobiles, which made their homes less remote. There were regular requests to buy in, or get on a waiting list.

A terrible war in Europe was at first seen as a simple task for military assistance. It turned out to be a huge source of broken men, many of whom came to Hospitality House, hoping to find renewed health and strength. In 1919, legislators passed the eighteenth Amendment to the Constitution, forbidding the making or selling beverage alcohol, so the Grove House shut down the distillery for four years until the twenty third amendment repealed the restriction. There was a joke at the Grove House because the hotel purchased all the barrels of rum that were still aging. They sequestered them away so well that the hotel enjoyed a constant supply of dark rum, while the rest of the town was bone dry.

Cars and trucks at first seemed like novelties of the city, until Miss Molly realized they were a source of travel that made it possible to get from Grove House to Lafayette and back in less than two hours. She soon wondered how she could function without them. One day in March of '29, at the Federal Bank, she was chatting with the newest vice president, Gerald Greenleaf. He only knew her as a longtime customer of the bank with a thriving account. They were talking about the rapid change automobiles had brought when he gave her some valuable advice.

"Things are rolling along at a boom rate, Miss Molly. There are some of us in the finance world, who see this as a dangerous sign. We want to keep your business, so we are recommending to our larger accounts that they convert to Bearer Bonds and have at least a three month supply of operating cash on hand. It may not be as convenient, but it will get you through whatever adjustment is coming," he sort of grunted in discomfort, "we believe."

At the time, it seemed like such a simple thing to do. Molly was happy to convert both the Vermillion's and the Grove House accounts into Bearer Bonds and place them in the security boxes the bank provided. She also decided to hold off on making deposits of their income, to build a large cash nest egg. "Perhaps David could build a vault under our bed," she thought to herself.

In October, when the financial "adjustment" began, Hospitality House was completely insulated from the crisis, much to the gratitude of the bank. Even though guest requests were at about a quarter of their usual pace, Miss Molly kept her staff at full force. Salaries and bonuses were paid which meant that their little slice of heaven knew nothing of the financial hardship that was happening all around the country.

That same principle continued when the war broke out in Europe, and the radio reported that the Japanese nation had bombed

Pearl Harbor in Hawaii. Many of the husbands and sons living in Bethel marched off to serve their country, so the women filled the vacancies in the harvests. David wondered what the age limit might be for joining. Although he didn't understand how it was happening, he realized that however liberal it might be, at over one hundred, he was well beyond it. Hospitality House was at full staff regardless of the number of guests. Once again an increase of wounded and disabled warriors came to find hope in a visit to the beach. The Seerier were diligent in their applications and more stories of healing continued. Then there was a war in the mountains of South Korea.

Sea Wasp!

It was Sunday afternoon in May. Devotions had been well attended, the meal delicious as always. David and Molly followed their custom of visiting the beach, sitting in the comforting water. Remembering the chores achieved in the past week, and planning those that needed their attention, was a wonderful way to gain focus for the upcoming days. Finally, David said he needed to work off that pecan pie with some exercise. He asked if she wanted to come along on a swim. Molly understood that he was going to be aggressive in the swim and she was too comfortable for that. "But I'll watch you," she said cheerily. She did admire his strong untiring stroke that carried him about a quarter mile down the bay. Then he circled out into deeper water and was almost even with her again when suddenly she saw him splashing as though fending something away, and shouting in pain. Instantly, Molly started to join him to see if he was in distress. Instead, he waved her back, making his way toward the shore.

"I ran into something that looked like floating glass," he said as he waded toward her. "I don't think it cut me, because I can't find any blood." He raised his foot to examine his ankle. "It got me on the neck," he rubbed behind his ear, "and on the back of my leg. It burns like fire, but I can't see any wound." David was out of the water so Molly could join in the investigation. The areas were swelling and turning an angry shade of red. "I'm guessing my avoidance saved me from more bites. Whatever it was must have gone right over me."

Molly was on her way up to the Hospitality House. "Perhaps someone has a suggestion for how we can treat that," she said over her shoulder. "If you'll wait in the water to keep it cool, I'll be right back." Little did they understand that the Seerier had detected the presence of their arch enemy, the Box Jellyfish, and were in full retreat to the safety of the deeper water and sandy obscurity.

When Molly returned she shook her head in confusion. "No one had an idea what we should do. If there is no wound, and no stinger, they suggested a poultice of Mulberry leaves, or rub some Bay Rum aftershave on it." She shrugged in frustration; for she could see the areas were more swollen, and the discoloration was becoming dark purple "Someone remembered that the college has a Marine Biology Station down at Morgan City. If we leave first thing in the morning we can be back by suppertime. They might know what this is." Again she shrugged for lack of other suggestions.

"The fiery pain is not going away," David reported, "but it's not getting any worse, either. I'm just afraid one of our guests might happen to get stung, and we would be in big trouble." He didn't realize they were already in big trouble!

Invasion!

They stopped at the first gas station they came to in Morgan City. They were told that the Marine Biology Department was actually two miles further east in Wyandotte. "It's the cluster of white and green buildings out on the edge of Sweetbay Lake," they were told. At least the color of the buildings would be recognizable. Actually, with some helpful signage they were able to drive right to it. The main office told them where they could find Dr. Leon Proctor, the Director.

"So, you folks have Cubozoa trouble, huh?" the tanned and wrinkled man smiled. When David turned a questioning face toward him, the man explained, "Jellyfish, from the look of those marks I'd guess Chironex fleckeri, which has an almost transparent medusa with trailing tendrils. They are sometimes called 'sea wasps.' I'll bet you live right on the water and have a septic tank within fifty paces of the shore. Am I right?"

"We're from Vermillion Plantation and have four septic tanks about that close. Does that make a difference?" David had been told to do most of the talking, especially to white folks who might not appreciate Miss Molly's status.

"Well it sure does," the biologist said. "That close to the water lets the sandy soil perk down nitrites and sulfites into the bay, which act like fertilizer to sea grass. Where there is sea grass all sorts of new sea life start to show up, including jellyfish. They usually spawn in early spring, spreading their eggs along the sea grass, seven days after a full moon. There are many jellyfish that are harmless, but those sting marks on you say 'Box Jellyfish' to me. By the way, those marks will become scars that are permanent, but it is the only lasting effect you'll have. Down in Australia, their sting can take a man clear out of commission. And the biggest pain of it is we don't have any antitoxin to combat the rascal, although some folks have found some comfort in rubbing in Apple Cider vinegar. Folks might think you smell like a pickle. But that's not a real bad thing." They all chuckled what a large pickle David would be.

The Marine Biologist was quiet for just a moment before he asked, "Have you been taking less shrimp?"

"Yeah," David replied. "There was a time we could drag a sock for half an hour and fill two buckets. Now we work for a couple of hours for half a bucket."

"Yup," Dr. Proctor agreed. "Jellyfish love to dine on shrimp hatchlings. With their elongated envelope and eyes, they can out swim and out maneuver most any target. It's that way out front here in Atchafalaya Bay, up through Blanche Bay, and now you are telling me Vermillion is the same. It's like an infestation."

Molly couldn't remain quiet any longer. "We operate the Hospitality House on Vermillion Bay. Our business could be seriously jeopardized if there are more of these stinging jellyfish."

"I can understand your concern, sure enough. It is a Chamber of Commerce bad dream up and down the coast. It was bad when Mr. David got stung, but if Mr. Paying-Customer gets it you may have trouble in a heaping portion." Molly liked this down to earth man. With a wink, Dr. Proctor said, "We've been working on a solution of sorts because yours isn't the first, or only, place these rascals are showing up. We've been working on a hatching program to reintroduce some fingerling natural predators. Sea turtles would be our best friends, if they stayed around. The trouble with them is they eat a jellyfish meal or two and then swim away. They are always on the move, until it's time to build a nest, and then they don't eat much. But we have had an energetic program of propagation of Butterfish, which are aggressive jellyfish feeders; then there are the Batfish that patrol the deeper waters at night, also looking for jellyfish hatchlings. Finally we have had three doctoral programs raising Blue Tangs for reef control, only to discover that while they are primarily vegetarians, they are also terrific at feeding on jellyfish hatchlings. They nip the problem while it is still in the nursery. And all three of these fish will reproduce within the first year if there is plenty of food for them to eat."

He would have gone on but Molly interrupted, "How can we get some of those fingerlings?"

"I was about to suggest," Dr. Proctor answered with a smile, "if we can have close access to your beach, since we only have a hundred foot feeder pipe, and if you will pay for a tank of gas, we can drop about fifteen thousand fingerlings in Vermillion Bay."

Once again Molly interrupted, asking, "Would it be better to double the amount."

"Ooeee, you are in a big hurt, aren't you, Molly?" Then in a quieter voice he answered, "No, it doesn't work to overplant the fingerlings. If we stock more than the natural food supply can support, they just start feeding on one another. We lose much more than any gain. When there is an abundant food source, the fingerlings will quickly grow and reproduce to eat it all. Nature has a way of staying in balance. It is also a good idea for us to plant the fingerlings at night when the gulls are roosted so they don't take a tithe." When there were no more questions, and David was quietly stroking the tender area of his neck, Dr. Proctor concluded, "Well, think about it for a while. If you want to do that, just send me $20 dollars for gas, and we'll have a tanker at your place in a couple of days." Molly was already pulling a bill out of her purse.

On Saturday evening the tanker truck arrived, backed down the path to the beach, stretched out a black flex pipe into the water, and dumped more than fifteen thousand fingerlings that were hungry. The invasion had begun! The attacking horde came out of the shadows swiftly, without warning, feeding on anything in their path. They did not distinguish between jellyfish hatchlings, immature shrimp, or complex Seerier who were too slow to evade the onslaught. Nature was suddenly no longer in balance!

Some Seerier tried to find shelter by hiding, others attempted to escape by fleeing. Neither effort was successful as the voracious onslaught swept over them. Along the coast of Florida, Alabama,

Mississippi, Louisiana, and Texas, wherever tourism was challenged by jellyfish the same scenario was taking place. The Seerier attempted to find the safety of the deep Atlantic Trench, but found their way blocked by Puerto Rico's applications and the West Indies' addition to the increasing population of hungry fish. The stocking campaign spread from the east coast of Mexico to the west coast, Hawaii, and the Philippines. Within a couple months the beaches of the southern hemisphere and the Mediterranean were also being purified of jellyfish; and unknown to all, the Seerier as well.

Miss Molly had closed the Hospitality House following David's painful encounter. After a week, when no other jellyfish were detected, she reopened to eager visitors. The results of their visits were, however, immediately seen as disappointing. No healing, invigorating, cleansing accounts occurred. Miss Molly refunded all their money, and reclosed the Hospitality House. The Seerier were completely gone! But how could they grieve what they had never known they possessed?

After a month of cleaning inside and outside, she accepted another test group of guests, with the same sad results. There were no more miraculous stories to tell, no tales of wondrous invigoration. She closed the Hospitality House claiming changes in the sea currents had modified their ability to offer hope as they had in the past. She was diligent to oversee the Taro, sugar cane, and pecan harvests through two more crop seasons, but sadly realized that the once precious income from them had little significance now that Hospitality House was vacant.

Finally, with no other alternatives, in July of 1968, Molly advertised the plantation for sale. A group of businessmen purchased it, planning to use it as a seaside gaming resort. The funds were distributed to the surviving grandchildren of Becca, and Jonathan.

Through those two years, Molly had been aware of an ominous change that was rapidly happening to David, who was at least thirty years her junior. His hair was becoming snow white, and thinning. His face was lined with deep wrinkles. He walked with a slower stooped gate, and had difficulty with both his hearing and eyesight. When she first pointed that out to him, he asked if she had noticed the same thing about herself. Even though they swam daily, and drank from the pure spring water, without cell replacement boosts, they were aging at an alarming rate. Neither of them survived to celebrate glorious Easter. Born a slave one hundred and sixty years ago, she had become the guiding hand of a financial success, without ever knowing the source of that success, or her longevity. The grandchildren of Timothy, Tobias and Annie were astounded to receive a financial inheritance, and the grandchildren of Gracie also divided ownership of Grove House. The dreams of pioneers were finally and forever over.

Off the coast of what is now Libya, buried beneath meters of silt and six fathoms of water, where it was originally hidden, a tiny spacecraft awaits the return of the explorers, and the continuation of their search for a friendly planet with an oxygen based atmosphere. For where there was oxygen, and hydrogen, there would be a liquid base in which they might recover.